VERA

One sunny day, at noon, twenty-two-year-old Lucy Entwhistle stands leaning on a cottage garden gate, staring out at the sea. Her beloved father has died but three hours ago, and she is dazed with grief. Then middle-aged Everard Wemyss passes by, in a state of miserable distraction. Recently bereaved himself, he is drawn to Lucy by their mutual pain. Each seeking sanctuary in the other, the two are soon married. But one thing casts a shadow across their union: Vera, Everard's first wife, who died in a violent accident — in which Everard is suspected of being involved . . .

Books by Elizabeth von Arnim
Published by Ulverscroft:

ELIZABETH AND HER
GERMAN GARDEN
THE SOLITARY SUMMER

SPE ... DERS

THE ... ATION

(registered UK charity number 264873)
was established in 1972 to provide funds for
research, diagnosis and treatment of eye diseases.
Examples of major projects funded by
the Ulverscroft Foundation are:-

- The Children's Eye Unit at Moorfields Eye
  Hospital, London
- The Ulverscroft Children's Eye Unit at Great
  Ormond Street Hospital for Sick Children
- Funding research into eye diseases and
  ... ...gy,
- ... ...up,
- ... ...ern
- ... ...yal

You ... ...ion

Ev ... ...u
w ... ...r

T ...

we ... n

ELIZABETH VON ARNIM

VERA

Complete and Unabridged

ULVERSCROFT
Leicester

First published in Great Britain in 1921

This Large Print Edition
published 2017

The moral right of the author has been asserted

A catalogue record for this book is available
from the British Library.

ISBN 978–1–4448–3519–9

Published by
F. A. Thorpe (Publishing)
Anstey, Leicestershire

Set by Words & Graphics Ltd.
Anstey, Leicestershire
Printed and bound in Great Britain by
T. J. International Ltd., Padstow, Cornwall

This book is printed on acid-free paper

1

When the doctor had gone, and the two women from the village he had been waiting for were upstairs shut in with her dead father, Lucy went out into the garden and stood leaning on the gate staring at the sea.

Her father had died at nine o'clock that morning, and it was now twelve. The sun beat on her bare head; and the burnt-up grass along the top of the cliff, and the dusty road that passed the gate, and the glittering sea, and the few white clouds hanging in the sky, all blazed and glared in an extremity of silent, motionless heat and light.

Into this emptiness Lucy stared, motionless herself, as if she had been carved in stone. There was not a sail on the sea, nor a line of distant smoke from any steamer, neither was there once the flash of a bird's wing brushing across the sky. Movement seemed smitten rigid. Sound seemed to have gone to sleep.

Lucy stood staring at the sea, her face as empty of expression as the bright blank world before her. Her father had been dead three hours, and she felt nothing.

It was just a week since they had arrived in

Cornwall, she and he, full of hope, full of pleasure in the pretty little furnished house they had taken for August and September, full of confidence in the good the pure air was going to do him. But there had always been confidence; there had never been a moment during the long years of his fragility when confidence had even been questioned. He was delicate, and she had taken care of him. She had taken care of him and he had been delicate ever since she could remember. And ever since she could remember he had been everything in life to her. She had had no thought since she grew up for anybody but her father. There was no room for any other thought, so completely did he fill her heart. They had done everything together, shared everything together, dodged the winters together, settled in charming places, seen the same beautiful things, read the same books, talked, laughed, had friends — heaps of friends; wherever they were her father seemed at once to have friends, adding them to the mass he had already. She had not been away from him a day for years; she had had no wish to go away. Where and with whom could she be so happy as with him? All the years were years of sunshine. There had been no winters; nothing but summer, summer, and sweet scents and soft skies, and patient understanding with her slowness — for he had the nimblest mind — and love. He was the most amusing companion to her, the most generous friend, the most illuminating guide, the most adoring father; and now he was dead, and she felt nothing.

Her father. Dead. For ever.

She said the words over to herself. They meant nothing.

She was going to be alone. Without him. Always.

She said the words over to herself. They meant nothing.

Up in that room with its windows wide open, shut away from her with the two village women, he was lying dead. He had smiled at her for the last time, said all he was ever going to say to her, called her the last of the sweet, half-teasing names he loved to invent for her. Why, only a few hours ago they were having breakfast together and planning what they would do that day. Why, only yesterday they drove together after tea towards the sunset, and he had seen, with his quick eyes that saw everything, some unusual grasses by the road-side, and had stopped and gathered them, excited to find such rare ones, and had taken them back with him to study, and had explained them to her and made her see profoundly interesting, important things in them, in these grasses which, till he touched them, had seemed just grasses. That is what he did with everything — touched it into life and delight. The grasses lay in the dining-room now, waiting for him to work on them, spread out where he had put them on some blotting-paper in the window. She had seen them as she came through on her way to the garden; and she had seen, too, that the breakfast was still there, the breakfast they had had together, still as they had left it, forgotten by the servants in the surprise of death. He had fallen down as he got up from it. Dead. In an instant. No time for anything, for a cry, for a look. Gone. Finished. Wiped out.

What a beautiful day it was; and so hot. He loved heat. They were lucky in the weather . . .

Yes, there were sounds after all — she suddenly noticed them; sounds from the room upstairs, a busy moving about of discreet footsteps, the splash of water, crockery being carefully set down. Presently the women would come and tell her everything was ready, and she could go back to him again. The women had tried to comfort her when they arrived; and so had the servants, and so had the doctor. Comfort her! And she felt nothing.

4

Lucy stared at the sea, thinking these things, examining the situation as a curious one but unconnected with herself, looking at it with a kind of cold comprehension. Her mind was quite clear. Every detail of what had happened was sharply before her. She knew everything, and she felt nothing — like God, she said to herself; yes, exactly like God.

Footsteps came along the road, which was hidden by the garden's fringe of trees and bushes for fifty yards on either side of the gate, and presently a man passed between her eyes and the sea. She did not notice him, for she was noticing nothing but her thoughts, and he passed in front of her quite close, and was gone.

But he had seen her, and had stared hard at her for the brief instant it took to pass the gate. Her face and its expression had surprised him. He was not a very observant man, and at that moment was even less so than usual, for he was particularly and deeply absorbed in his own affairs; yet when he came suddenly on the motionless figure at the gate, with its wide-open eyes that simply looked through him as he went by, unconscious, obviously, that any one was going by, his attention was surprised away from himself and almost he had stopped to examine the strange creature more closely. His code, however, prevented that, and he continued along the further fifty yards of bushes and trees that hid the other half of the garden from the road, but more slowly, slower and slower, till at the end of the garden where the road left it behind and went on very solitarily over the bare grass on the top of the cliffs, winding in and out with the ins and outs of the coast for as far as one could see, he hesitated, looked back, went on a yard or two, hesitated again, stopped and took off his hot hat and wiped his forehead, looked at the bare country and the long twisting glare of the road ahead, and then very slowly turned and went past the belt of bushes towards the gate again.

He said to himself as he went: 'My God, I'm so lonely. I can't stand it. I must speak to some one. I shall go off my head — '

For what had happened to this man — his name was Wemyss — was that public opinion was forcing him into retirement and inactivity at the very time when he most needed company and distraction. He had to go away by himself, he had to withdraw for at the very least a week from his ordinary life, from his house on the river where he had just begun his summer holiday, from his house in London where at least there were his clubs, because of this determination on the part of public opinion that he should for a space be alone with his sorrow. Alone with sorrow — of all ghastly things for a man to be alone with! It was an outrage, he felt, to condemn a man to that; it was the cruellest form of solitary confinement. He had come to Cornwall because it took a long time to get to, a whole day in the train there and a whole day in the train back, clipping the week, the minimum of time public opinion insisted on for respecting his bereavement, at both ends; but still that left five days of awful loneliness, of wandering about the cliffs by himself trying not to think, without a soul to speak to, without a thing to do. He couldn't play bridge because of public opinion. Everybody knew what had happened to him. It had been in all the papers. The moment he said his name they would know. It was so recent. Only last week . . .

No, he couldn't bear this, he must speak to some one. That girl — with those strange eyes she wasn't just ordinary. She wouldn't mind letting him talk to her for a little, perhaps sit in the garden with her a little. She would understand.

Wemyss was like a child in his misery. He very nearly cried outright when he got to the gate and took off his hat, and the girl looked at him blankly just as if she still didn't see him and hadn't heard him when he said, 'Could you let me have a glass of water? I — it's so hot — '

He began to stammer because of her eyes. 'I — I'm horribly thirsty — the heat — '

He pulled out his handkerchief and mopped his forehead. He certainly looked very hot. His face was red and distressed, and his forehead dripped. He was all puckered, like an unhappy baby. And the girl looked so cool, so bloodlessly cool. Her hands, folded on the top bar of the gate, looked more than cool, they looked cold; like hands in winter, shrunk and small with cold. She had bobbed hair, he noticed, so that it was impossible to tell how old she was, brown hair from which the sun was beating out bright lights; and her small face had no colour except those wide eyes fixed on his and the colour of her rather big mouth; but even her mouth seemed frozen.

'Would it be much bother — ' began Wemyss again; and then his situation overwhelmed him.

'You would be doing a greater kindness than you know,' he said, his voice trembling with unhappiness, 'if you would let me come into the garden a minute and rest.'

At the sound of the genuine wretchedness in his voice Lucy's blank eyes became a little human. It got through to her consciousness that this distressed warm stranger was appealing to her for something.

'Are you so hot?' she asked, really seeing him for the first time.

'Yes, I'm hot,' said Wemyss. 'But it isn't that. I've had a misfortune — a terrible misfortune — '

He paused, overcome by the remembrance of it, by the unfairness of so much horror having overtaken him.

'Oh, I'm sorry,' said Lucy vaguely, still miles away from him, deep in indifference. 'Have you lost anything?'

'Good God, not that sort of misfortune!' cried Wemyss. 'Let me come in a minute — into the garden a minute — just to sit a minute with a human being. You would be doing a great kindness. Because you're a stranger I can talk to you about it if you'll let me. Just because we're strangers I could talk. I haven't spoken to a soul but servants and official people since — since it happened. For two days I haven't spoken at all to a living soul — I shall go mad — '

His voice shook again with his unhappiness, with his astonishment at his unhappiness.

Lucy didn't think two days very long not to speak to anybody in, but there was something overwhelming about the strange man's evident affliction that roused her out of her apathy; not much — she was still profoundly detached, observing from another world, as it were, this extreme heat and agitation, but at least she saw him now, she did with a faint curiosity consider him. He was like some elemental force in his directness. He had the quality of an irresistible natural phenomenon. But she did not move from her position at the gate, and her eyes continued, with the unwaveringness he thought so odd, to stare into his.

'I would gladly have let you come in,' she said, 'if you had come yesterday, but to-day my father died.'

Wemyss looked at her in astonishment. She had said it in as level and ordinary a voice as if she had been remarking, rather indifferently, on the weather.

Then he had a moment of insight. His own calamity had illuminated him. He who had never known pain, who had never let himself be worried, who had never let himself be approached in his life by a doubt, had for the last week lived in an atmosphere of worry and pain, and of what, if he allowed himself to think, to become morbid, might well grow into a most unfair, tormenting doubt. He understood, as he would not have understood a week ago, what her whole attitude, her rigidity meant. He stared at her a moment while she stared straight back at him, and then his big warm hands dropped on to the cold ones folded on the top bar of the gate, and he said, holding them firmly though they made no attempt to move, 'So that's it. So that's why. Now I know.'

And then he added, with the simplicity his own situation was putting into everything he did, 'That settles it. We two stricken ones must talk together.'

And still covering her hands with one of his, with the other he unlatched the gate and walked in.

2

There was a seat under a mulberry tree on the little lawn, with its back to the house and the gaping windows, and Wemyss, spying it out, led Lucy to it as if she were a child, holding her by the hand.

She went with him indifferently. What did it matter whether she sat under the mulberry tree or stood at the gate? This convulsed stranger — was he real? Was anything real? Let him tell her whatever it was he wanted to tell her, and she would listen, and get him his glass of water, and then he would go his way and by that time the women would have finished upstairs and she could be with her father again.

'I'll fetch the water,' she said when they got to the seat.

'No. Sit down,' said Wemyss.

She sat down. So did he, letting her hand go. It dropped on the seat, palm upwards, between them.

'It's strange our coming across each other like this,' he said, looking at her while she looked indifferently straight in front of her at the sun on the grass beyond the shade of the mulberry tree, at a mass of huge fuchsia bushes a little way off. 'I've been going through hell — and so must you have been. Good God, what hell! Do you mind if I tell you? You'll understand because of your own — '

Lucy didn't mind. She didn't mind anything. She merely vaguely wondered that he should think she had been going through hell. Hell and her darling father; how quaint it sounded. She began to suspect that she was asleep. All this wasn't really happening. Her father wasn't dead. Presently the housemaid would come in with the hot water and wake her to the usual cheerful day. The man sitting beside her — he seemed rather vivid for a dream, it was true; so detailed, with his flushed face and the perspiration on his forehead, besides the feel of his big warm hand a moment ago and the small puffs of heat that came from his clothes when he moved. But it was so unlikely . . . everything that had happened since breakfast was so *unlikely*. This man, too, would resolve himself soon into just something she had had for dinner last night, and she would tell her father about her dream at breakfast, and they would laugh.

She stirred uneasily. It wasn't a dream. It was real.

'The story is unbelievably horrible,' Wemyss was saying in a high aggrievement, looking at her little head with the straight cut hair, and her grave profile. How old was she? Eighteen? Twenty-eight? Impossible to tell exactly with hair cut like that, but young anyhow compared to him; very young perhaps compared to him who was well over forty, and so much scarred, so deeply scarred, by this terrible thing that had happened to him.

'It's so horrible that I wouldn't talk about it if you were going to mind,' he went on, 'but you can't mind because you're a stranger, and it may help you with your own trouble, because whatever you may suffer I'm suffering much worse, so then you'll see yours isn't so bad. And besides I must talk to some one or I should go mad — '

This was certainly a dream, thought Lucy. Things didn't happen like this when one was awake — grotesque things.

She turned her head and looked at him. No, it wasn't a dream. No dream could be so solid as the man beside her. What was he saying?

He was saying in a tormented voice that he was Wemyss.

'You are Wemyss,' she repeated gravely.

It made no impression on her. She didn't

mind his being Wemyss.

'I'm the Wemyss the newspapers were full of last week,' he said, seeing that the name left her unmoved. 'My God,' he went on, again wiping his forehead, but as fast as he wiped it more beads burst out, 'those posters to see one's own name staring at one everywhere on posters!'

'Why was your name on posters?' said Lucy.

She didn't want to know; she asked mechanically, her ear attentive only to the sounds from the open windows of the room upstairs.

'Don't you read newspapers here?' was his answer.

'I don't think we do,' she said, listening. 'We've been settling in. I don't think we've remembered to order any newspapers yet.'

A look of some, at any rate, relief from the pressure he was evidently struggling under came into Wemyss's face. 'Then I can tell you the real version,' he said, 'without you're being already filled up with the monstrous suggestions that were made at the inquest. As though I hadn't suffered enough as it was! As though it hadn't been terrible enough already — '

'The inquest?' repeated Lucy.

Again she turned her head and looked at

15

him. 'Has your trouble anything to do with death?'

'Why, you don't suppose anything else would reduce me to the state I'm in?'

'Oh, I'm sorry,' she said; and into her eyes and into her voice came a different expression, something living, something gentle. 'I hope it wasn't anybody you — loved?'

'It was my wife,' said Wemyss.

He got up quickly, so near was he to crying at the thought of it, at the thought of all he had endured, and turned his back on her and began stripping the leaves off the branches above his head.

Lucy watched him, leaning forward a little on both hands. 'Tell me about it,' she said presently, very gently.

He came back and dropped down heavily beside her again, and with many interjections of astonishment that such a ghastly calamity could have happened to him, to him who till now had never —

'Yes,' said Lucy, comprehendingly and gravely, 'yes — I know — '

— had never had anything to do with — well, with calamities, he told her the story.

They had gone down, he and his wife, as they did every 25th of July, for the summer to their house on the river, and he had been

16

looking forward to a glorious time of peaceful doing nothing after months of London, just lying about in a punt and reading and smoking and resting — London was an awful place for tiring one out — and they hadn't been there twenty-four hours before his wife — before his wife —

The remembrance of it was too grievous to him. He couldn't go on.

'Was she — very ill?' asked Lucy gently, to give him time to recover. 'I think that would almost be better. One would be a little, at least one would be a little prepared — '

'She wasn't ill at all,' cried Wemyss. 'She just — died.'

'Oh like father!' exclaimed Lucy, roused now altogether. It was she now who laid her hand on his.

Wemyss seized it between both his, and went on quickly.

He was writing letters, he said, in the library at his table in the window where he could see the terrace and the garden and the river; they had had tea together only an hour before; there was a flagged terrace along that side of the house, the side the library was on and all the principal rooms; and all of a sudden there was a great flash of shadow between him and the light; come and gone instantaneously; and instantaneously then

17

there was a thud; he would never forget it, that thud; and there outside his window on the flags —

'Oh don't — oh don't — ' gasped Lucy.

'It was my wife,' Wemyss hurried on, not able now to stop, looking at Lucy while he talked with eyes of amazed horror. 'Fallen out of the top room of the house her sitting-room because of the view — it was in a straight line with the library window — she dropped past my window like a stone — she was smashed — smashed — '

'Oh, don't — oh — '

'Now can you wonder at the state I'm in?' he cried. 'Can you wonder if I'm nearly off my head? And forced to be by myself — forced into retirement for what the world considers a proper period of mourning, with nothing to think of but that ghastly inquest.'

He hurt her hand, he gripped it so hard.

'If you hadn't let me come and talk to you,' he said, 'I believe I'd have pitched myself over the cliff there this afternoon and made an end of it.'

'But how — but why — how could she fall?' whispered Lucy, to whom poor Wemyss's misfortune seemed more frightful than anything she had ever heard of.

She hung on his words, her eyes on his face, her lips parted, her whole body an agony of sympathy. Life — how terrible it was, and how unsuspected. One went on and on, never dreaming of the sudden dreadful day when the coverings were going to be dropped and one would see it was death after all, that it had been death all the time, death pretending, death waiting. Her father, so full of love and interests and plans — gone, finished, brushed away as if he no more mattered than some insect one unseeingly treads on as one walks; and this man's wife, dead in an instant, dead so far more cruelly, so horribly . . .

'I had often told her to be careful of that window,' Wemyss answered in a voice that almost sounded like anger; but all the time his tone had been one of high anger at the wanton, outrageous cruelty of fate. 'It was a very low one, and the floor was slippery. Oak. Every floor in my house is polished oak. I had them put in myself. She must have been leaning out and her feet slipped away behind her. That would make her fall head foremost — '

'Oh — oh — ' said Lucy, shrinking. What could she do, what could she say to help him, to soften at least these dreadful memories?

'And then,' Wemyss went on after a moment, as unaware as Lucy was that she was tremblingly stroking his hand, 'at the inquest, as though it hadn't all been awful enough for me already, the jury must actually get wrangling about the cause of death.'

'The cause of death?' echoed Lucy. 'But — she fell.'

'Whether it were an accident or done on purpose.'

'Done on — ?'

'Suicide.'

'Oh — '

She drew in her breath quickly.

'But — it wasn't?'

'How could it be? She was my wife, without a care in the world, everything done for her, no troubles, nothing on her mind, nothing wrong with her health. We had been married fifteen years, and I was devoted to her — devoted to her.'

He banged his knee with his free hand. His voice was full of indignant tears.

'Then why did the jury — '

'My wife had a fool of a maid — I never could stand that woman — and it was something she said at the inquest, some invention or other about what my wife had said to her. You know what servants are. It upset some of the jury. You know juries are made up of anybody and everybody — butcher, baker, and candle-stick-maker — quite uneducated most of them, quite at the mercy of any suggestion. And so instead of a verdict of death by misadventure, which would have been the right one, it was an open verdict.'

'Oh, how terrible — how terrible for you,' breathed Lucy, her eyes on his, her mouth twitching with sympathy.

'You'd have seen all about it if you had read the papers last week,' said Wemyss, more quietly. It had done him good to get it out and talked over.

He looked down at her upturned face with its horror-stricken eyes and twitching mouth. 'Now tell me about yourself,' he said, touched with compunction; nothing that had happened to her could be so horrible as what had happened to him, still she too was newly smitten, they had met on a common ground of disaster, Death himself had been their introducer.

'Is life all — only death?' she breathed, her horror-stricken eyes on his.

Before he could answer — and what was there to answer to such a question except that of course it wasn't, and he and she were just victims of a monstrous special unfairness — he certainly was; her father had probably died as fathers did, in the usual way in his bed — before he could answer, the two women came out of the house, and with small discreet steps proceeded down the path to the

21

gate. The sun flooded their spare figures and their decent black clothes, clothes kept for these occasions as a mark of respectful sympathy.

One of them saw Lucy under the mulberry tree and hesitated, and then came across the grass to her with the mincing steps of tact.

'Here's somebody coming to speak to you,' said Wemyss, for Lucy was sitting with her back to the path.

She started and looked round.

The woman approached hesitatingly, her head on one side, her hands folded, her face pulled into a little smile intended to convey encouragement and pity.

'The gentleman's quite ready, miss,' she said softly.

3

All that day and all the next day Wemyss was Lucy's tower of strength and rock of refuge. He did everything that had to be done of the business part of death — that extra wantonness of misery thrown in so grimly to finish off the crushing of a mourner who is alone. It is true the doctor was kind and ready to help, but he was a complete stranger; she had never seen him till he was fetched that dreadful morning; and he had other things to see to besides her affairs — his own patients, scattered widely over a lonely countryside. Wemyss had nothing to see to. He could concentrate entirely on Lucy. And he was her friend, linked to her so strangely and so strongly by death. She felt she had known him for ever. She felt that since the beginning of time she and he had been advancing hand in hand towards just this place, towards just this house and garden, towards just this year, this August, this moment of existence.

Wemyss dropped quite naturally into the place a near male relative would have been in if there had been a near male relative within reach; and his relief at having something to do, something practical and immediate, was so immense that never were funeral arrangements made with greater zeal and energy — really one might almost say with greater gusto. Fresh from the horrors of those other funeral arrangements, clouded as they had been by the silences of friends and the averted looks of neighbours — all owing to the idiotic jurors and their hesitations, and the vindictiveness of that woman because, he concluded, he had refused to raise her wages the previous month — what he was arranging now was so simple and straightforward that it positively was a pleasure. There were no anxieties, there were no worries, and there was a grateful little girl. After each fruitful visit to the undertaker, and he paid several in his zeal, he came back to Lucy and she was grateful; and she was not only grateful, but very obviously glad to get him back.

He saw she didn't like it when he went away, off along the top of the cliff on his various business visits, purpose in each step, a different being from the indignantly miserable person who had dragged about that very cliff killing time such a little while before; he could see she didn't like it. She knew he had to go, she was grateful and immensely expressive of her gratitude — Wemyss thought he had never met any one so expressively grateful — that he should so diligently go, but she didn't like it. He saw she didn't like it; he saw that she clung to him; and it pleased him.

'Don't be long,' she murmured each time, looking at him with eyes of entreaty; and when he got back, and stood before her again mopping his forehead, having triumphantly advanced the funeral arrangements another stage, a faint colour came into her face and she had the relieved eyes of a child who has been left alone in the dark and sees its mother coming in with a candle. Vera usedn't to look like that. Vera had accepted everything he did for her as a matter of course.

Naturally he wasn't going to let the poor little girl sleep alone in that house with a dead body, and the strange servants who had been hired together with the house and knew nothing either about her or her father probably getting restive as night drew on, and as likely as not bolting to the village; so he fetched his things from the primitive hotel down in the cove about seven o'clock and announced his intention of sleeping on the drawing-room sofa. He had lunched with her, and had had tea with her, and now was going to dine with her. What she would have done without him Wemyss couldn't think.

He felt he was being delicate and tactful in

this about the drawing-room sofa. He might fairly have claimed the spare-room bed; but he wasn't going to take any advantage, not the smallest, of the poor little girl's situation. The servants, who supposed him to be a relation and had supposed him to be that from the first moment they saw him, big and middle-aged, holding the young lady's hand under the mulberry tree, were surprised at having to make up a bed in the drawing-room when there were two spare-rooms with beds already in them upstairs, but did so obediently, vaguely imagining it had something to do with watchfulness and French windows; and Lucy, when he told her he was going to stay the night, was so grateful, so really thankful, that her eyes, red from the waves of grief that had engulfed her at intervals during the afternoon — ever since, that is, the sight of her dead father lying so remote from her, so wrapped, it seemed, in a deep, absorbed attentiveness, had unfrozen her and swept her away into a sea of passionate weeping — filled again with tears.

'Oh,' she murmured, 'how *good* you are — '

It was Wemyss who had done all the thinking for her, and in the spare moments between his visits to the undertaker about the arrangements, and to the doctor about the certificate, and to the vicar about the burial, had telegraphed to her only existing relative, an aunt, had sent the obituary notice to *The Times*, and had even reminded her that she had on a blue frock and asked if she hadn't better put on a black one; and now this last instance of his thoughtfulness overwhelmed her.

She had been dreading the night, hardly daring to think of it so much did she dread it; and each time he had gone away on his errands, through her heart crept the thought of what it would be like when dusk came and he went away for the last time and she would be alone, all alone in the silent house, and upstairs that strange, wonderful, absorbed thing that used to be her father, and whatever happened to her, whatever awful horror overcame her in the night, whatever danger, he wouldn't hear, he wouldn't know, he would still lie there content, content . . .

'How *good* you are!' she said to Wemyss, her red eyes filling. 'What would I have done without you?'

'But what would I have done without *you*?' he answered; and they stared at each other, astonished at the nature of the bond between them, at its closeness, at the way it seemed almost miraculously to have been arranged that they should meet on the crest of despair and save each other.

Till long after the stars were out they sat together on the edge of the cliff, Wemyss smoking while he talked, in a voice subdued by the night and the silence and the occasion, of his life and of the regular healthy calm with which it had proceeded till a week ago. Why this calm should have been interrupted, and so cruelly, he couldn't imagine. It wasn't as if he had deserved it. He didn't know that a man could ever be justified in saying he had done good, but he, Wemyss, could at least fairly say that he hadn't done any one any harm.

'Oh, but you have done good,' said Lucy, her voice, too, dropped into more than ordinary gentleness by the night, the silence, and the occasion; besides which it vibrated with feeling, it was lovely with seriousness, with simple conviction. 'Always, always I know that you've been doing good,' she said, 'being kind. I can't imagine you anything else but a help to people and a comfort.'

And Wemyss said, Well, he had done his best and tried, and no man could say more, but judging from what — well, what people had said to him, it hadn't been much of a success sometimes, and often and often he had been hurt, deeply hurt, by being misunderstood.

And Lucy said, How was it possible to misunderstand him, to misunderstand any one so transparently good, so evidently kind?

And Wemyss said, Yes, one would think he was easy enough to understand; he was a very natural, simple sort of person, who had only all his life asked for peace and quiet. It wasn't much to ask. Vera —

'Who is Vera?' asked Lucy.

'My wife.'

'Ah, don't,' said Lucy earnestly, taking his hand very gently in hers. 'Don't talk of that to-night, please don't let yourself think of it. If I could only, only find the words that would comfort you — '

And Wemyss said that she didn't need words, that just her being there, being with him, letting him help her, and her not having been mixed up with anything before in his life, was enough.

'Aren't we like two children,' he said, his voice, like hers, deepened by feeling, 'two scared, unhappy children, clinging to each other alone in the dark.'

So they talked on in subdued voices as people do who are in some holy place, sitting close together, looking out at the starlit sea, darkness and coolness gathering round them, and the grass smelling sweetly after the hot day, and the little waves, such a long way down, lapping lazily along the shingle, till Wemyss said it must be long past bedtime, and she, poor girl, must badly need rest.

'How old are you?' he asked suddenly, turning to her and scrutinising the delicate faint outline of her face against the night.

'Twenty-two,' said Lucy.

'You might just as easily be twelve,' he said, 'except for the sorts of things you say.'

'It's my hair,' said Lucy. 'My father liked — he liked — '

'Don't,' said Wemyss, in his turn taking her hand. 'Don't cry again. Don't cry any more to-night. Come — we'll go in. It's time you were in bed.'

And he helped her up, and when they got into the light of the hall he saw that she had, this time, successfully strangled her tears.

'Good-night,' she said, when he had lit her candle for her, 'good-night, and — God bless you.'

'God bless *you*,' said Wemyss solemnly, holding her hand in his great warm grip.

'He has,' said Lucy. 'Indeed He has already, in sending me you.' And she smiled up at him.

For the first time since he had known her — and he too had the feeling that he had known her ever since he could remember — he saw her smile, and the difference it made to her marred, stained face surprised him.

'Do that again,' he said, staring at her, still holding her hand.

'Do what?' asked Lucy.

'Smile,' said Wemyss.

Then she laughed; but the sound of it in the silent, brooding house was shocking.

'*Oh*,' she gasped, stopping short, hanging her head appalled by what it had sounded like.

'Remember you're to go to sleep and not think of anything,' Wemyss ordered as she went slowly upstairs.

And she did fall asleep at once, exhausted but protected, like some desolate baby that had cried itself sick and now had found its mother.

4

All this, however, came to an end next day
when towards evening Miss Entwhistle,
Lucy's aunt, arrived.

Wemyss retired to his hotel again and did
not reappear till next morning, giving Lucy
time to explain him; but either the aunt was
inattentive, as she well might be under the
circumstances in which she found herself so
suddenly, so lamentably placed, or Lucy's
explanations were vague, for Miss Entwhistle
took Wemyss for a friend of her dear Jim's,
one of her dear, dear brother's many friends,
and accepted his services as natural and
himself with emotion, warmth, and reminis-
cences.

Wemyss immediately became her rock as
well as Lucy's, and she in her turn clung to
him. Where he had been clung to by one he
was now clung to by two, which put an end to
talk alone with Lucy. He did not see Lucy
alone again once before the funeral, but at
least, owing to Miss Entwhistle's inability to
do without him, he didn't have to spend any
more solitary hours. Except breakfast, he had
all his meals up in the little house on the cliff,

and in the evenings smoked his pipe under the mulberry tree till bedtime sent him away, while Miss Entwhistle in the darkness gently and solemnly reminisced, and Lucy sat silent, as close to him as she could get.

The funeral was hurried on by the doctor's advice, but even so the short notice and the long distance did not prevent James Entwhistle's friends from coming to it. The small church down in the cove was packed; the small hotel bulged with concerned, grave-faced people. Wemyss, who had done everything and been everything, disappeared in this crowd. Nobody noticed him. None of James Entwhistle's friends happened — luckily, he felt, with last week's newspapers still fresh in the public mind — to be his. For twenty-four hours he was swept entirely away from Lucy by this surge of mourners, and at the service in the church could only catch a distant glimpse, from his seat by the door, of her bowed head in the front pew.

He felt very lonely again. He wouldn't have stayed in the church a minute, for he objected with a healthy impatience to the ceremonies of death, if it hadn't been that he regarded himself as the stage-manager, so to speak, of these particular ceremonies, and that it was in a peculiarly intimate sense his funeral. He took a pride in it. Considering the shortness of the time it really was a remarkable achievement, the way he had done it, the smooth way the whole thing was going. But to-morrow — what would happen to-morrow, when all these people had gone away again? Would they take Lucy and the aunt with them? Would the house up there be shut, and he, Wemyss, left alone again with his bitter, miserable recollections? He wouldn't, of course, stay on in that place if Lucy were to go, but wherever he went there would be emptiness without her, without her gratefulness, and gentleness, and clinging. Comforting and being comforted — that is what he and she had been doing to each other for four days, and he couldn't but believe she would feel the same emptiness without him that he knew he was going to feel without her.

In the dark under the mulberry tree, while her aunt talked softly and sadly of the past, Wemyss had sometimes laid his hand on Lucy's, and she had never taken hers away. They had sat there, content and comforted to be hand in hand. She had the trust in him, he felt, of a child; the confidence, and the knowledge that she was safe. He was proud and touched to know it, and it warmed him through and through to see how her face lit up whenever he appeared. Vera's face hadn't done that. Vera had never understood him, not with fifteen years to do it in, as this girl had in half a day. And the way Vera had died — it was no use mincing matters when it came to one's own thoughts, and it had been all of a piece with her life: the disregard for others and of anything said to her for her own good, the determination to do what suited her, to lean out of dangerous windows if she wished to, for instance, not to take the least trouble, the least thought . . . Imagine bringing such horror on him, such unforgettable horror, besides worries and unhappiness without end, by deliberately disregarding his warnings, his orders indeed, about that window. Wemyss did feel that if one looked at the thing dispassionately it would be difficult to find indifference to the wishes and feelings of others going further.

Sitting in the church during the funeral service, his arms folded on his chest and his mouth grim with these thoughts, he suddenly caught sight of Lucy's face. The priest was coming down the aisle in front of the coffin on the way out to the grave, and Lucy and her aunt were following first behind it.

Man that is born of a woman hath but a short time to live, and is full of misery. He cometh up, and is cut down, like a flower; he fleeth as it were a shadow, and never continueth in one stay . . .

The priest's sad, disillusioned voice recited the beautiful words as he walked, the afternoon sun from the west window and the open west door pouring on his face and on the faces of the procession that seemed all black and white — black clothes, white faces.

The whitest face was Lucy's, and when Wemyss saw the look on it his mouth relaxed and his heart went soft within him, and he came impulsively out of the shadow and joined her, boldly walking on her other side at the head of the procession, and standing beside her at the grave; and at the awful moment when the first earth was dropped on to the coffin he drew her hand, before everybody, through his arm and held it there tight.

Nobody was surprised at his standing there with her like that. It was taken quite for granted. He was evidently a relation of poor Jim's. Nor was anybody surprised when Wemyss, not letting her go again, took her home up the cliff, her arm in his just as though he were the chief mourner, the aunt following with some one else.

He didn't speak to her or disturb her with any claims on her attention, partly because the path was very steep and he wasn't used to cliffs, but also because of his feeling that he and she, isolated together by their sorrows, understood without any words. And when they reached the house, the first to reach it from the church just as if, he couldn't help thinking, they were coming back from their wedding, he told her in his firmest voice to go straight up to her room and lie down, and she obeyed with the sweet obedience of perfect trust.

'Who is that?' asked the man who was helping Miss Entwhistle up the cliff.

'Oh, a very old friend of darling Jim's,' she sobbed — she had been sobbing without stopping from the first words of the burial service, and was quite unable to leave off. 'Mr. — Mr. — We — We — Wemyss — '

'Wemyss? I don't remember coming across him with Jim.'

'Oh, one of his — his *oldest* — f — fr — friends,' sobbed poor Miss Entwhistle, got completely out of control.

Wemyss, continuing in his rôle of chief mourner, was the only person who was asked to spend the evening up at the bereaved house.

'I don't wonder,' said Miss Entwhistle to him at dinner, still with tears in her voice, 'at my dear brother's devotion to you. You have been the greatest help, the greatest com-fort — '

And neither Wemyss nor Lucy felt equal to explanation.

What did it matter? Lucy, fatigued by emotions, her mind bruised by the violent demands that had been made on it the last four days, sat drooping at the table, and merely thought that if her father had known Wemyss it would certainly have been true that he was devoted to him. He hadn't known him; he had missed him by — yes, by just three hours; and this wonderful friend of hers was the very first good thing that she and her father hadn't shared. And Wemyss's attitude was simply that if people insist on jumping at conclusions, why, let them. He couldn't anyhow begin to expound himself in the middle of a meal, with a parlourmaid handing dishes round and listening.

But there was an awkward little moment when Miss Entwhistle tearfully wondered — she was eating blanc-mange, the last of a series of cold and pallid dishes with which the imaginative cook, a woman of Celtic origin, had expressed her respectful appreciation of the occasion — whether when the will was read it wouldn't be found that Jim had appointed Mr. Wemyss poor Lucy's guardian.

'I am — dear me, how very hard it is to remember to say I was — my dear brother's only relative. We belong — belonged — to an exiguous family, and naturally I'm no longer as young as I was. There is only — was only — a year between Jim and me, and at any moment I may be — '

Here Miss Entwhistle was interrupted by a sob, and had to put down her spoon.

' — taken,' she finished after a moment, during which the other two sat silent.

'When this happens,' she went on presently, a little recovered, 'poor Lucy will be without any one, unless Jim thought of this and has appointed a guardian. You, Mr. Wemyss, I hope and expect.'

Neither Lucy nor Wemyss spoke. There was the parlourmaid hovering, and one couldn't anyhow go into explanations now which ought to have been made four days ago.

A dead-white cheese was handed round — something local probably, for it wasn't any form of cheese with which Wemyss was acquainted, and the meal ended with cups of intensely black cold coffee. And all these carefully thought-out expressions of the cook's sympathy were lost on the three, who noticed nothing; certainly they noticed nothing in the way the cook had intended. Wemyss was privately a little put out by the coffee being cold. He had eaten all the other clammy things patiently, but a man likes his after-dinner coffee hot, and it was new in his experience to have it served cold. He did notice this, and was surprised that neither of his companions appeared to. But there — women were notoriously insensitive to food; on this point the best of them were unintelligent, and the worst of them were impossible. Vera had been awful about it; he had had to do all the ordering of the meals himself at last, and also the engaging of the cooks.

He got up from the table to open the door for the ladies feeling inwardly chilled, feeling, as he put it to himself, slabby inside; and, left alone with a dish of black plums and some sinister-looking wine in a decanter, which he avoided because when he took hold of it ice clinked, he rang the bell as unobtrusively as he could and asked the parlourmaid in a subdued voice, the French window to the garden being open and in the garden being Lucy and her aunt, whether there were such a thing in the house as a whisky and soda.

The parlourmaid, who was a nice-looking girl and much more at home, as she herself was the first to admit, with gentlemen than with ladies, brought it him, and inquired how he had liked the dinner.

'Not at all,' said Wemyss, whose mind on that point was clear.

'No sir,' said the parlourmaid, nodding

sympathetically. 'No sir.'

She then explained in a discreet whisper, also with one eye on the open window, how the dinner hadn't been an ordinary dinner and it wasn't expected that it should be enjoyed, but it was the cook's tribute to her late master's burial day — a master they had only known a week, sad to say, but to whom they had both taken a great fancy, he being so pleasant-spoken and all for giving no trouble.

Wemyss listened, sipping the comforting drink and smoking a cigar.

Very different, said the parlourmaid, who seemed glad to talk, would the dinner have been if the cook hadn't liked the poor gentleman. Why, in one place where she and the cook were together, and the lady was taken just as the cook would have given notice if she hadn't been because she was such a very dishonest and unpunctual lady, besides not knowing her place — no lady, of course, and never was — when she was taken, not sudden like this poor gentleman but bit by bit, on the day of her funeral the cook sent up a dinner you'd never think of — she was like that, all fancy. Lucky it was that the family didn't read between the lines, for it began with fried soles —

The parlourmaid paused, her eye anxiously on the window. Wemyss sat staring at her.

'Did you say fried soles?' he asked, staring at her.

'Yes sir. Fried soles. I didn't see anything in that either at first. It's how you spell it makes the difference, Cook said. And the next course was' — her voice dropped almost to inaudibleness — 'devilled bones.'

Wemyss hadn't so much as smiled for nearly a fortnight, and now to his horror, for what could it possibly sound like to the two mourners on the lawn, he gave a sudden dreadful roar of laughter. He could hear it sounding hideous himself.

The noise he made horrified the parlour-maid as much as it did him. She flew to the window and shut it. Wemyss, in his effort to strangle the horrid thing, choked and coughed, his table-napkin up to his face, his body contorted. He was very red, and the parlourmaid watched him in terror. He had seemed at first to be laughing, though what Uncle Wemyss (thus did he figure in the conversations of the kitchen) could see to laugh at in the cook's way of getting her own back, the parlourmaid, whose flesh had crept when she first heard the story, couldn't understand; but presently she feared he wasn't laughing at all but was being, in some very robust way, ill. Dread seized her, deaths being on her mind, lest perhaps here in the chair, so convulsively struggling behind a table-napkin, were the beginnings of yet another corpse. Having flown to shut the window she now flew to open it, and ran out panic-stricken into the garden to fetch the ladies.

This cured Wemyss. He got up quickly, leaving his half-smoked cigar and his half-drunk whisky, and followed her out just in time to meet Lucy and her aunt hurrying across the lawn towards the dining-room window.

'I choked,' he said, wiping his eyes, which indeed were very wet.

'Choked?' repeated Miss Entwhistle anxiously. 'We heard a most strange noise — '

'That was me choking,' said Wemyss. 'It's all right — it's nothing at all,' he added to Lucy, who was looking at him with a face of extreme concern.

But he felt now that he had had about as much of the death and funeral atmosphere as he could stand. Reaction had set in, and his reactions were strong. He wanted to get away from woe, to be with normal, cheerful people again, to have done with conditions in which a laugh was the most improper of sounds. Here he was, being held down by the head, he felt, in a black swamp — first that ghastly business of Vera's, and now this

43

woebegone family.

Sudden and violent was Wemyss's reaction, let loose by the parlourmaid's story. Miss Entwhistle's swollen eyes annoyed him. Even Lucy's pathetic face made him impatient. It was against nature, all this. It shouldn't be allowed to go on, it oughtn't to be encouraged. Heaven alone knew how much he had suffered, how much more he had suffered than the Entwhistles with their perfectly normal sorrow, and if he could feel it was high time now to think of other things surely the Entwhistles could. He was tired of funerals. He had carried this one through really brilliantly from start to finish, but now it was over and done with, and he wished to get back to naturalness. Death seemed to him highly unnatural. The mere fact that it only happened once to everybody showed how exceptional it was, thought Wemyss, thoroughly disgusted with it. Why couldn't he and the Entwhistles go off somewhere to-morrow, away from this place altogether, go abroad for a bit, to somewhere cheerful, where nobody knew them and nobody would expect them to go about with long faces all day? Ostend, for instance? His mood of sympathy and gentleness had for the moment quite gone. He was indignant that there should be circumstances under which a man felt as guilty over a laugh as over a crime. A natural person like himself looked at things whole-somely. It was healthy and proper to forget horrors, to dismiss them from one's mind. If convention, that offspring of cruelty and hypocrisy, insisted that one's misfortunes should be well rubbed in, that one should be forced to smart under them, and that the more one was seen to wince the more one was regarded as behaving creditably — if convention insisted on this, and it did insist, as Wemyss had been experiencing himself since Vera's accident, why then it ought to be defied. He had found he couldn't defy it by himself, and came away solitary and wretched in accordance with what it expected, but he felt quite different now that he had Lucy and her aunt as trusting friends who looked up to him, who had no doubts of him and no criticisms. Health of mind had come back to him — his own natural wholesomeness, which had never deserted him in his life till this shocking business of Vera's.

'I'd like to have some sensible talk with you,' he said, looking down at the two small black figures and solemn tired faces that were growing dim and wraith-like in the failing light of the garden.

'With me or with Lucy?' asked Miss Entwhistle.

By this time they both hung on his possible wishes, and watched him with the devout attentiveness of a pair of dogs.

'With you and with Lucy,' said Wemyss, smiling at the upturned faces. He felt very conscious of being the male, of being in command.

It was the first time he had called her Lucy. To Miss Entwhistle it seemed a matter of course, but Lucy herself flushed with pleasure, and again had the feeling of being taken care of and safe. Sad as she was at the end of that sad day, she still was able to notice how nice her very ordinary name sounded in this kind man's voice. She wondered what his own name was, and hoped it was something worthy of him — not Albert, for instance.

'Shall we go into the drawing-room?' asked Miss Entwhistle.

'Why not to the mulberry tree?' said Wemyss, who naturally wished to hold Lucy's little hand if possible, and could only do that in the dark.

So they sat there as they had sat other nights, Wemyss in the middle, and Lucy's hand, when it got dark enough, held close and comfortingly in his.

'This little girl,' he began, 'must get the roses back into her cheeks.'

'Indeed, indeed she must,' agreed Miss Entwhistle, a catch in her voice at the mere reminder of the absence of Lucy's roses, and consequently of what had driven them away.

'How do you propose to set about it?' asked Wemyss.

'Time,' gulped Miss Entwhistle.

'Time?'

'And patience. We must wait we must both wait p-patiently till time has s-softened — '

She hastily pulled out her handkerchief.

'No, no,' said Wemyss, 'I don't at all agree. It isn't natural, it isn't reasonable to prolong sorrow. You'll forgive plain words, Miss Entwhistle, but I don't know any others, and I say it isn't right to wallow — yes, wallow — in sorrow. Far from being patient one should be impatient. One shouldn't wait resignedly for time to help one, one should up and take time by the forelock. In cases of this kind, and believe me I know what I'm talking about' — it was here that his hand, the one on the further side from Miss Entwhistle, descended gently on Lucy's, and she made a little movement closer up to him — 'it is due to oneself to refuse to be knocked out. Courage, spirit, is what one must aim at — setting an example.'

Ah, how wonderful he was, thought Lucy; so big, so brave, so simple, and so tragically recently himself the victim of the most awful of catastrophes. There was something burly about his very talk. Her darling father and his friends had talked quite differently. Their talk used to seem as if it ran about the room like liquid fire, it was so quick and shining; often it was quite beyond her till her father afterwards, when she asked him, explained it, put it more simply for her, eager as he always was that she should share and understand. She could understand every word of Wemyss's. When he spoke she hadn't to strain, to listen with all her might; she hardly had to think at all. She found this immensely reposeful in her present state.

'Yes,' murmured Miss Entwhistle into her handkerchief, 'yes — you're quite right, Mr. Wemyss — one ought — it would be more — more heroic. But then if one — if one has loved some one very tenderly — as I did my dear brother — and Lucy her most precious father — '

She broke off and wiped her eyes.

'Perhaps,' she finished, 'you haven't ever loved anybody very — very particularly and lost them.'

'Oh,' breathed Lucy at that, and moved still closer to him.

Wemyss was deeply injured. Why should Miss Entwhistle suppose he had never particularly loved anybody? He seemed, on looking back, to have loved a great deal. Certainly he had loved Vera with the utmost devotion till she herself wore it down. He indignantly asked himself what this maiden lady could know of love.

But there was Lucy's little hand, so clinging, so understanding, nestling in his. It soothed him.

There was a pause. Then he said, very gravely, 'My wife died only a fortnight ago.'

Miss Entwhistle was crushed. 'Ah,' she cried, 'but you must forgive me — '

5

Nevertheless he was not able to persuade her to join him, with Lucy, in a trip abroad. She was tirelessly concerned to do and say everything she could that showed her deep sympathy with him in his loss — he had told her nothing beyond the bare fact, and she was not one to read about inquests — and her deep sense of obligation to him that he, labouring under so great a burden of sorrow of his own, should have helped them with such devotion and unselfishness in theirs; but she wouldn't go abroad. She was going, she said, to her little house in London with Lucy.

'What, in August?' exclaimed Wemyss.

Yes, they would be quiet there, and indeed they were both worn out and only wished for solitude.

'Then why not stay here?' asked Wemyss, who now considered Lucy's aunt selfish. 'This is solitary enough, in all conscience.'

No, they neither of them felt they could bear to stay in that house. Lucy must go to the place least connected in her mind with her father. Indeed, indeed it was best. She did so understand and appreciate Mr. Wemyss's wonderful and unselfish motives in suggesting the continent, but she and Lucy were in that state when the idea of an hotel and waiters and a band was simply impossible to them, and all they wished was to creep into the quiet and privacy of their own nest — 'Like wounded birds,' said poor Miss Entwhistle, looking up at him with much the piteous expression of a dog lifting an injured paw.

'It's very bad for Lucy to be encouraged to think she's a wounded bird,' said Wemyss, controlling his disappointment as best he could.

'You must come and see us in London and help us to feel heroic,' said Miss Entwhistle, with a watery smile.

'But I can come and see you much better and easier if you're here,' persisted Wemyss.

Miss Entwhistle, however, though watery, was determined. She refused to stay where she so conveniently was, and Wemyss now considered Lucy's aunt obstinate as well as selfish. Also he thought her very ungrateful. She had made use of him, and now was going to leave him, without apparently giving him a thought, in the lurch.

He was having a good deal of Miss Entwhistle, because during the two days that came after the funeral Lucy was practically invisible, engaged in collecting and packing

51

her father's belongings. Wemyss hung about the garden, not knowing when these activities mightn't suddenly cease and not wishing to miss her if she did come out, and Miss Entwhistle, who couldn't help Lucy in this — no one could help her in the heart-breaking work — naturally joined him.

He found these two days long. Miss Entwhistle felt there was a great bond between herself and him, and Wemyss felt there wasn't. When she said there was he had difficulty in not contradicting her. Not only, Miss Entwhistle felt, and also explained, was there the bond of their dear Jim, whom both she and Mr. Wemyss had so much loved, but there was this communion of sorrow — the loss of his wife, the loss of her brother, within the same fortnight.

Wemyss shut his mouth tight at this and said nothing.

How natural for her, feeling so sorry for him, feeling so grateful to him, when from a window during those two days she beheld him sitting solitary beneath the mulberry tree, to go down and sit there with him; how natural that, when he got up, made restless, she supposed, by his memories, and began to pace the lawn, she should get up and sympathetically pace it too. She could not let this kind, tender-hearted man — he must be that, or Jim wouldn't have been fond of him, besides she had seen it for herself in the way he had helped her and Lucy — she could not let him be alone with his sad thoughts. And he had a double burden of sad thoughts, a double loss to bear, for he had lost her dear brother as well as his poor wife.

All Entwhistles were compassionate, and as she and Wemyss sat together or together paced, she kept up a flow of gentle loving-kindness. Wemyss smoked his pipe in practically unbroken silence. This was his way when he was holding on to himself. Miss Entwhistle of course didn't know he was holding on to himself, and taking his silence for the inarticulateness of deep unhappiness was so much touched that she would have done anything for him, anything that might bring this poor, kind, suffering fellow-creature comfort — except go to Ostend. From that dreadful suggestion she continued to shudder away; nor, though he tried again, even after all arrangements for leaving Cornwall had been made, would she be persuaded to stay where she was.

Therefore Wemyss was forced to conclude that she was obstinate as well as selfish; and if it hadn't been for the brief moments at meals when Lucy appeared, and through her unhappiness — what she was doing was obviously depressing her very much — smiled faintly at him and always went and sat as near him as she could, he would have found these two days intolerable.

How atrocious, he thought, while he smoked in silence and held on to himself, that Lucy should be taken away from him by a mere maiden lady, an aunt, an unmarried aunt — weakest and most negligible, surely, of all relatives. How atrocious that such a person should have any right to come between him and Lucy, to say she wouldn't do this, that, or the other that Wemyss proposed, and thus possess the power to make him unhappy. Miss Entwhistle was so little that he could have brushed her aside with the back of one hand; yet here again the strong monster public opinion stepped in and forced him to acquiesce in any plan she chose to make for Lucy, however desolate it left him, merely because she stood to her in the anæmic relationship of aunt.

During two mortal days, as he waited about in that garden so grievously infested by Miss Entwhistle, sounds of boxes being moved and drawers being opened and shut came through the windows, but except at meals there was no Lucy. He could have borne it if he hadn't known they were the very last days he would be with her, but as things were it seemed cruel that he should be left like that to be miserable. Why should he be left like that to be miserable, just because of a lot of clothes and papers? he asked himself; and he felt he was getting thoroughly tired of Jim.

'Haven't you done yet?' he said at tea on the second afternoon of this sorting out and packing, when Lucy got up to go indoors again, leaving him with Miss Entwhistle, even before he had finished his second cup of tea.

'You've no idea what a lot there is,' she said, her voice sounding worn out; and she lingered a moment, her hand on the back of her aunt's chair. 'Father brought all his notes with him, and heaps and heaps of letters from people he was consulting, and I'm trying to get them straight — get them as he would have wished — '

Miss Entwhistle put up her hand and stroked Lucy's arm.

'If you weren't in this hurry to go away you'd have had more time and done it comfortably,' said Wemyss.

'Oh, but I don't want more time,' said Lucy quickly.

'Lucy means she couldn't bear it drawn out,' said Miss Entwhistle, leaning her thin cheek against Lucy's sleeve. 'These things — they tear one's heart. And nobody can help her. She has to go through with it alone.' And she drew Lucy's face down to hers and held it there a moment, gently stroking it, the tears brimming up again in the eyes of both.

Always tears, thought Wemyss. Yes, and there always would be tears as long as that aunt had hold of Lucy. She was the arch-wallower, he told himself, filling his pipe in silence after Lucy had gone in.

He got up and went out at the gate and crossed the road and stood staring at the evening sea. Should he hear steps coming after him and Miss Entwhistle were to follow him even beyond the garden, he would proceed without looking round down to the cove and to the inn, where she must needs leave him alone. He had had enough. That Miss Entwhistle should explain to him what Lucy meant, he considered to be the last straw of her behaviour. Barging in, he said indignantly to himself; barging in when nobody had asked her opinion or explanation of anything. And she had stroked Lucy's face as though Lucy and her face and everything about her belonged to her, merely because she happened to be her aunt. Fancy explaining to him what Lucy really meant, taking upon herself the functions of inter-preter, of go-between, when for a whole day and a half before she appeared on the scene

— and she had only appeared on it at all thanks to his telegram — Lucy and he had been in the closest fellowship, the closest communion . . .

Well, things couldn't go on like this. He was not the man to be dominated by a relative. If he had lived in those sensible ancient days when people behaved wholesomely, he would have flung Lucy over his shoulder and walked off with her to Ostend or Paris and laughed at such insects as aunts. He couldn't do that unfortunately, though where the harm would be in two mourners like himself and Lucy going together in search of relief he must say he was unable to see. Why should they be condemned to search for relief separately? Their sorrows, surely, would be their chaperone, especially his sorrow. Nobody would object to Lucy's nursing him, supposing he were dangerously ill; why should she not be equally beyond the reach of tongues if she nursed the bitter wounds of his spirit?

He heard steps coming down the garden path to the gate. There, he thought, was the aunt again, searching for him, and he stood squarely and firmly with his back to the road, smoking his pipe and staring at the sea. If he heard the gate open and she dared to come through it he would instantly walk away. In the garden he had to endure being joined by her, because there he was in the position of guest; but let her try to join him on the King's highway!

Nobody opened the gate, however, and, as he heard no retreating footsteps either, after a minute he began to want to look round. He struggled against this wish, because the moment Miss Entwhistle caught his eye she would come out to him, he felt sure. But Wemyss was not much good at struggling against his wishes — he usually met with defeat; and after briefly doing so on this occasion he did look round. And what a good thing he did, for it was Lucy.

There she was, leaning on the gate just as she had been that first morning, but this time her eyes instead of being wide and blank were watching him with a deep and touching interest.

He got across the road in one stride. 'Lucy!' he exclaimed. 'You? Why didn't you call me? We've wasted half an hour — '

'About two minutes,' she said, smiling up at him as he, on the other side of the gate, folded both her hands in his just as he had done that first morning; and the relief it was to Wemyss to see her again alone, to see that smile of trust and — surely — content in getting back to him!

Then her face went grave again. 'I've finished father's things now,' she said, 'and so I came to look for you.'

'Lucy, how can you leave me,' was Wemyss's answer to that, his voice vibrating, 'how can you go away from me to-morrow and hand me over again to the torments — yes, torments, I was in before?'

'But I have to go,' she said, distressed. 'And you mustn't say that. You mustn't let yourself be like that again. You won't be, I know — you're so brave and strong.'

'Not without you. I'm nothing without you,' said Wemyss; and his eyes, as he searched hers, were full of tears.

At this Lucy flushed, and then, staring at him, her face went slowly white. These words of his, the way he said them, reminded her — oh no, it wasn't possible; he and she stood in a relationship to each other like none, she was sure, that had ever yet been. It was an intimacy arrived at at a bound, with no preliminary steps. It was a holy thing, based on mutual grief, protected from everything ordinary by the great wings of Death. He was her wonderful friend, big in his simplicity, all care for her and goodness, a very rock of refuge and shelter in the wilderness she had been flung into when he found her. And that he, bleeding as he was himself from the lacerations of the violent rending asunder from his wife to whom he had been, as he had told her, devoted, that he should — oh no, it wasn't possible; and she hung her head, shocked at her thoughts. For the way he had said those words, and the words themselves had reminded her — no, she could hardly bear to think it, but they *had* reminded her of the last time she had been proposed to. The man — he was a young man; she had never been proposed to by any one even approximately Wemyss's age — had said almost exactly that: Without you I am nothing. And just in that same deep, vibrating voice.

How dreadful thoughts could be, Lucy said to herself, overcome that such a one at such a moment should thrust itself into her mind. Hateful of her, hateful . . .

She hung her head in shame; and Wemyss, looking down at the little bobbed head with its bright, thick young hair bent over their folded hands as though it were saying its prayers — Wemyss, not having his pipe in his mouth to protect him and help him to hold on to himself, for he had hastily stuffed it in his pocket, all alight as it was, when he saw her at the gate, and there at that moment it was burning holes — Wemyss, after a brief struggle with his wishes, in which as usual he was defeated, stooped and began to kiss

Lucy's hair. And having begun, he continued.

She was horrified. At the first kiss she started as if she had been hit, and then, clinging to the gate, she stood without moving, without being able to think or lift her head, in the same attitude bowed over his and her own hands, while this astonishing thing was being done to her hair. Death all round them, death pervading every corner of their lives, death in its blackest shape brooding over him, and — kisses. Her mind, if anything so gentle could be said to be in anything that sounds so loud, was in an uproar. She had had the complete, guileless trust in him of a child for a tender and sympathetic friend — a friend, not a father, though he was old enough to be her father, because in a father, however much hidden by sweet comradeship as it had been in hers, there always at the back of everything was, after all, authority. And it had been even more than the trust of a child in its friend: it had been the trust of a child in a fellow-child hit by the same punishment — a simple fellowship, a wordless understanding.

She hung on to the gate while her thoughts flew about in confusion within her. These kisses — and his wife just dead — and dead so terribly — how long would she have to stand there with this going on — she couldn't lift up her head, for then she felt it would only get worse — she couldn't turn and run into the house, because he was holding her hands. He oughtn't to have — oh, he oughtn't to have — it wasn't fair . . .

Then — what was he saying? She heard him say, in an absolutely broken voice, laying his head on hers, 'We two poor things — we two poor things' — and then he said and did nothing more, but kept his head like that, and presently, thick though her hair was, through it came wetness.

At that Lucy's thoughts suddenly stopped flying about and were quite still. Her heart went to wax within her, melted again into pity, into a great flood of pitiful understanding. The dreadfulness of lonely grief . . . Was there anything in the world so blackly desolate as to be left alone in grief? This poor broken fellow-creature — and she herself, so lost, so lost in loneliness — they were two half-drowned things, clinging together in a shipwreck — how could she let him go, leave him to himself — how could she be let go, left to herself . . .

'Lucy,' he said, 'look at me — '

She lifted her head. He loosed her hands, and put his arms round her shoulders.

'Look at me,' he said; for though she had lifted her head she hadn't lifted her eyes.

She looked at him. Tears were on his face. When she saw them her mouth began to quiver and twitch. She couldn't bear that.

'Lucy — ' he said again.

She shut her eyes. 'Yes' — she breathed, 'yes.' And with one hand she felt along up his coat till she reached his face, and shakingly tried to brush away its tears.

6

After that, for the moment anyhow, it was all over with Lucy. She was engulfed. Wemyss kissed her shut eyes, he kissed her parted lips, he kissed her dear, delightful bobbed hair. His tears dried up; or rather, wiped away by her little blind, shaking hand, there were no more of them. Death for Wemyss was indeed at that moment swallowed up in victory. Instantly he passed from one mood to the other, and when she finally did open her eyes at his orders and look at him, she saw bending over her a face she hardly recognised, for she had not yet seen him happy. Happy! How could he be happy, as happy as that all in a moment? She stared at him, and even through her confusion, her bewilderment, was frankly amazed.

Then the thought crept into her mind that it was she who had done this, it was she who had transformed him, and her stare softened into a gaze almost of awe, with something of the look in it of a young mother when she first sees her new-born baby. 'So that is what it is like,' the young mother whispers to herself in a sort of holy surprise, 'and I have made it, and it is mine'; and so, gazing at this new, effulgent Wemyss, did Lucy say to herself with the same feeling of wonder, of awe at her own handiwork, 'So that is what he is like.'

Wemyss's face was indeed one great beam. He simply at that moment couldn't remember that he had ever been miserable. He seemed to have his arms round Love itself; for never did any one look more like the very embodiment of his idea of love than Lucy then as she gazed up at him, so tender, so resistless. But there were even more wonderful moments after dinner in the darkening garden, while Miss Entwhistle was upstairs packing ready to start by the early train next morning, and they hadn't got the gate between them, and Lucy of her own accord laid her cheek against his coat, nestling her head into it as though there indeed she knew that she was safe.

'My baby — my baby,' Wemyss murmured, in an ecstasy of passionate protectiveness, in his turn flooded by maternal feeling. 'You shall never cry again never, never.'

It irked him that their engagement — Lucy demurred at first to the word engagement, but Wemyss, holding her tight in his arms, said he would very much like to know, then, by what word she would describe her position at that moment — it irked him that it had to be a secret. He wanted instantly to shout out to the whole world his glory and his pride. But this under the tragic circumstances of their mourning was even to Wemyss clearly impossible. Generally he brushed aside the word impossible if it tried to come between him and the smallest of his wishes, but that inquest was still too vividly in his mind, and the faces of his so-called friends. What the faces of his so-called friends would look like if he, before Vera had been dead a fortnight, should approach them with the news of his engagement even Wemyss, a person not greatly imaginative, could picture. And Lucy, quite overwhelmed, first by his tears and then by his joy, no longer could judge anything. She no longer knew whether it were very awful to be love-making in the middle of death, or whether it were, as Wemyss said, the natural glorious self-assertiveness of life. She knew nothing any more except that he and she, shipwrecked, had saved each other, and that for the moment nothing was required of her, no exertion, nothing at all, except to sit passive with her head on his breast, while he called her his baby and softly, wonderfully, kissed her closed eyes. She couldn't think; she needn't think; oh, she was tired — and this was rest.

But after he had gone that night, and all the next day in the train without him, and for the first few days in London, misgivings laid hold of her.

That she should be being made love to, be engaged, as Wemyss insisted, within a week of her father's death, could not, she thought, be called anything worse than possibly and at the outside an irrelevance. It did no harm to her father's dear memory; it in no way encroached on her adoration of him. He would have been the first to be pleased that she should have found comfort. But what worried her was that Everard — Wemyss's Christian name was Everard — should be able to think of such things as love and more marriage when his wife had just died so awfully, and he on the very spot, and he the first to rush out and see . . .

She found that the moment she was away from him she couldn't get over this. It went round and round in her head as a thing she was unable, by herself, to understand. While she was with him he overpowered her into a torpor, into a shutting of her eyes and her thoughts, into just giving herself up, after the shocks and agonies of the week, to the blessedness of a soothed and caressed semi-consciousness; and it was only when his first letters began to come, such simple, adoring letters, taking the situation just as it was, just as life and death between them had offered it, untroubled by questioning, undimmed by doubt, with no looking backward but with a touching, thankful acceptance of the present, that she gradually settled down into that placidity which was at once the relief and the astonishment of her aunt. And his letters were so easy to understand. They were so restfully empty of the difficult thoughts and subtle, half-said things her father used to write and all his friends. His very handwriting was the round, slow handwriting of a boy. Lucy had loved him before; but now she fell in love with him, and it was because of his letters.

7

Miss Entwhistle lived in a slim little house in Eaton Terrace. It was one of those little London houses where you go in and there's a dining-room, and you go up and there's a drawing-room, and you go up again and there's a bedroom and a dressing-room, and you go up yet more and there's a maid's room and a bathroom, and then that's all. For one person it was just enough; for two it was difficult. It was so difficult that Miss Entwhistle had never had any one stay with her before, and the dressing-room had to be cleared out of all her clothes and toques, which then had nowhere to go to and became objects that you met at night hanging over banisters or perched with an odd air of dashingness on the ends of the bath, before Lucy could go in.

But no Entwhistle ever minded things like that. No trouble seemed to any of them too great to take for a friend; while as for one's own dear niece, if only she could have been induced to take the real bedroom and let her aunt, who knew the dressing-room's ways, sleep there instead, that aunt — on such liberal principles was this family constructed — would have been perfectly happy.

Lucy, of course, only smiled at that suggestion, and inserted herself neatly into the dressing-room, and the first weeks of their mourning, which Miss Entwhistle had dreaded for them both, proceeded to flow by with a calm, an unruffledness, that could best be described by the word placid.

In that small house, unless the inhabitants were accommodating and adaptable, daily life would be a trial. Miss Entwhistle well knew Lucy would give no trouble that she could help, but their both being in such trouble themselves would, at such close quarters, she had been afraid, inevitably keep their sorrow raw by sheer rubbing against each other.

To her surprise and great relief nothing of the sort happened. There seemed to be no rawness to rub. Not only Lucy didn't fret — her white face and heavy eyes of the days in Cornwall had gone — but she was almost from the first placid. Just on leaving Cornwall, and for a day or two after, she was a little *bouleversée*, and had a curious kind of timidity in her manner to her aunt, and crept rather than walked about the house, but this gradually disappeared; and if Miss Entwhistle hadn't known her, hadn't known of her terrible loss, she would have said that here was some one who was quietly happy. It was subdued, but there it was, as if she had some private source of confidence and warmth. Had she by any chance got religion? wondered her aunt, who herself had never had it, and neither had Jim, and neither had any Entwhistles she had ever heard of. She dismissed that. It was too unlikely for one of their breed. But even the frequent necessary visits to the house in Bloomsbury she and her father had lived in so long didn't quite blot out the odd effect Lucy produced of being somehow inwardly secure. Presently, when these sad settlings up were done with, and the books and furniture stored, and the house handed over to the landlord, and she no longer had to go to it and be among its memories, her face became what it used to be — delicately coloured, softly rounded, ready to light up at a word, at a look.

Miss Entwhistle was puzzled. This serenity of the one who was, after all, chief mourner, made her feel it would be ridiculous if she outdid Lucy in grief. If Lucy could pull herself together so marvellously — and she supposed it must be that, it must be that she was heroically pulling herself together — she for her part wouldn't be behindhand. Her darling Jim's memory should be honoured, then, like this: she would bless God for him, bless God that she had had him, and in a high thankfulness continue cheerfully on her way.

Such were some of Miss Entwhistle's reflections and conclusions as she considered Lucy. She seemed to have no thought of the future — again to her aunt's surprise and relief, who had been afraid she would very soon begin to worry about what she was to do next. She never talked of it; she never apparently thought of it. She seemed to be — yes, that was the word, decided Miss Entwhistle observing her — resting. But resting on what? A second time Miss Entwhistle dismissed the idea of religion. Impossible, she thought, that Jim's girl — yet it did look very like religion.

There was, it appeared, enough money left scraped together by Jim for Lucy in case of his death to produce about two hundred pounds a year. This wasn't much; but Lucy apparently didn't give it a thought. Probably she didn't realise what it meant, thought her aunt, because of her life with her father having been so easy, surrounded by all those necessities for an invalid which were, in fact, to ordinary people luxuries. No one had been appointed her guardian. There was no mention of Mr. Wemyss in the will. It was a very short will, leaving everything to Lucy.

This, as far as it went, was admirable, thought Miss Entwhistle, but unfortunately there was hardly anything to leave. Except books; thousands of books, and the old charming furniture of the Bloomsbury house. Well, Lucy should live with her for as long as she could endure the dressing-room, and perhaps they might take a house together a little less tiny, though Miss Entwhistle had lived in the one she was in for so long that it wouldn't be very easy for her to leave it.

Meanwhile the first weeks of mourning slid by in an increasing serenity, with London empty and no one to intrude on what became presently distinctly recognisable as happiness. She and Lucy agreed so perfectly. And they weren't altogether alone either, for Mr. Wemyss came regularly twice a week, coming on the same days, and appearing so punctually on the stroke of five that at last she began to set her clocks by him.

He, too, poor man, seemed to be pulling himself together. He had none of the air of the recently bereaved, either in his features or his clothes. Not that he wore coloured ties or anything like that, but he certainly didn't produce an effect of blackness. His trousers, she observed, were grey; and not a particularly dark grey either. Well, perhaps it was no longer the fashion, thought Miss Entwhistle, eyeing these trousers with some doubt, to be very unhappy. But she couldn't help thinking there ought to be a band on his left arm to counteract the impression of light-heartedness in his legs; a crape band, no matter how narrow, or a band of black anything, not necessarily crape, such as she was sure it was usual in these circumstances to wear.

However, whatever she felt about his legs she welcomed him with the utmost cordiality, mindful of his kindness to them down in Cornwall and of how she had clung to him there as her rock; and she soon got to remember the way he liked his tea, and had the biggest chair placed comfortably ready for him — the chairs were neither very big nor numerous in her spare little drawing-room — and did all she could in the way of hospitality and pleasant conversation. But the more she saw of him, and the more she heard of his talk, the more she wondered at Jim.

Mr. Wemyss was most good-natured, and she was sure, and as she knew from experience, was most kind and thoughtful; but the things he said were so very unlike the things Jim said, and his way of looking at things was so very unlike Jim's way. Not that there wasn't room in the world for everybody, Miss Entwhistle reminded herself, sitting at her tea-table observing Wemyss, who looked particularly big and prosperous in her small frugal room, and no doubt one star differed from another in glory; still, she did wonder at Jim. And if Mr. Wemyss could bear the loss of his wife to the extent of grey trousers, how was it he couldn't bear Jim's name so much as mentioned? Whenever the talk got on to Jim — it couldn't be kept off him in a circle composed of his daughter and his sister and his friend — she noticed that Mr. Wemyss went silent. She would have taken this for excess of sensibility and the sign of a deep capacity for faithful devotion if it hadn't been for those trousers. Faced by them, it perplexed her.

While Miss Entwhistle was thinking like this and observing Wemyss, who never observed her at all after a first moment of surprise that she should look and behave so differently from the liquid lady of the cottage in Cornwall, that she should sit so straight and move so briskly, he and Lucy were, though present in the body, absent in love. Round them was drawn that magic circle through which nobody and nothing can penetrate, and within it they sat hand in hand and safe. Lucy's whole heart was his. He only had to come into the room for her to feel content. There was a naturalness, a bigness about his way of looking at things that made intricate, tormenting feelings shrink away in his presence ashamed. Quite apart from her love for him, her gratitude, her longing that he should go on now being happy and forget his awful tragedy, he was so very comfortable. She had never met any one so comfortable to lean on mentally. Bodily, on the few occasions on which her aunt was out of the room, he was comfortable too; he reminded her of the very nicest of sofas — expensive ones, all cushions. But mentally he was more than comfortable, he was positively luxurious. Such perfect rest, listening to his talk. No thinking needed. Things according to him were either so, or so. With her father things had never been either so, or so; and one had had to frown, and concentrate, and make efforts to follow and understand his distinctions, his infinitely numerous, delicate, difficult distinctions. Everard's plain division of everything into two categories only, snow-white and jet-black, was as reposeful as the Roman church. She hadn't got to strain or worry, she had only to surrender. And to what love, to what safety! At night she couldn't go to bed for thinking of how happy she was. She would sit quite still in the little dressing-room, her hands in her lap, and a proverb she had read somewhere running in her head:

When God shuts the door He opens the window.

Not for a moment, hardly, had she been left alone to suffer. Instantly, almost, Everard had come into her life and saved her. Lucy had indeed, as her aunt had twice suspected, got religion, but her religion was Wemyss. Ah, how she loved him! And every night she slept with his last letter under her pillow on the side of her heart.

As for Wemyss, if Lucy couldn't get over having got him he couldn't get over having got Lucy. He hadn't had such happiness as this, of this quality of tenderness, of goodness, in his life before. What he had felt for Vera had not at any time, he was sure, even at the beginning, been like this. While for the last few years — oh, well. Wemyss, when he found himself thinking of Vera, pulled up short. He declined to think of her now. She had filled his thoughts enough lately, and how terribly. His little angel Lucy had healed that wound, and there was no use in thinking of an old wound; nobody healthy ever did that. He had explained to Lucy, who at first had been a little morbid, how wrong it is, how really wicked, besides being intensely stupid, not to get over things. Life, he had said, is for the living; let the dead have death. The present is the only real possession a man has, whatever clever people may say; and the wise man, who is also the natural man of simple healthy instincts and a proper natural shrinking from death and disease, does not allow the past, which after all anyhow is done for, to intrude upon, much less spoil, the present. That is what, he explained, the past will always do if it can. The only safe way to deal with it is to forget it.

'But I don't want to forget mine,' Lucy had said at that, opening her eyes, which as usual had been shut, because the commas of Wemyss's talk with her when they chanced to be alone were his soothing, soporific kisses dropped gently on her closed eyelids. 'Father — '

'Oh, you may remember yours,' he had answered, smiling tenderly down at the head lying on his breast. 'It's such a little one. But you'll see when you're older if your Everard wasn't right.'

To Wemyss in his new happiness it seemed that Vera had belonged to another life altogether, an elderly, stale life from which, being healthy-minded, he had managed to unstick himself and to emerge born again all new and fresh and fitted for the present. She was forty when she died. She had started life five years younger than he was, but had quickly caught him up and passed him, and had ended, he felt, by being considerably his senior. And here was Lucy, only twenty-two anyhow, and looking like twelve. The contrast never ceased to delight him, to fill him with pride. And how pretty she was, now that she had left off crying. He adored her bobbed hair that gave her the appearance of a child or a very young boy, and he adored the little delicate lines of her nose and nostrils, and her rather big, kind mouth that so easily smiled, and her sweet eyes, the colour of Love-in-a-Mist. Not that he set any store by prettiness, he told himself; all he asked in a woman was devotion. But her being pretty would make it only the more exciting when the moment came to show her to his friends, to show his little girl to those friends who had dared slink away from him after Vera's death, and say, 'Look here — look at this perfect little thing — *she* believes in me all right!'

8

London being empty, Wemyss had it all his own way. No one else was there to cut him out, as his expression was. Lucy had many letters with offers of every kind of help from her father's friends, but naturally she needed no help and had no wish to see anybody in her present condition of secret contentment, and she replied to them with thanks and vague expressions of hope that later on they might all meet. One young man — he was the one who often proposed to her — wasn't to be put off like that, and journeyed all the way from Scotland, so great was his devotion, and found out from the caretaker of the Bloomsbury house that she was living with her aunt, and called at Eaton Terrace. But that afternoon Lucy and Miss Entwhistle were taking the air in a car Wemyss had hired, and at the very moment the young man was being turned away from the Eaton Terrace door Lucy was being rowed about the river at Hampton Court — very slowly, because of how soon Wemyss got hot — and her aunt, leaning on the stone parapet at the end of the Palace gardens, was observing her. It was a good thing the young man wasn't observing her too, for it wouldn't have made him happy.

'What is Mr. Wemyss?' asked Miss Entwhistle unexpectedly that evening, just as they were going to bed.

Lucy was taken aback. Her aunt hadn't asked a question or said a thing about him up to then, except general comments on his kindness and good-nature.

'What is Mr. Wemyss?' she repeated stupidly; for she was not only taken aback, but also, she discovered, she had no idea. It had never occurred to her even to wonder what he was, much less to ask. She had been, as it were, asleep the whole time in a perfect contentment on his breast.

'Yes. What is he besides being a widower?' said Miss Entwhistle. 'We know he's that, but it is hardly a profession.'

'I — don't think I know,' said Lucy, looking and feeling very stupid.

'Oh well, perhaps he isn't anything,' said her aunt, kissing her good-night. 'Except punctual,' she added, smiling, pausing a moment at her bedroom door.

And two or three days later, when Wemyss had again hired a car to take them for an outing to Windsor, while she and Lucy were tidying themselves for tea in the ladies' room of the hotel she turned from the looking-glass in the act of pinning back some hair loosened by motoring, and in spite of having a hairpin in her mouth said, again suddenly, 'What did Mrs. Wemyss die of?'

This unnerved Lucy. If she had stared stupidly at her aunt at the other question she stared aghast at her at this one.

'What did she die of?' she repeated, flushing.

'Yes. What illness was it?' asked her aunt, continuing to pin.

'It — wasn't an illness,' said Lucy helplessly.

'Not an illness?'

'I — believe it was an accident.'

'An accident?' said Miss Entwhistle, taking the hairpin out of her mouth and in her turn staring. 'What sort of an accident?'

'I think a rather serious one,' said Lucy, completely unnerved.

How could she bear to tell that dreadful story, the knowledge of which seemed somehow so intimately to bind her and Everard together with a sacred, terrible tie?

At that her aunt remarked that an accident resulting in death would usually be described as serious, and asked what its nature, apart from its seriousness, had been; and Lucy, driven into a corner, feeling instinctively that her aunt, who had already once or twice expressed what she said was her surprised admiration for Mr. Wemyss's heroic way of bearing his bereavement, might be too admiringly surprised altogether if she knew how tragically much he really had to bear, and might begin to inquire into the reasons of this heroism, took refuge in saying what she now saw she ought to have begun by saying, even though it wasn't true, that she didn't know.

'Ah,' said her aunt. 'Well — poor man. It's wonderful how he bears things.' And again in her mind's eye, and with an increased doubt, she saw the grey trousers.

That day at tea Wemyss, with the simple naturalness Lucy found so restful, the almost bald way he had of talking frankly about things more sophisticated people wouldn't have mentioned, began telling them of the last time he had been at Windsor.

It was the summer before, he said, and he and his wife — at this Miss Entwhistle became attentive — had motored down one Sunday to lunch in that very room, and it had been so much crowded, and the crowding had been so monstrously mismanaged, that positively they had had to go away without having had lunch at all.

'Positively without having had any lunch at all,' repeated Wemyss, looking at them with a face full of astonished aggrievement at the mere recollection.

'Ah,' said Miss Entwhistle, leaning across to him, 'don't let us revive sad memories.'

Wemyss stared at her. Good heavens, he thought, did she think he was talking about Vera? Any one with a grain of sense would know he was only talking about the lunch he hadn't had.

He turned impatiently to Lucy, and addressed his next remark to her. But in another moment there was her aunt again.

'Mr. Wemyss,' she said, 'I've been dying to ask you — '

Again he was forced to attend. The pure air and rapid motion of the motoring intended to revive and brace his little love were apparently reviving and bracing his little love's aunt as well, for lately he had been unable to avoid noticing a tendency on her part to assert herself. During his first eight visits to Eaton Terrace — that made four weeks since his coming back to London and six since the funeral in Cornwall — he had hardly known she was in the room; except, of course, that she *was* in the room, completely hindering his courting. During those eight visits his first impression of her remained undisturbed in his mind: she was a wailing creature who had hung round him in Cornwall in a constant state of tears. Down there she had behaved exactly like the traditional foolish woman when there is a death about — no common sense, no grit, crying if you looked at her, and keeping up a continual dismal recital of the virtues of the departed. Also she had been obstinate; and she had, besides, shown unmistakable signs of selfishness. When he paid his first call in Eaton Terrace he did notice that she had considerably, indeed completely, dried up, and was therefore to that extent improved, but she still remained for him just Lucy's aunt — somebody who poured out the tea, and who unfortunately hardly ever went out of the room; a necessary, though luckily a transitory, evil. But now it was gradually being borne in on him that she really existed, on her own account, independently. She asserted herself. Even when she wasn't saying anything — and often she said hardly a word during an entire outing — she still somehow asserted herself.

And here she was asserting herself very much indeed, and positively asking him across a tea-table which was undoubtedly for the moment his, asking him straight out what, if anything, he did in the way of a trade, profession or occupation.

She was his guest, and he regarded it as less than seemly for a guest to ask a host what he did. Not that he wouldn't gladly have told her if it had come from him of his own accord. Surely a man has a right, he thought, to his own accord. At all times Wemyss disliked being asked questions. Even the most innocent, ordinary question appeared to him to be an encroachment on the right he surely had to be let alone.

Lucy's aunt between sips of tea — his tea — pretended, pleasantly it is true, and clothing what could be nothing but idle curiosity in words that were not disagreeable, that she was dying to know what he was. She could see for herself, she said, smiling down at the leg nearest her, that he wasn't a bishop, she was sure he wasn't either a painter, musician or writer, but she wouldn't be in the least surprised if he were to tell her he was an admiral.

Wemyss thought this intelligent of the aunt. He had no objection to being taken for an admiral; they were an honest, breezy lot.

Placated, he informed her that he was on the Stock Exchange.

'Ah,' nodded Miss Entwhistle, looking wise because on this subject she so completely wasn't, the Stock Exchange being an institution whose nature and operations were alien to anything the Entwhistles were familiar with; 'ah yes. Quite. Bulls and bears.

86

Now I come to look at it, you have the Stock Exchange eye.'

'Foolish woman,' thought Wemyss, who for some reason didn't like being told before Lucy that he had the Stock Exchange eye; and he dismissed her impatiently from his mind and concentrated on his little love, asking himself while he did so how short he could, with any sort of propriety, cut this unpleasant time of restricted courting, of never being able to go anywhere with her unless her tiresome aunt came too.

Nearly two months now since both those deaths; surely Lucy's aunt might soon be told now of the engagement. It was after this outing that he began in his letters, and in the few moments he and she were alone, to urge Lucy to tell her aunt. Nobody else need know, he wrote; it could go on being kept secret from the world; but the convenience of her aunt's knowing was so obvious — think of how she would then keep out of the way, think of how she would leave them to themselves, anyhow indoors, anyhow in the house in Eaton Terrace.

Lucy, however, was reluctant. She demurred. She wrote begging him to be patient. She said that every week that passed would make their engagement less a thing that need surprise. She said that at present it would take too much explaining, and she wasn't sure that even at the end of the explanation her aunt would understand.

Wemyss wrote back brushing this aside. He said her aunt would have to understand, and if she didn't what did it matter so long as she knew? The great thing was that she should know. Then, he said, she would leave them alone together, instead of for ever sticking; and his little love must see how splendid it would be for him to come and spend happy hours with her quite alone. What was an aunt after all? he asked. What could she possibly be, compared to Lucy's own Everard? Besides, he disliked secrecy, he said. No honest man could stand an atmosphere of concealment. His little girl must make up her mind to tell her aunt, and believe that her Everard knew best; or, if she preferred it, he would tell her himself.

Lucy didn't prefer it, and was beginning to feel worried, because as the days went on Wemyss grew more and more persistent the more he became bored by Miss Entwhistle's development of an independent and inquiring mind, and she hated having to refuse or even to defer doing anything he asked, when her aunt one morning at breakfast, in the very middle of apparent complete serene absorption in her bacon, looked up suddenly over the coffee-pot and said, 'How long had your father known Mr. Wemyss?'

This settled things. Lucy felt she could bear no more of these shocks. A clean breast was the only thing left for her.

'Aunt Dot,' she stammered — Miss Entwhistle's Christian name was Dorothy — 'I'd like — I've got — I want to tell you — '

'After breakfast,' said Miss Entwhistle briskly. 'We shall need lots of time, and to be undisturbed. We'll go up into the drawing-room.'

And immediately she began talking about other things.

Was it possible, thought Lucy, her eyes carefully on her toast and butter, that Aunt Dot suspected?

9

It was not only possible, but the fact. Aunt Dot had suspected, only she hadn't suspected anything like all that was presently imparted to her, and she found great difficulty in assimilating it. And two hours later Lucy, standing in the middle of the drawing-room, was still passionately saying to her, and saying it for perhaps the tenth time, 'But don't you see? It's just *because* what happened to him was so awful. It's nature asserting itself. If he couldn't be engaged now, if he couldn't reach up out of such a pit of blackness and get into touch with living things again and somebody who sympathises and — is fond of him, he would die, die or go mad; and oh, what's the *use* to the world of somebody good and fine being left to die or go mad? Aunt Dot, what's the *use*?'

And her aunt, sitting in her customary chair by the fireplace, continued to assimilate with difficulty. Also her face was puckered into folds of distress. She was seriously upset.

Lucy, looking at her, felt a kind of despair that she wasn't being able to make her aunt, whom she loved, see what she saw, understand what she understood, and so be, as she was, filled with confidence and happiness. Not that she was happy at that moment; she, too, was seriously upset, her face flushed, her eyes bright with effort to get Wemyss as she knew him, as he so simply was, through into her aunt's consciousness.

She had made her clean breast with a completeness that had included the confession that she did know what Mrs. Wemyss's accident had been, and she had described it. Her aunt was painfully shocked. Anything so horrible as that hadn't entered her mind. To fall past the very window her husband was sitting at . . . it seemed to her dreadful that Lucy should be mixed up in it, and mixed up so instantly on the death of her of her natural protector — of her two natural protectors, for hadn't Mrs. Wemyss as long as she existed also been one? She was bewildered, and couldn't understand the violent reactions that Lucy appeared to look upon as so natural in Wemyss. She would have concluded that she didn't understand because she was too old, because she was out of touch with the elasticities of the younger generation, but Wemyss must be very nearly as old as herself. Certainly he was of the same generation; and yet behold him, within a fortnight of his wife's most shocking death, able to forget her, able to fall in love —

'But that's *why* — that's *why*,' Lucy cried when Miss Entwhistle said this. 'He *had* to forget, or die himself. It was beyond what anybody could bear and stay sane — '

'I'm sure I'm very glad he should stay sane,' said Miss Entwhistle, more and more puckered, 'but I can't help wishing it hadn't been you, Lucy, who are assisting him to stay it.'

And then she repeated what at intervals she had kept on repeating with a kind of stubborn helplessness, that her quarrel with Mr. Wemyss was that he had got happy so very quickly.

'Those grey trousers,' she murmured.

No; Miss Entwhistle couldn't get over it. She couldn't understand it. And Lucy, expounding and defending Wemyss in the middle of the room with all the blaze and emotion of what was only too evidently genuine love, was to her aunt an astonishing sight. That little thing, defending that enormous man. Jim's daughter; Jim's cherished little daughter . . .

Miss Entwhistle, sitting in her chair, struggled among other struggles to be fair, and reminded herself that Mr. Wemyss had proved himself to be most kind and eager to help down in Cornwall — though even on this there was shed a new and disturbing light, and that now that she knew everything, and the doubts that had made her perhaps be a little unjust were out of the way and she could begin to consider him impartially, she would probably very soon become sincerely attached to him. She hoped so with all her heart. She was used to being attached to people. It was normal to her to like and be liked. And there must be something more in him than his fine appearance for Lucy to be so very fond of him.

She gave herself a shake. She told herself she was taking this thing badly; that she ought not, just because it was an unusual situation, be so ready to condemn it. Was she really only a conventional spinster, shrinking back shocked at a touch of naked naturalness? Wasn't there much in what that short-haired child was so passionately saying about the rightness, the saneness, of reaction from horror? Wasn't it nature's own protection against too much death? After all, what was the good of doubling horror, of being so much horrified at the horrible that you stayed rooted there and couldn't move, and became, with your starting eyes and bristling hair, a horror yourself?

Better, of course, to pass on, as Lucy was explaining, to get on with one's business, which wasn't death but life. Still — there were the decencies. However desolate one would be in retirement, however much one would suffer, there was a period, Miss Entwhistle felt, during which the bereaved withdrew. Instinctively. The really bereaved *would* want to withdraw —

'Ah, but don't you *see*,' Lucy once more tried despairingly to explain, 'this wasn't just being bereaved — this was something simply too awful. Of course Everard would have behaved in the ordinary way if it had been an ordinary death.'

'So that the more terrible one's sorrow the more cheerfully one goes out to tea,' said Miss Entwhistle, the remembrance of the light trousers at one end of Wemyss and the unmistakably satisfied face at the other being for a moment too much for her.

'Oh,' almost moaned Lucy at that, and her head drooped in a sudden fatigue.

Miss Entwhistle got up quickly and put her arms round her. 'Forgive me,' she said. 'That was just stupid and cruel. I think I'm hide-bound. I think I've probably got into a rut. Help me out of it, Lucy. You shall teach me to take heroic views — '

And she kissed her hot face tenderly, holding it close to her own.

'But if I could only make you *see*,' said

Lucy, clinging to her, tears in her voice.

'But I do see that you love him very much,' said Miss Entwhistle gently, again very tenderly kissing her.

That afternoon when Wemyss appeared at five o'clock, it being his bi-weekly day for calling, he found Lucy alone.

'Why, where — ? How — ?' he asked, peeping round the drawing-room as though Miss Entwhistle must be lurking behind a chair.

'I've told,' said Lucy, who looked tired.

Then he clasped her with a great hug to his heart. 'Everard's own little love,' he said, kissing and kissing her. 'Everard's own good little love.'

'Yes, but — ' began Lucy faintly. She was, however, so much muffled and engulfed that her voice didn't get through.

'Now wasn't I right?' he said triumphantly, holding her tight. 'Isn't this as it should be? Just you and me, and nobody to watch or interfere?'

'Yes, but — ' began Lucy again.

'What do you say? 'Yes, but?'' laughed Wemyss, bending his ear. 'Yes without any but, you precious little thing. Buts don't exist for us — only yeses.'

And on these lines the interview continued for quite a long time before Lucy succeeded in telling him that her aunt had been much upset.

Wemyss minded that so little that he didn't even ask why. He was completely incurious about anything her aunt might think. 'Who cares?' he said, drawing her to his heart again. 'Who cares? We've got each other. What does anything else matter? If you had fifty aunts, all being upset, what would it matter? What can it matter to us?'

And Lucy, who was exhausted by her morning, felt too as she nestled close to him that nothing did matter so long as he was there. But the difficulty was that he wasn't there most of the time, and her aunt was, and she loved her aunt and did very much hate that she should be upset.

She tried to convey this to Wemyss, but he didn't understand. When it came to Miss Entwhistle he was as unable to understand Lucy as Miss Entwhistle was unable to understand her when it came to Wemyss. Only Wemyss didn't in the least mind not understanding. Aunts. What were they? Insects. He laughed, and said his little love couldn't have it both ways; she couldn't eat her cake, which was her Everard, and have it too, which was her aunt; and he kissed her hair and asked who was a complicated little baby, and rocked her gently to and fro in his arms, and Lucy was amused at that and laughed too, and forgot her aunt, and forgot everything except how much she loved him.

Meanwhile Miss Entwhistle was spending a diligent afternoon in the newspaper room of the British Museum. She was reading *The Times* report of the Wemyss accident and inquest; and if she had been upset by what Lucy told her in the morning she was even more upset by what she read in the afternoon. Lucy hadn't mentioned that suggestion of suicide. Perhaps he hadn't told her. Suicide. Well, there had been no evidence. There was an open verdict. It had been a suggestion made by a servant, perhaps a servant with a grudge. And even if it had been true, probably the poor creature had discovered she had some incurable disease, or she may have had some loss that broke her down temporarily, and — oh, there were many explanations; respectable, ordinary explanations.

Miss Entwhistle walked home slowly, loitering at shop windows, staring at hats and blouses that she never saw, spinning out her walk to its utmost, trying to think. Suicide. How desolate it sounded on that beautiful afternoon. Such a giving up. Such a defeat. Why should she have given up? Why should she have been defeated? But it wasn't true.

The coroner had said there was no evidence to show how she came by her death.

Miss Entwhistle walked slower and slower. The nearer she got to Eaton Terrace the more unwillingly did she advance. When she reached Belgrave Square she went right round it twice, lingering at the garden railings studying the habits of birds. She had been out all the afternoon, and, as those who have walked it know, it is a long way from the British Museum to Eaton Terrace. Also it was a hot day and her feet ached, and she very much would have liked to be in her own chair in her cool drawing-room having her tea. But there in that drawing-room would probably still be Mr. Wemyss, no longer now to be Mr. Wemyss for her — would she really have to call him Everard? — or she might meet him on the stairs — narrow stairs; or in the hall — also narrow, which he would fill up; or on her doorstep she might meet him, filling up her doorstep; or, when she turned the corner into her street, there, coming towards her, might be the triumphant trousers.

No, she felt she couldn't stand seeing him that day. So she lingered forlornly watching the sparrows inside the garden railings of Belgrave Square, balancing first on one and then on the other of those feet that ached.

This was only the beginning, she thought;

this was only the first of many days for her of wandering homelessly round. Her house was too small to hold both herself and love-making. If it had been the slender love-making of the young man who was so doggedly devoted to Lucy, she felt it wouldn't have been too small. He would have made love youthfully, shyly. She could have sat quite happily in the dining-room while the suitably paired young people dallied delicately together overhead. But she couldn't bear the thought of being cramped up so near Mr. Wemyss's — no, Everard's; she had better get used to that at once — love-making. His way of courting wouldn't be — she searched about in her uneasy mind for a word, and found vegetarian. Yes; that word sufficiently indicated what she meant: it wouldn't be vegetarian.

Miss Entwhistle drifted away from the railings, and turning her back on her own direction wandered towards Sloane Street. There she saw an omnibus stopping to let some one out. Wanting very much to sit down she made an effort and caught it, and squeezing herself into its vacant seat gave herself up to wherever it should take her.

It took her to the City; first to the City, and then to strange places beyond. She let it take her. Her clothes became steadily more fashionable the farther the omnibus went. She ended by being conspicuous and stared at. But she was determined to give the widest margin to the love-making and go the whole way, and she did.

For an hour and a half the omnibus went on and on. She had no idea omnibuses did such things. When it finally stopped she sat still; and the conductor, who had gradually come to share the growing surprise of the relays of increasingly poor passengers, asked her what address she wanted.

She said she wanted Sloane Street.

He was unable to believe it, and tried to reason with her, but she sat firm in her place and persisted.

At nine o'clock he put her down where he had taken her up. She disappeared into the darkness with the movements of one who is stiff, and he winked at the passenger nearest the door and touched his forehead.

But as she climbed wearily and hungrily up her steps and let herself in with her latchkey, she felt it had been well worth it; for that one day at least she had escaped Mr. We — no, Everard.

10

Miss Entwhistle, however, made up her mind very firmly that after this one afternoon of giving herself up to her feelings she was going to behave in the only way that is wise when faced by an inevitable marriage, the way of sympathy and friendliness.

Too often had she seen the first indignation of disappointed parents at the marriages of their children harden into a matter of pride, a matter of doggedness and principle, and finally become an attitude unable to be altered, long after years had made it ridiculous. If the marriages turned out happy, how absurd to persist in an antiquated disapproval; if they turned out wretched, then how urgent the special need for love.

Thus Miss Entwhistle reasoned that first sleepless night in bed, and on these lines she proceeded during the next few months. They were trying months. She used up all she had of gallantry in sticking to her determination. Lucy's instinct had been sound, that wish to keep her engagement secret from her aunt for as long as possible. Miss Entwhistle, always thin, grew still more thin in her constant daily and hourly struggle to be pleased, to enter into Lucy's happiness, to make things easy for her, to protect her from the notice and inquiry of their friends, to look hopefully and with as much of Lucy's eyes as she could at Everard and at the future.

'She isn't simple enough,' Wemyss would say to Lucy if ever she said anything about her aunt's increasing appearance of strain and overwork. 'She should take things more naturally. Look at us.' For it was the one fly in Lucy's otherwise perfect ointment, this intermittent consciousness that her aunt wasn't altogether happy.

And then he would ask her, laying his head on hers as he stood with his arms about her, who had taught his little girl to be simple; and they would laugh, and kiss, and talk of other things.

Miss Entwhistle was unable to be simple in Wemyss's sense. She tried to; for when she saw his fresh, unlined face, his forehead without a wrinkle on it, and compared it in the glass with her own which was only three years older, she thought there must be a good deal to be said for single-mindedness. It was Lucy who told her Everard was so single-minded. He took one thing at a time, she said, concentrating quietly. When he had completely finished it off then, and not till then, he went on to the next. He knew his own mind. Didn't Aunt Dot think it was a great thing to know one's own mind? Instead of wobbling about, wasting one's thoughts and energies on side-shows?

This was the very language of Wemyss; and Miss Entwhistle, after having been listening to him in the afternoon — for every time he came she put in a brief appearance just for the look of the thing, and on the Saturday and Sunday outings she was invariably present the whole time — felt it a little hard that when at last she had reached the end of the day and the harbour of her empty drawing-room she should, through the mouth of Lucy, have to listen to him all the evening as well.

But she always agreed, and said Yes, he was a great dear; for when an only and much-loved niece is certainly going to marry, the least a wise aunt can call her future nephew is a great dear. She will make this warmer and more varied if she can, but at least she will say that much. Miss Entwhistle tried to think of variations, afraid Lucy might notice a certain sameness, and once with an effort she faltered out that he seemed to be a — a real darling; but it had a hollow sound, and she didn't repeat it. Besides, Lucy was quite satisfied with the other.

She used, sitting at her aunt's feet in the evenings — Wemyss never came in the evenings because he distrusted the probable dinner — sometimes to make her aunt say it again, by asking a little anxiously, 'But you *do* think him a great dear, don't you, Aunt Dot?'

Whereupon Miss Entwhistle, afraid her last expression of that opinion may have been absent-minded, would hastily exclaim with almost excess of emphasis, 'Oh, a *great* dear.'

Perhaps he was a dear. She didn't know. What had she against him? She didn't know. He was too old, that was one thing; but the next minute, after hearing something he had said or laughed at, she thought he wasn't old enough. Of course what she really had against him was that he had got over his wife's shocking death so quickly. Yet she admitted there was much in Lucy's explanation of this as a sheer instinctive gesture of self-defence. Besides, she couldn't keep it up as a grudge against him for ever; with every day it mattered less. And sometimes Miss Entwhistle even doubted whether it was this that mattered to her at all — whether it was not rather some quite small things that she really objected to: a want of fastidiousness, for instance, a forgetfulness of the minor courtesies — the objections, in a word, she told herself smiling, of an old maid. Lucy seemed not to mind his blunders in these directions in the least. She seemed positively, thought her aunt, to take a kind of pride in them, delighting in everything he said or did with the adoring tenderness of a young mother watching the pranks of her first-born. She laughed gaily; she let him caress her openly. She too, thought Miss Entwhistle, had become what she no doubt would say was single-minded. Well, perhaps all this was a spinster's way of feeling about a type not previously met with, and she had got — again she reproached herself — into an elderly groove. Jim's friends — well, they had been different, but not necessarily better. Mr. Wemyss would call them, she was sure, a finicking lot.

When in October London began to fill again, and Jim's friends came to look her and Lucy up and showed a tendency, many of them, to keep on doing it, a new struggle was added to her others, the struggle to prevent their meeting Wemyss. He wouldn't, she was convinced, be able to hide his proprietorship in Lucy, and Lucy wouldn't ever get that look of tenderness out of her eyes when they rested on him. Questions as to who he was would naturally be asked, and one or other of Jim's friends would be sure to remember the affair of Mrs. Wemyss's death; indeed, that day she went to the British Museum and read the report of it she had been amazed that she hadn't seen it at the time. It took up so much of the paper that she was bound to have seen it if she had seen a paper at all. She could only suppose that as she was visiting friends just then, she chanced that day to have been in the act of leaving or arriving, and that if she bought a paper on the journey she had looked, as was sometimes her way in trains, not at it but out of the window.

She felt she hadn't the strength to support being questioned, and in her turn have to embark on the explanation and defence of Wemyss. There was too much of him, she felt, to be explained. He ought to be separated into sections, and taken gradually and bit by bit — but far best not to produce him, to keep him from meeting her friends. She therefore arranged a day in the week when she would be at home, and discouraged every one from the waste of time of trying to call on her on other days. Then presently the afternoon became an evening once a week, when whoever liked could come in after dinner and talk and drink coffee, because the evening was safer; made safe by Wemyss's conviction — he hadn't concealed it — that the dinners of maiden ladies were notoriously both scanty and bad.

Lucy would have preferred never to see a soul except Wemyss, who was all she wanted, all she asked for in life; but she did see her aunt's point, that only by pinning their friends to a day and an hour could the risk of their overflowing into precious moments be avoided. This is how Miss Entwhistle put it to her, wondering as she said it at her own growing ability in artfulness.

She had an old friend living in Chesham Street, a widow full of that ripe wisdom that sometimes comes at the end to those who have survived marriage; and to her, when the autumn brought her back to London, Miss Entwhistle went occasionally in search of comfort.

'What in the whole world puts such a gulf between two affections and comprehensions as a new love?' she asked one day, freshly struck, because of something Lucy had said, by the distance she had travelled. Lucy was quite a tiny figure now, so far away from her had she moved; she couldn't even get her voice to carry to her, much less still hold on to her with her hands.

And the friend, made brief of speech by wisdom, said: 'Nothing.'

About Wemyss's financial position Miss Entwhistle could only judge from appearances, for it wouldn't have occurred to him that it might perhaps be her concern to know, and she preferred to wait till later, when the engagement could be talked about, to ask some old friend of Jim's to make the proper inquiries; but from the way he lived it seemed to be an easy one. He went freely in taxis, he hired cars with a reasonable frequency, he inhabited one of the substantial houses of Lancaster Gate, and also, of course, he had The Willows, the house on the river near Strorley where his wife had died. After all, what could be better than two houses, Miss Entwhistle thought, congratulating herself, as it were, on Lucy's behalf that this side of Wemyss was so satisfactory. Two houses, and no children; how much better than the other way about. And one day, feeling almost hopeful about Lucy's prospects, on the advantages of which she had insisted that her mind should dwell, she went round again to the widow in Chesham Street and said suddenly to her, who was accustomed to these completely irrelevant exclamatory inquiries from her friend, and who being wise was also incurious, 'What can be better than two houses?'

To which the widow, whose wisdom was more ripe than comforting, replied disappointingly: 'One.'

Later, when the marriage loomed very

near, Miss Entwhistle, who found that she was more than ever in need of reassurance instead of being, as she had hoped to become, more reconciled, went again, in a kind of desperation this time, to the widow, seeking some word from her who was so wise that would restore her to tranquillity, that would dispel her absurd persistent doubts. 'After all,' she said almost entreatingly, 'what can be better than a devoted husband?'

And the widow, who had had three and knew what she was talking about, replied with the large calm of those who have finished and can in leisure weigh and reckon up: 'None.'

11

The Wemyss-Entwhistle engagement proceeded on its way of development through the ordinary stages of all engagements: secrecy complete, secrecy partial, semi-publicity, and immediately after that entire publicity, with its inevitable accompanying uproar. The uproar, always more or less audible to the protagonists, of either approval or disapproval, was in this case one of unanimous disapproval. Lucy's father's friends protested to a man. The atmosphere at Eaton Terrace was convulsed; and Lucy, running as she always did to hide from everything upsetting into Wemyss's arms, was only made more certain than ever that there alone was peace.

This left Miss Entwhistle to face the protests by herself. There was nothing for it but to face them. Jim had had so many intimate, devoted friends, and each of them apparently regarded his daughter as his special care and concern. One or two of the younger ones, who had been disciples rather than friends, were in love with her themselves, and these were specially indignant and vocal in their indignation. Miss Entwhistle found herself in the position she had tried so hard to avoid, that of defending and explaining Wemyss to a highly sceptical, antagonistic audience. It was as if, forced to fight for him, she was doing so with her back to her drawing-room wall.

Lucy couldn't help her, because though she was distressed that her aunt should be being worried because of her affairs, yet she did feel that Everard was right when he said that her affairs concerned nobody in the world but herself and him. She, too, was indignant, but her indignation was because her father's friends, who had been ever since she could remember always good and kind, besides perfectly intelligent and reasonable, should with one accord, and without knowing anything about Everard except that story of the accident, be hostile to her marrying him. The ready unfairness, the willingness immediately to believe the worst instead of the best, astonished and shocked her. And then the way they all talked! Everlasting arguments and reasoning and hair-splitting; so clever, so impossible to stand up against, and yet so surely, she was certain, if only she had been clever too and able to prove things, wrong. All their multitudinous points of view — why, there was only one point of view about a

111

thing, Everard said, and that was the right one. Ah, but what a woman wanted wasn't this; she didn't want this endless thinking and examining and dissecting and considering. A woman — her very thoughts were now dressed in Wemyss's words — only wanted her man. ''Hers not to reason why,'' Wemyss had quoted one day, and both of them had laughed at his parody, ''hers but to love and — not die, but live.''

The most that could be said for her father's friends was that they meant well; but oh, what trouble the well-meaning could bring into an otherwise simple situation! From them she hid — it was inevitable — in Wemyss's arms. Here were no arguments; here were no misgivings and paralysing hesitations. Here was just simple love, and the feeling — delicious to her whose mother had died in the very middle of all the sweet early petting, and whose whole life since had been spent entirely in the dry and bracing company of unusually inquisitive-minded, clever men — of being a baby again in somebody's big, comfortable, uncritical lap.

The engagement hadn't leaked out so much as flooded out. It would have continued secret for quite a long time, known only to the three and to the maids — who being young women themselves, and well acquainted with the symptoms of the condition, were sure of it before Miss Entwhistle had even begun to suspect — if Wemyss hadn't taken to dropping in, contrary to expectations, on the Thursday evenings. Lucy's descriptions of these evenings and of the people who came, and of how very kind they were to her aunt and herself, and how anxious they were to help her, they of course supposing that she was, actually, the lonely thing she would have been if she hadn't had Everard as the dear hidden background to her life — at this point they embraced — at first amused him, then made him curious, and finally caused him to come and see for himself.

He didn't tell Lucy he was coming, he just came. It had taken him five Thursday evenings of playing bridge as usual at his club, playing it with one hand, as he said to her afterwards, and thinking of her with the other — 'You know what I mean,' he said, and they laughed and embraced — before it slowly oozed into and pervaded his mind that there was his little girl, surrounded by people fussing over her and making love to her (because, said Wemyss, everybody would naturally want to make love to her), and there was he, the only person who had a right to do this, somewhere else.

So he walked in; and when he walked in, the group standing round Lucy with their backs to the door saw her face, which had been gently attentive, suddenly flash into colour and light; and turning with one accord to see what it was she was looking at behind them with parted lips and eyes of startled joy, beheld once more the unknown chief mourner of the funeral in Cornwall.

Down there they had taken for granted that he was a relation of Jim's, the kind of relative who in a man's life appears only three times, the last of which is his funeral; here in Eaton Terrace they were immediately sure he was not, anyhow, that, because for relatives who only appear those three times a girl's face doesn't change in a flash from gentle politeness to tremulous, shining life. They all stared at him astonished. He was so different from the sorts of people they had met at Jim's. For one thing he was so well dressed — in the mating season, thought Miss Entwhistle, even birds dress well — and in his impressive evening clothes, with what seemed a bigger and more spotless shirt-front than any shirt-front they could have imagined, he made them look and feel what they actually were, a dingy, shabby lot.

Wemyss was good-looking. He might be middle-aged, but he was good-looking enough frequently to eclipse the young. He might have a little too much of what tailors call a fine presence, but his height carried this off. His features were regular, his face care-free and healthy, his brown hair sleek with no grey in it, he was clean-shaven, and his mouth was the kind of mouth sometimes described by journalists as mobile, sometimes as determined, but always as well cut. One could visualise him in a fur-lined coat, thought a young man near Lucy, considering him; and one couldn't visualise a single one of the others, including himself, in the room that evening in a fur-lined coat. Also, thought this same young man, one could see railway porters and taxi-drivers and waiters hurrying to be of service to him; and one not only couldn't imagine them taking any notice that wasn't languid and reluctant of the others, including himself, but one knew from personal distressing experience that they didn't.

'My splendid lover!' Lucy's heart cried out within her when the door opened and there he stood. She had not seen him before in the evening, and the contrast between him and the rest of the people there was really striking.

Miss Entwhistle had been right: there was no hiding the look in Lucy's eyes or Wemyss's proprietary manner. He hadn't meant to take any but the barest notice of his little girl, he had meant to be quite an ordinary guest — just shake hands and say 'Hasn't it been wet to-day' — that sort of thing; but his pride and love were too much for him, he couldn't hide them. He thought he did, and was sure he was behaving beautifully and with the easiest unconcern, but the mere way he looked at her and stood over her was enough. Also there was the way she looked at him. The intelligences in that room were used to drawing more complicated inferences than this. They were outraged by its obviousness. Who was this middle-aged, prosperous outsider who had got hold of Jim's daughter? What had her aunt been about? Where had he dropped from? Had Jim known?

Miss Entwhistle introduced him. 'Mr. Wemyss,' she said to them generally, with a vague wave of her hand; and a red spot appeared and stayed on each of her cheekbones.

Wemyss held forth. He stood on the hearthrug filling his pipe — he was used to smoking in that room when he came to tea with Lucy, and forgot to ask Miss Entwhistle if it mattered — and told everybody what he thought. They were talking about Ireland when he came in, and after the disturbance of his arrival had subsided he asked them not to

116

mind him but to go on. He then proceeded to go on himself, telling them what he thought; and what he thought was what *The Times* had thought that morning. Wemyss spoke with the practised fluency of a leading article. He liked politics and constantly talked them at his club, and it created vacancies in the chairs near him. But Lucy, who hadn't heard him on politics before and found that she could understand every word, listened to him with parted lips. Before he came in they had been saying things beyond her quickness in following, eagerly discussing Sinn Fein, Lloyd George, the outrageous cost of living — it was the autumn of 1920 — turning everything inside out, upside down, being witty, being surprising, being tremendously eager and earnest. It had been a kind of restless flashing round and catching fire from each other — a kind of kick, and flick, and sparks, and a burst of laughter, and then on to something else just as she was laboriously getting under weigh to follow the last sentence but six. She had been missing her father, who took her by the hand on these occasions when he saw her lagging behind, and stopped a moment to explain to her, and held up the others while she got her breath.

But now came Everard, and in a minute everything was plain. He had the effect on her of a window being thrown open and fresh air and sunlight being let in. He was so sensible, she felt, compared to these others; so healthy and natural. The Government, he said, only had to do this and that, and Ireland and the cost of living would immediately, regarded as problems, be solved. He explained the line to be taken. It was a very simple line. One only needed goodwill and a little common sense. Why, thought Lucy, unconsciously nodding proud agreement, didn't people have goodwill and a little common sense?

At first there was a disposition to interrupt, to heckle, but it grew fainter and soon gave way to complete silence. The other guests might have been stunned, Miss Entwhistle thought, so motionless did they presently sit. And when they went away, which they seemed to do earlier than usual and in a body, Wemyss was still standing on the hearthrug explaining the points of view of the ordinary, sensible business man.

'Mind you,' he said, pointing at them with his pipe, 'I don't pretend to be a great thinker. I'm just a plain business man, and as a plain business man I know there's only one way of doing a thing, and that's the right way. Find out what that way is, and go and do it. There's too much arguing altogether and asking other people what they think. We don't want talk, we want action. I agree with Napoleon, who said concerning the French Revolution, '*Il aurait fallu mitrailler cette canaille.*' We're not simple enough.'

This was the last the others heard as they trooped in silence down the stairs. Outside they lingered for a while in little knots on the pavement talking, and then they drifted away to their various homes, where most of them spent the rest of the evening writing to Miss Entwhistle.

The following Thursday evening, her letters in reply having been vague and evasive, they came again, each hoping to get Lucy's aunt to himself, and on the ground of being Jim's most devoted friend ask her straight questions such as who and what was Wemyss. Also, more particularly, why. Who and what he was was of no sort of consequence if he would only be and do it somewhere else; but they arrived determined to get an answer to the third question: Why Wemyss? And when they got there, there he was again; there before them this time, standing on the hearthrug as if he had never moved off it since the week before and had gone on talking ever since.

This was the end of the Thursday evenings. The next one was unattended, except by Wemyss; but Miss Entwhistle had been forced to admit the engagement, and from then on right up to the marriage her life was a curse to her and a confusion. Just because Jim had appointed no guardian in his will for Lucy, every single one of his friends felt bound to fill the vacancy. They were indignant when they discovered that almost before they had begun Lucy was being carried off, but they were horrified when they discovered what Wemyss it was who was carrying her off. Most of them quite well remembered the affair of Mrs. Wemyss's death a few weeks before, and those who did not went, as Miss Entwhistle had gone, to the British Museum and read it up. They also, though they themselves were chiefly unworldly persons who lost money rather than made it, instituted the most searching private inquiries into Wemyss's business affairs, hoping that he might be caught out as such a rascal or so penniless, or, preferably, both, that no woman could possibly have anything to do with him. But Wemyss's business record, the solicitor they employed informed them, was quite creditable. Everything about it was neat and in order. He was not what the City would call a wealthy man, but if you went out say to Ealing, said the solicitor, he would be called wealthy. He was solid, and he was certainly more than able to support a wife and family. He could have been quite wealthy if he had not adopted a principle to which he had adhered for years of knocking off work early and leaving his office at an hour when other men did not — the friends were obliged to admit that this, at least, seemed sensible. There had been, though, a very sad occurrence recently in his private life — 'Oh, thank you,' interrupted the friends, 'we have heard about that.'

But however good Wemyss's business record might be, it couldn't alter their violent objection to Jim's daughter marrying him. Apart from the stuff he talked, there was the inquest. They were aware that in this they were unreasonable, but they were all too much attached to Jim's memory to be able to be reasonable about a man they felt so certain he wouldn't have liked. Singly and in groups they came at safe times, such as after breakfast, to Eaton Terrace to reason with Lucy, too much worried to remember that you cannot reason with a person in love. Less wise than Miss Entwhistle, they tried to dissuade her from marrying this man, and the more they tried the tighter she clung to him. To the passion of love was added, by their attitudes, the passion of protectiveness, of flinging her body between him and them.

And all the while, right inside her innermost soul, in spite of her amazement at them and her indignation, she was smiling to herself; for it was really very funny, the superficial judgments of these clever people when set side by side with what she alone knew — the tenderness, the simple goodness of her heart's beloved.

Lucy laughed to herself in her happy sureness. She had miraculously found not only a lover she could adore and a guide she could follow and a teacher she could look up to and a sufferer who without her wouldn't have been healed, but a mother, a nurse, and a playmate. In spite of his being so much older and so extraordinarily wise, he was yet her contemporary — sometimes hardly even that, so boyish was he in his talk and jokes. Lucy had never had a playmate. She had spent her life sitting, as it were, bolt upright mentally behaving, and she hadn't known till Wemyss came on the scene how delicious it was to relax. Nonsense had delighted her father, it is true, but it had to be of a certain kind; never the kind to which the adjective 'sheer' would apply. With Wemyss she could say whatever nonsense came into her head, sheer or otherwise. He laughed consumedly at her when she talked it. She loved to make him laugh. They laughed together. He understood her language. He was her playmate. Those people outside, old and young, who didn't know what playing was and were trying to get her away from him, might beat at the door behind which he and she sat listening, amused, as long as they liked.

'How they all try to separate us,' she said to him one day, sitting as usual safe in the circle of his arm, her head on his breast.

'You can't separate unity,' remarked Wemyss comfortably.

She wanted to tell them that answer, confront them with it next time they came after breakfast, as a discouragement to useless further effort, but she had learned that they somehow always knew when what she said was Everard's and not hers, and then, of course, prejudiced as they were, they wouldn't listen.

'Now, Lucy, that's pure Wemyss,' they would say. 'For heaven's sake say something of your own.'

At Christmas Wemyss had an encounter with Miss Entwhistle, who ever since she had been told of the engagement had been so quiet and inoffensive that he quite liked her. She had seemed to recognise her position as a side-show, and had accepted it without a word. She no longer asked him questions, and she made no difficulties. She left him alone with Lucy in Eaton Terrace, and though she had to go with them on the outings she asserted herself so little that he forgot she was there. But when towards the middle of December he remarked one afternoon that he always spent Christmas at The Willows, and what day would she and Lucy come down, Christmas Eve or the day before, to his astonishment she looked astonished, and after a silence said it was most kind of him, but they were going to spend Christmas where they were.

'I had hoped you would join us,' she said. 'Must you really go away?'

'But — ' began Wemyss, incredulous, doubting his ears.

It was, however, the fact that Miss Entwhistle wouldn't go to The Willows; and of course if she wouldn't Lucy couldn't either. Nothing that he said could shake her determination. Here was a repetition, only how much worse — fancy spoiling his Christmas — of her conduct in Cornwall when she insisted on going away from that nice little house where they were all so comfortably established, and taking Lucy up to London. He had forgotten, so acquiescent had she been for weeks, that down there he had discovered she was obstinate. It was a shock to him to realise that her obstinacy, the most obstinate obstinacy he had ever met, might be going to upset his plans. He couldn't believe it. He couldn't believe he wasn't going to be able to have what he wished, and only because an old maid said 'No.' Was the story of Balaam to be reversed, and the angel be held up by the donkey? He refused to believe such a thing possible.

Wemyss, who made his plans first and talked about them afterwards, hadn't mentioned Christmas even to Lucy. It was his habit to settle what he wished to do, arrange all the details, and then, when everything was ready, inform those who were to take part. It hadn't occurred to him that over the Christmas question there would be trouble. He had naturally taken it for granted that he would spend Christmas with his little girl, and of course as he always spent it at The Willows she would spend it there too. All his arrangements were made, and the servants, who looked surprised, had been told to get the spare-rooms ready for two ladies. He had begun to feel seasonable as early as the first week in December, and had bespoken two big turkeys instead of one, because this was to be his first real Christmas at The Willows — Vera had been without the Christmas spirit — and he felt it couldn't be celebrated lavishly enough. Two where there had in previous years been one — that was the turkeys; four where there had been two — that was the plum puddings. He doubled everything. Doubling seemed the proper, even the symbolic expression of his feelings, for wasn't he soon going to be doubled himself? And how sweetly.

Then suddenly, having finished his preparations and proceeding, the time being ripe, to the question of the day of arrival, he found himself up against opposition. Miss Entwhistle wouldn't go to The Willows — incredible, impossible, and insufferable — while Lucy, instead of instantly insisting and joining with him in a compelling majority, sat as quiet as a mouse.

'But Lucy — ' Wemyss having stared speechless at her aunt, turned to her. 'But of course we must spend Christmas together.'

'Oh yes,' said Lucy, leaning forward, 'of course — '

'But of course you must come down. Why, any other arrangement is unthinkable. My house is in the country, which is the proper place for Christmas, and it's your Everard's house, and you haven't seen it yet — why, I would have taken you down long ago, but I've been saving up for this.'

'We hoped,' said Miss Entwhistle, 'you

would join us here.'

'Here! But there isn't room to swing a turkey here. I've ordered two, and each of them is twice too big to get through your front door.'

'Oh, Everard — have you actually ordered turkeys?' said Lucy.

She wanted to laugh, but she also wanted to cry. His simplicity was too wonderful. In her eyes it set him apart from criticism and made him sacred, like the nimbus about the head of a saint.

That he should have been secretly busy making preparations, buying turkeys, planning a surprise, when all this time she had been supposing that why he never mentioned The Willows was because he shrank both for himself and for her from the house of his tragedy! There had never been any talk of showing it to her, as there had about the house in Lancaster Gate, and she had imagined he would never go near it again and was probably quietly getting rid of it. He would want to get rid of it, of course — that house of unbearable memories. To the other one, the house in Lancaster Gate, he had insisted on taking them to tea, and in spite of a great desire not to go, plainly visible on her aunt's face and felt too by herself, it had seemed after all a natural and more or less inevitable thing, and they had gone. At least that poor Vera had only lived there, and not died there. It was a gloomy house, and Lucy had wanted him to give it up and start life with her in a place without associations, but he had been so much astonished at the idea — 'Why,' he had cried, 'it was my father's house and I was born in it!' — that she couldn't help laughing at his dismay, and was ashamed of herself for having thought of uprooting him. Besides, she hadn't known he had been born in it.

The Willows, however, was different. Of that he never spoke, and Lucy had been sure of the pitiful, the delicate reason. Now it appeared that all this time he had just been saving it up as a Christmas treat.

'Oh, Everard — !' she said, with a gasp. She hadn't reckoned with The Willows. That The Willows should still be in Everard's life, and actively so, not just lingering on while house agents were disposing of it, but visited and evidently prized, came upon her as an immense shock.

'I think we can achieve a happy little Christmas for you here,' said her aunt, smiling the smile she smiled when she found difficulty in smiling. 'Of course you and Lucy would want to be together. I ought to have told you earlier that we were counting on you, but somehow Christmas comes on one so unexpectedly.'

'Perhaps you'll tell me why you won't come to The Willows,' said Wemyss, holding on to himself as she used to make him hold on to himself in Cornwall. 'You realise, of course, that if you persist you spoil both Lucy's and my Christmas.'

'Ah, but you mustn't put it that way,' said Miss Entwhistle, gentle but determined. 'I promise you that you and Lucy shall be very happy here.'

'You haven't answered my question,' said Wemyss, slowly filling his pipe.

'I don't think I'm going to,' said Miss Entwhistle, suddenly flaring up. She hadn't flared up since she was ten, and was instantly ashamed of herself, but there was something about Mr. Wemyss —

'I think,' she said, getting up and speaking very gently, 'you'll like to be alone together now.' And she crossed to the door.

There she wavered, and turning round said more gently still, even penitentially, 'If Lucy wishes to go to The Willows I'll — I'll accept your kind invitation and take her. I leave it to her.'

Then she went out.

'That's all right then,' said Wemyss with a great sigh of relief, smiling broadly at Lucy.

'Come here, little love — come to your Everard, and we'll fix it all up. Lord, what a kill-joy that woman is!'

And he put out his arms and drew her to him.

12

But Christmas was spent after all at Eaton Terrace, and they lived on Wemyss's turkeys and plum puddings for a fortnight.

It was not a very successful Christmas, because Wemyss was so profoundly disappointed, and Miss Entwhistle had the apologeticness of those who try to make up for having got their own way, and Lucy, who had shrunk from The Willows far more than her aunt, wished many times before it was over that they had after all gone there. It would have been much simpler in the long run, and much less painful than having to look on at Everard being disappointed; but at the time, and taken by surprise, she had felt that she couldn't have borne festivities, and still less could she have borne seeing Everard bearing festivities in that house.

'This is morbid,' he said, when in answer to his questioning she at last told him it was poor Vera's dreadful death there that made her feel she couldn't go; and he explained, holding her in his arms, how foolish it was to be morbid, and how his little girl, who was marrying a healthy, sensible man who, God knew, had had to fight hard enough to keep so — she pressed closer — and yet had succeeded, must be healthily sensible too. Otherwise, if she couldn't do this and couldn't do that because it reminded her of something sad, and couldn't go here and couldn't go there because of somebody's having died, he was afraid she would make both herself and him very unhappy.

'Oh, Everard — ' said Lucy at that, holding him tight, the thought of making him unhappy, him, her own beloved who had been through such terrible unhappiness already, giving her heart a stab.

His little girl must know, he continued, speaking with the grave voice that was natural to him when he was serious, the voice not of the playmate but of the man she adored, the man she was in love with, in whose hands she could safely leave her earthly concerns — his little girl must know that somebody had died everywhere. There wasn't a spot, there wasn't a house, except quite new ones —

'Oh yes, I know — but — ' Lucy tried to interrupt.

And The Willows was his home, the home he had looked forward to and worked for and had at last been able to afford to rent on a long lease, a lease so long that it made it practically his very own, and he had spent the last ten years developing and improving it, and there wasn't a brick or a tree in it in which he didn't take an interest, really an almost personal interest, and his one thought all these months had been the day when he would show it to her, to its dear future mistress.

'Oh, Everard — yes — you shall — I want to — ' said Lucy incoherently, her cheek against his, 'only not yet — not festivities — please — I won't be so morbid — I promise not to be morbid — but — please — '

And just when she was wavering, just when she was going to give in, not because of his reasoning, for her instincts were stronger than his reasoning, but because she couldn't bear his disappointment, Miss Entwhistle, sure now of Lucy's dread of Christmas at The Willows, suddenly turned firm again and announced that they would spend it in Eaton Terrace.

So Wemyss was forced to submit. The sensation was so new to him that he couldn't get over it. Once it was certain that his Christmas was, as he insisted, spoilt, he left off talking about it and went to the other extreme and was very quiet. That his little love should be so much under the influence of her aunt saddened him, he told her. Lucy tried to bring gaiety into this attitude by pointing out the proof she was giving him of how very submissive she was to the person she happened to live with — 'And presently all my submissiveness will be concentrated on you,' she said gaily.

But he wouldn't be gay. He shook his head in silence and filled his pipe. He was too deeply disappointed to be able to cheer up. And the expression 'happen to live with,' jarred a little. There was an airy carelessness about the phrase. One didn't happen to live with one's husband; yet that had been the implication.

Every year in April Wemyss had a birthday; that is, unlike most people of his age, he regularly celebrated it. Christmas and his birthday were the festivals of the year for him, and were always spent at The Willows. He regarded his birthday, which was on the 4th of April, as the first day of spring, defying the calendar, and was accustomed to find certain yellow flowers in blossom down by the river on that date supporting his contention. If these flowers came out before his birthday he took no notice of them, treating them as non-existent, nor did he ever notice them afterwards, for he did not easily notice flowers; but his gardener had standing orders to have a bunch of them on the table that one

134

morning in the year to welcome him with their bright shiny faces when he came down to his birthday breakfast, and coming in and seeing them he said, 'My birthday and Spring's'; whereupon his wife — up to now it had been Vera, but from now it would be Lucy — kissed him and wished him many happy returns. This was the ritual; and when one year of abnormal cold the yellow flowers weren't there at breakfast, because neither by the river's edge nor in the most sheltered of the swamps had the increasingly frantic gardener been able to find them, the entire birthday was dislocated. He couldn't say on entering the room and beholding them, 'My birthday and Spring's,' because he didn't behold them; and his wife — that year Vera — couldn't kiss him and wish him many happy returns because she hadn't the cue. She was so much used to the cue that not having it made her forget her part — forget, indeed, his birthday altogether; and consequently it was a day of the extremest spiritual chill and dinginess, matching the weather without. Wemyss had been terribly hurt. He hoped never to spend another birthday like it. Nor did he, for Vera remembered it after that.

Birthdays being so important to him, he naturally reflected after Miss Entwhistle had spoilt his Christmas that she would spoil his birthday too if he let her. Well, he wasn't going to let her. Not twice would he be caught like that; not twice would he be caught in a position of helplessness on his side and power on hers. The way to avoid it was very simple: he would marry Lucy in time for his birthday. Why should they wait any longer? Why stick to that absurd convention of the widower's year? No sensible man minded what people thought. And who were the people? Surely one didn't mind the opinions of those shabby weeds he had met on the two Thursday evenings at Lucy's aunt's. The little they had said had been so thoroughly unsound and muddled and yet dangerous, that if they one and all emigrated tomorrow England would only be the better. After meeting them he had said to Lucy, who had listened in some wonder at this new light thrown on her father's friends, that they were the very stuff of which successful segregation was made. In an island by themselves, he told her, they would be quite happy undermining each other's backbones, and the backbone of England, which consisted of plain unspoilt patriots, would be let alone. They, certainly, didn't matter; while as for his own friends, those friends who had behaved badly to him on Vera's death, not only didn't he care twopence for their criticisms but he could hardly wait for the moment when he would confound them by producing for their inspection this sweetest of little girls, so young, so devoted to him, Lucy his wife.

He accordingly proceeded to make all the necessary arrangements for being married in March, for going for a trip to Paris, and for returning to The Willows for the final few days of his honeymoon on the very day of his birthday. What a celebration that would be! Wemyss, thinking of it, shut his eyes so as to dwell upon it undisturbed. Never would he have had a birthday like this next one. He might really quite fairly call it his First, for he would be beginning life all over again, and entering on years that would indeed be truthfully described as tender.

So much was it his habit to make plans privately and not mention them till they were complete, that he found it difficult to tell Lucy of this one in spite of the important part she was to play in it. But, after all, some preparing would, he admitted to himself, be necessary even for the secret marriage he had decided on at a registrar's office. She would have to pack a bag; she would have to leave her belongings in order. Also he might perhaps have to use persuasion. He knew his little girl well enough to be sure she would relinquish church and white satin without a murmur at his request, but she might want to tell her aunt of the marriage's imminence, and then the aunt would, to a dead certainty, obstruct, and either induce her to wait till the year was out, or, if Lucy refused to do this, make her miserable with doubts as to whether she had been right to follow her lover's wishes. Fancy making a girl miserable because she followed her lover's wishes! What a woman, thought Wemyss, filling his pipe. In his eyes Miss Entwhistle had swollen since her conduct at Christmas to the bulk of a monster.

Having completed his preparations, and fixed his wedding day for the first Saturday in March, Wemyss thought it time he told Lucy; so he did, though not without a slight fear at the end that she might make difficulties.

'My little love isn't going to do anything that spoils her Everard's plans after all the trouble he has taken?' he said, seeing that with her mouth slightly open she gazed at him in an obvious astonishment and didn't say a word.

He then proceeded to shut the eyes that were gazing up into his, and the surprised parted lips, with kisses, for he had discovered that gentle, lingering kisses hushed Lucy quiet when she was inclined to say, 'But — ' and brought her back quicker than anything to the mood of tender, half-asleep acquiescence in which, as she lay in his arms, he most loved her; then indeed she was his baby, the object of the passionate protectiveness he felt he was naturally filled with, but for the exercise of which circumstances up to now had given him no scope. You couldn't passionately protect Vera. She was always in another room.

Lucy, however, did say, 'But — ' when she recovered from her first surprise, and did presently — directly, that is, he left off kissing her and she could speak — make difficulties. Her aunt; the secrecy; why secrecy; why not wait; it was so necessary under the circumstances to wait.

And then he explained about his birthday.

At that she gazed at him again with a look of wonder in her eyes, and after a moment began to laugh. She laughed a great deal, and with her arm tight round his neck, but her eyes were wet. 'Oh, Everard,' she said, her cheek against his, 'do you think we're really old enough to marry?'

This time, however, he got his way. Lucy found she couldn't bring herself to spoil his plans a second time; the spectacle of his prolonged silent disappointment at Christmas was still too vividly before her. Nor did she feel she could tell her aunt. She hadn't the courage to face her aunt's expostulations and final distressed giving in. Her aunt, who loomed so enormous in Wemyss's eyes, seemed to Lucy to be only half the size she used to be. She seemed to have been worried small by her position, like a bone among contending dogs, in the middle of different indignations. What would be the effect on her of this final blow? The thought of it haunted Lucy and spoilt all the last days before her marriage, days which she otherwise would have loved, because she very quickly became infected by the boyish delight and excitement over their secret that made Wemyss hardly able to keep still in his chair. He didn't keep still in it. Once at least he got up and did some slow steps about the room, moving with an apparent solemnity because of not being used to such steps, which he informed her presently were a dance. Till he told her this she watched him too much surprised to say anything. So did penguins dance in pictures. She couldn't think what was the matter with him. When he had done, and told her, breathing a little hard, that it was a dance symbolic of married happiness, she laughed and laughed, and flew to hug him.

'Baby, oh, baby!' she said, rubbing her cheek up and down his coat.

'Who's another baby?' he asked, breathless but beaming.

Such was their conversation.

But poor Aunt Dot . . .

Lucy couldn't bear to think of poor little kind Aunt Dot. She had been so wonderful, so patient, and she would be deeply horrified by a runaway marriage. Never, never would she understand the reason for it. She didn't a bit understand Everard, didn't begin to understand him, and that his birthday should be a reason for breaking what she would regard as the common decencies would of course only seem to her too childish to be even discussed. Lucy was afraid Aunt Dot was going to be very much upset, poor darling little Aunt Dot. Conscience-stricken, she couldn't do enough for Aunt Dot now that the secret date was fixed. She watched for every possible want during their times alone, flew to fetch things, darted at dropped handkerchiefs, kissed her not only at bedtime and in the morning but whenever there was the least excuse and with the utmost tenderness; and every kiss and every look seemed to say, 'Forgive me.'

'Are they going to run away?' wondered Miss Entwhistle presently.

Lucy would have been immensely taken aback, and perhaps, such is one's perversity, even hurt, if she could have seen the ray of hope which at this thought lit her Aunt Dot's exhausted mind; for Miss Entwhistle's life, which had been a particularly ordered and calm one up to the day when Wemyss first called at Eaton Terrace, had since then been nothing but just confused clamour. Everybody was displeased with her, and each for directly opposite reasons. She had fallen on evil days, and they had by February been going on so long that she felt worn out. Wemyss, she was quite aware, disliked her heartily; her Jim was dead; Lucy, her one living relation, so tenderly loved, was every day disappearing further before her very eyes into Wemyss's personality, into what she sometimes was betrayed by fatigue and impatience into calling to herself the Wemyss maw; and her little house, which had always been so placid, had become, she wearily felt, the cockpit of London. She used to crawl back to it with footsteps that lagged more and more the nearer she got, after her enforced prolonged daily outings — enforced and prolonged because the house couldn't possibly hold both herself and Wemyss except for the briefest moments — and drearily wonder what letters she would find from Jim's friends scolding her, and what fresh arrangements in the way of tiring motor excursions, or invitations to tea at that dreadful house in Lancaster Gate, would be sprung upon her. Did all engagements pursue such a turbulent course? she asked herself — she had given up asking the oracle of Chesham Street anything because of her disconcerting answers. How glad she was she had never been engaged; how glad she was she had refused the offers she had had when she was a girl. Quite recently she had met one of those would-be husbands in an omnibus, and how glad she was when she looked at him that she had refused him. People don't keep well, mused Miss Entwhistle. If Lucy would only refuse Wemyss now, how glad she would be that she had when she met him in ten years' time in an omnibus.

But these, of course, were merely the reflections of a tired-out spinster, and she still had enough spirit to laugh at them to herself. After all, whatever she might feel about Wemyss Lucy adored him, and when anybody adores anybody as much as that, Miss Entwhistle thought, the only thing to do is to marry and have done with it. No; that was cynical. She meant, marry and not have done with it. Ah, if only the child were marrying that nice young Teddy Trevor, her own age and so devoted, and with every window-sill throughout his house in Chelsea the proper height . . .

Miss Entwhistle was very unhappy all this time, besides having feet that continually ached. Though she dreaded the marriage, yet she couldn't help feeling that it would be delicious to be able once more to sit down. How enchanting to sit quietly in her own empty drawing-room, and not to have to walk about London any more. How enchanting not to make any further attempts to persuade herself that she enjoyed Battersea Park, and liked the Embankment, and was entertained by Westminster Abbey. What she wanted with an increasing longing that amounted at last to desperation as the winter dragged on, was her own chair by the fire and an occasional middle-aged crony to tea. She had reached the time of life when one likes sitting down. Also she had definitely got to the period of cronies. One's contemporaries — people who had worn the same kinds of clothes as oneself in girlhood, who remembered bishop's sleeves and could laugh with one about bustles — how very much one longed for one's contemporaries.

When, then, Lucy's behaviour suddenly became so markedly attentive and so very tender, when she caught her looking at her with wistful affection and flushing on being caught, when her good-nights and good-mornings were many kisses instead of one, and she kept on jumping up and bringing her teaspoons she hadn't asked for and sugar she didn't want, Miss Entwhistle began to revive.

'Is it possible they're going to run away?' she wondered; and so much reduced was she that she very nearly hoped so.

13

Lucy had meant to do exactly as Wemyss said and keep her marriage secret, creeping out of the house quietly, going off with him abroad after the registrar had bound them together, and telegraphing or writing to her aunt from some safe distant place *en route* like Boulogne; but on saying good-night the evening before the wedding day, to her very great consternation her aunt, whom she was in the act of kissing, suddenly pushed her gently a little away, looked at her a moment, and then holding her by both arms said with conviction, 'It's to-morrow.'

Lucy could only stare. She stared idiotically, open-mouthed, her face scarlet. She looked and felt both foolish and frightened. Aunt Dot was uncanny. If she had discovered, how had she discovered? And what was she going to do? But had she discovered, or was it just something she chanced to remember, some engagement Lucy had naturally forgotten, or perhaps only somebody coming to tea?

She clutched at this straw. 'What is to-morrow?' she stammered, scarlet with fright and guilt.

And her aunt made herself perfectly clear by replying, 'Your wedding.'

Then Lucy fell on her neck and cried and told her everything, and her wonderful, unexpected, uncanny, adorable little aunt, instead of being upset and making her feel too wicked and ungrateful to live, was full of sympathy and understanding. They sobbed together, sitting on the sofa locked in each other's arms, but it was a sweet sobbing, for they both felt at this moment how much they loved each other. Miss Entwhistle wished she had never had a single critical impatient thought of the man this darling little child so deeply loved, and Lucy wished she had never had a single secret from this darling little aunt Everard so blindly didn't love. Dear, dear little Aunt Dot. Lucy's heart was big with gratitude and tenderness and pity — pity because she herself was so gloriously happy and surrounded by love, and Aunt Dot's life seemed, compared to hers, so empty, so solitary, and going to be like that till the end of her days; and Miss Entwhistle's heart was big with yearning over this lamb of Jim's who was giving herself with such fearlessness, all lit up by radiant love, into the hands of a strange husband. Presently, of course, he wouldn't be a strange husband, he would be a familiar husband; but would he be any the better for that, she wondered? They sobbed, and kissed, and sobbed again, each keeping half her thoughts to herself.

This is how it was that Miss Entwhistle walked into the registrar's office with Lucy next morning and was one of the witnesses of the marriage.

Wemyss had a very bad moment when he saw her come in. His heart gave a great thump, such as it had never done in his life before, for he thought there was to be a hitch and that at the very last minute he was somehow not going to get his Lucy. Then he looked at Lucy and was reassured. Her face was like the morning of a perfect day in its cloudlessness, her Love-in-a-Mist eyes were dewy with tenderness as they rested on him, and her mouth was twisted up by happiness into the sweetest, funniest little crooked smile. If only she would take off her hat, thought Wemyss, bursting with pride, so that the registrar could see how young she looked with her short hair — why, perhaps the old boy might think she was too young to be married and start asking searching questions! What fun that would be.

He himself produced the effect on Miss Entwhistle, as he stood next to Lucy being married, of an enormous schoolboy who has just won some silver cup or other for his

House after immense exertions. He had exactly that glowing face of suppressed triumph and pride; he was red with delighted achievement.

'Put the ring on your wife's finger,' ordered the registrar when, having got through the first part of the ceremony, Wemyss, busy beaming down at Lucy, forgot there was anything more to do. And Lucy stuck up her hand with all the fingers spread out and stiff, and her face beamed too with happiness at the words, 'Your wife.'

"'Nothing is here for tears',' quoted Miss Entwhistle to herself, watching the blissful absorption with which they were both engaged in getting the ring successfully over the knuckle of the proper finger. 'He really *is* a-a dear. Yes. Of course. But how queer life is. I wonder what he was doing this day last year, he and that poor other wife of his.'

When it was over and they were outside on the steps, with the taxi Wemyss had come in waiting to take them to the station, Miss Entwhistle realised that here was the place and moment of good-bye, and that not only could she go no further with Lucy but that from now on she could do nothing more for her. Except love her. Except listen to her. Ah, she would always be there to love and listen to her; but happiest of all it would be for the

149

little thing if she never, from her, were to need either of those services.

At the last moment she put her hand impulsively on Wemyss's breast and looked up into his triumphant, flushed face and said, 'Be kind to her.'

'Oh, Aunt Dot!' laughed Lucy, turning to hug her once more.

'Oh, Aunt Dot!' laughed Wemyss, vigorously shaking her hand.

They went down the steps, leaving her standing alone on the top, and she watched the departing taxi with the two heads bobbing up and down at the window and the four hands waving good-byes. That taxi window could never have framed in so much triumph, so much radiance before. Well, well, thought Aunt Dot, going down in her turn when the last glimpse of them had disappeared, and walking slowly homeward; and she added, after a space of further reflection, 'He really *is* a — a dear.'

14

Marriage, Lucy found, was different from what she had supposed; Everard was different; everything was different. For one thing she was always sleepy. For another she was never alone. She hadn't realised how completely she would never be alone, or, if alone, not sure for one minute to the other of going on being alone. Always in her life there had been intervals during which she recuperated in solitude from any strain; now there were none. Always there had been places she could go to and rest in quietly, safe from interruption; now there were none. The very sight of their room at the hotels they stayed at, with Wemyss's suitcases and clothes piled on the chairs, and the table covered with his brushes and shaving things, for he wouldn't have a dressing-room, being too natural and wholesome, he explained, to want anything separate from his own woman — the very sight of this room fatigued her. After a day of churches, pictures and restaurants — he was a most conscientious sightseer, besides being greatly interested in his meals — to come back to this room wasn't rest but further fatigue. Wemyss, who was never tired and slept wonderfully — it was the soundness of his sleep that kept her awake, because she wasn't used to hearing sound sleep so close — would fling himself into the one easy-chair and pull her on to his knee, and having kissed her a great many times he would ruffle her hair, and then when it was all on ends like a boy's coming out of a bath, look at her with the pride of possession and say, 'There's a wife for a respectable British business man to have! Mrs. Wemyss, aren't you ashamed of yourself?' And then there would be more kissing — jovial, gluttonous kisses, that made her skin rough and chapped.

'Baby,' she would say, feebly struggling, and smiling a little wearily.

Yes, he was a baby, a dear, high-spirited baby, but a baby now at very close quarters and one that went on all the time. You couldn't put him in a cot and give him a bottle and say, 'There now,' and then sit down quietly to a little sewing; you didn't have Sundays out; you were never, day or night, an instant off duty. Lucy couldn't count the number of times a day she had to answer the question, 'Who's my own little wife?' At first she answered it with laughing ecstasy, running into his outstretched arms, but very soon that fatal sleepiness set in and remained with her for the whole of her honeymoon, and she really felt too tired sometimes to get the ecstasy she quickly got to know was expected of her into her voice. She loved him, she was indeed his own little wife, but constantly to answer this and questions like it satisfactorily was a great exertion. Yet if there was a shadow of hesitation before she answered, a hair's-breadth of delay owing to her thoughts having momentarily wandered, Wemyss was upset, and she had to spend quite a long time reassuring him with the fondest whispers and caresses. Her thoughts mustn't wander, she had discovered; her thoughts were to be his as well as all the rest of her. Was ever a girl so much loved? she asked herself, astonished and proud; but, on the other hand, she was dreadfully sleepy.

Any thinking she did had to be done at night, when she lay awake because of the immense emphasis with which Wemyss slept, and she hadn't been married a week before she was reflecting what a bad arrangement it was, the way ecstasy seemed to have no staying power. Also it oughtn't to begin, she considered, at its topmost height and accordingly not be able to move except downwards. If one could only start modestly in marriage with very little of it and work steadily upwards, taking one's time, knowing there was more and more to come, it would be much better she thought. No doubt it would go on longer if one slept better and hadn't, consequently, got headaches. Everard's ecstasy went on. Perhaps by ecstasy she really meant high spirits, and Everard was beside himself with high spirits.

Wemyss was indeed the typical bridegroom of the Psalms, issuing forth rejoicing from his chamber. Lucy wished she could issue forth from it rejoicing too. She was vexed with herself for being so stupidly sleepy, for not being able to get used to the noise beside her at night and go to sleep as naturally as she did in Eaton Terrace, in spite of the horns of taxis. It wasn't fair to Everard, she felt, not to find a wife in the morning matching him in spirits. Perhaps, however, this was a condition peculiar to honeymoons, and marriage, once the honeymoon was over, would be a more tranquil state. Things would settle down when they were back in England, to a different, more separated life in which there would be time to rest, time to think; time to remember, while he was away at his office, how deeply she loved him. And surely she would learn to sleep; and once she slept properly she would be able to answer his loving questions throughout the day with more real *élan*.

But — there in England waiting for her, inevitable, no longer to be put off or avoided, was The Willows. Whenever her thoughts reached that house they gave a little jump and tried to slink away. She was ashamed of herself, it was ridiculous, and Everard's attitude was plainly the sensible one, and if he could adopt it surely she, who hadn't gone through that terrible afternoon last July, could; yet she failed to see herself in The Willows, she failed altogether to imagine it. How, for instance, was she going to sit on that terrace — 'We always have tea in fine weather on the terrace,' Wemyss had casually remarked, apparently quite untouched by the least memory — how was she going to have tea on the very flags perhaps where . . . Her thoughts slunk away; but not before one of them had sent a curdling whisper through her mind, '*The tea would taste of blood.*'

Well, this was sleeplessness. She never in her life had had that sort of absurd thought. It was just that she didn't sleep, and so her brain was relaxed and let the reins of her thinking go slack. The day her father died, it's true, when it began to be evening and she was afraid of the night alone with him in his mysterious indifference, she had begun thinking absurdly, but Everard had come and saved her. He could save her from this too if she could tell him; only she couldn't tell him. How could she spoil his joy in his home? It was the thing he loved next best to her.

As the honeymoon went on and Wemyss's ecstasies a little subsided, as he began to tire of so many trains — after Paris they did the châteaux country — and hotels and waiters and taxis and restaurants, and the cooking which he had at first enjoyed now only increased his longing at every meal for a plain English steak and boiled potatoes, he talked more and more of The Willows. With almost the same eagerness as that which had so much enchanted and moved her before their marriage when he talked of their wedding day, he now talked of The Willows and the day when he would show it to her. He counted the days now to that day. The 4th of April; his birthday; on that happy day he would lead his little wife into the home he loved. How could she, when he talked like that, do anything but pretend enthusiasm and looking forward? He had apparently entirely forgotten what she had told him about her reluctance to go there at Christmas. She was astonished that, when the first bliss of being married to her had worn off and his thoughts were free for this other thing he so much loved, his home, he didn't approach it with more care for what he must know was her feeling about it. She was still more astonished when she realised that he had entirely forgotten her feeling about it. It would be, she felt, impossible to shadow his happiness at the prospect of showing her his home by any reminder of her reluctance. Besides, she was certainly going to have to live at The Willows, so what was the use of talking?

'I suppose,' she did say hesitatingly one day when he was describing it to her for the hundredth time, for it was his habit to describe the same thing often, 'you've changed your room — ?'

They were sitting at the moment, resting after the climb up, on one of the terraces of the Château of Amboise, with a view across the Loire of an immense horizon, and Wemyss had been comparing it, to its disadvantage, when he recovered his breath, with the view from his bedroom window at The Willows. It wasn't very nice weather, and they both were cold and tired, and it was still only eleven o'clock in the morning.

'Change my room? What room?' he asked.

'Your — the room you and — the room you slept in.'

'My bedroom? I should think not. It's the best room in the house. Why do you think

I've changed it?' And he looked at her with a surprised face.

'Oh, I don't know,' said Lucy, taking refuge in stroking his hand. 'I only thought — '

An inkling of what was in her mind penetrated into his, and his voice went grave.

'You mustn't think,' he said. 'You mustn't be morbid. Now Lucy, I can't have that. It will spoil everything if you let yourself be morbid. And you promised me before our marriage you wouldn't be. Have you forgotten?'

He turned to her and took her face in both his hands and searched her eyes with his own very solemn ones, while the woman who was conducting them over the castle went to the low parapet, and stood with her back to them studying the view and yawning.

'Oh, Everard — of course I haven't forgotten. I've not forgotten anything I promised you, and never will. But — have I got to go into that bedroom too?'

He was really astonished. 'Have you got to go into that bedroom too?' he repeated, staring at the face enclosed in his two big hands. It looked extraordinarily pretty like that, like a small flower in its delicate whiteness next to his discoloured, middle-aged hands, and her mouth since her marriage seemed to have become an even more vivid red than it used to be, and her eyes were young enough to be made more beautiful instead of less by the languor of want of sleep. 'Well, I should think so. Aren't you my wife?'

'Yes,' said Lucy. 'But — '

'Now, Lucy, I'll have no buts,' he said, with his most serious air, kissing her on the cheek, she had discovered that just that kind of kiss was a rebuke. 'Those buts of yours butt in — '

He stopped, struck by what he had said.

'I think that was rather amusing — don't you?' he asked, suddenly smiling.

'Oh yes — very,' said Lucy eagerly, smiling too, delighted that he should switch off from solemnity.

He kissed her again — this time a real kiss, on her funny, charming mouth.

'I suppose you'll admit,' he said, laughing and squeezing up her face into a quaint crumpled shape, 'that either you're my wife or not my wife, and that if you're my wife — '

'Oh, I'm *that* all right,' laughed Lucy.

'Then you share my room. None of these damned new-fangled notions for me, young woman.'

'Oh, but I didn't mean — '

'What? Another but?' he exclaimed, pouncing down on to her mouth and stopping it with an enormous kiss.

'*Monsieur et Madame se refroidiront*,' said the woman, turning round and drawing her shawl closer over her chest as a gust of chilly wind swept over the terrace.

They were honeymooners, poor creatures, and therefore one had patience; but even honeymooners oughtn't to wish to embrace in a cold wind on an exposed terrace of a château round which they were being conducted by a woman who was in a hurry to return to the preparation of her Sunday dinner. For such purposes hotels were provided, and the shelter of a comfortable warm room. She had supposed them to be *père et fille* when first she admitted them, but was soon aware of their real relationship. '*Il doit être bien riche*,' had been her conclusion.

'Come along, come along,' said Wemyss, getting up quickly, for he too felt the gust of cold wind. 'Let's finish the château or we'll be late for lunch. I wish they hadn't preserved so many of these places — one would have been quite enough to show us the sort of thing.'

'But we needn't go and look at them all,' said Lucy.

'Oh yes we must. We've arranged to.'

'But Everard — ' began Lucy, following

after him as he followed after the conductress, who had a way of darting out of sight round corners.

'This woman's like a lizard,' panted Wemyss, arriving round a corner only to see her disappear through an arch. 'Won't we be happy when it's time to go back to England and not have to see any more sights.'

'But why don't we go back now, if you feel like it?' asked Lucy, trotting after him as he on his big legs pursued the retreating conductress, and anxious to show him, by eagerness to go sooner to The Willows than was arranged, that she wasn't being morbid.

'Why, you know we can't leave before the 3rd of April,' said Wemyss, over his shoulder. 'It's all settled.'

'But can't it be unsettled?'

'What, and upset all the plans, and arrive home before my birthday?' He stopped and turned round to stare at her. 'Really, my dear — ' he said.

She had discovered that my dear was a term of rebuke.

'Oh yes — of course,' she said hastily, 'I forgot about your birthday.'

At that Wemyss stared at her harder than ever; incredulously, in fact. Forgot about his birthday? *Lucy* had forgotten? If it had been Vera, now — but Lucy? He was deeply hurt.

He was so much hurt that he stood quite still, and the conductress was obliged, on discovering that she was no longer being followed, to wait once more for the honeymooners; which she did, clutching her shawl round her abundant French chest and shivering.

What had she said, Lucy hurriedly asked herself, nipping over her last words in her mind, for she had learned by now what he looked like when he was hurt. Oh yes — the birthday. How stupid of her. But it was because birthdays in her family were so unimportant, and nobody had minded whether they were remembered or not.

'I didn't mean that,' she said earnestly, laying her hand on his breast. 'Of course I hadn't forgotten anything so precious. It only had — well, you know what even the most wonderful things do sometimes — it — it had escaped my memory.'

'Lucy! Escaped your memory? The day to which you owe your husband?'

Wemyss said this with such an exaggerated solemnity, such an immense pomposity, that she thought he was in fun and hadn't really minded about the birthday at all; and, eager to meet every mood of his, she laughed. Relieved, she was so unfortunate as to laugh merrily.

To her consternation, after a moment's

further stare he turned his back on her without a word and walked on.

Then she realised what she had done, that she had laughed — oh, how dreadful! — in the wrong place, and she ran after him and put her arm through his, and tried to lay her cheek against his sleeve, which was difficult because of the way their paces didn't match and also because he took no notice of her, and said, 'Baby — baby — were his dear feelings hurt, then?' and coaxed him.

But he wouldn't be coaxed. She had wounded him too deeply — laughing, he said to himself, at what was to him the most sacred thing in life, the fact that he was her husband, that she was his wife.

'Oh, Everard,' she murmured at last, withdrawing her arm, giving up, 'don't spoil our day.'

Spoil their day? He? That finished it.

He didn't speak to her again till night. Then, in bed, after she had cried bitterly for a long while, because she couldn't make out what really had happened, and she loved him so much, and wouldn't hurt him for the world, and was heart-broken because she had, and anyhow was tired out, he at last turned to her and took her to his arms again and forgave her.

'I can't live,' sobbed Lucy, 'I can't live — if

you don't go on loving me — if we don't understand — '

'My little Love,' said Wemyss, melted by the way her small body was shaking in his arms, and rather frightened, too, at the excess of her woe. 'My little Love don't. You mustn't. Your Everard loves you, and you mustn't give way like this. You'll be ill. Think how miserable you'd make him then.'

And in the dark he kissed away her tears, and held her close till her sobbing quieted down; and presently, held close like that, his kisses shutting her smarting eyes, she now the baby comforted and reassured, and he the soothing nurse, she fell asleep, and for the first time since her marriage slept all night.

15

Early in their engagement Wemyss had expounded his theory to Lucy that there should be the most perfect frankness between lovers, while as for husband and wife there oughtn't to be a corner anywhere about either of them, mind, body, or soul, which couldn't be revealed to the other one.

'You can talk about everything to your Everard,' he assured her. 'Tell him your innermost thoughts, whatever they may be. You need no more be ashamed of telling him than of thinking them by yourself. He *is* you. You and he are one in mind and soul now, and when he is your husband you and he will become perfect and complete by being one in body as well. Everard — Lucy. Lucy — Everard. We shan't know where one ends and the other begins. That, little Love, is real marriage. What do you think of it?'

Lucy thought so highly of it that she had no words with which to express her admiration, and fell to kissing him instead. What ideal happiness, to be for ever removed from the fear of loneliness by the simple expedient of being doubled; and who so happy as herself to have found the exactly right person for this doubling, one she could so perfectly agree with and understand? She felt quite sorry she had nothing in her mind in the way of thoughts she was ashamed of to tell him then and there, but there wasn't a doubt, there wasn't a shred of anything a little wrong, not even an unworthy suspicion. Her mind was a chalice filled only with love, and so clear and bright was the love that even at the bottom, when she stirred it up to look, there wasn't a trace of sediment.

But marriage — or was it sleeplessness? — completely changed this, and there were perfect crowds of thoughts in her mind that she was thoroughly ashamed of. Remembering his words, and whole-heartedly agreeing that to be able to tell each other everything, to have no concealments, was real marriage, the day after her wedding she first of all reminded him of what he had said, then plunged bravely into the announcement that she'd got a thought she was ashamed of.

Wemyss pricked up his ears, thinking it was something interesting to do with sex, and waited with an amused, inquisitive smile. But Lucy in such matters was content to follow him, aware of her want of experience and of the abundance of his, and the thought that was worrying her only had to do with a waiter. A waiter, if you please.

Wemyss's smile died away. He had had occasion to reprimand this waiter at lunch for gross negligence, and here was Lucy alleging he had done so without any reason that she could see, and anyhow roughly. Would he remove the feeling of discomfort she had at being forced to think her own heart's beloved, the kindest and gentlest of men, hadn't been kind and gentle but unjust, by explaining?

Well, that was at the very beginning. She soon learned that a doubt in her mind was better kept there. If she brought it out to air it and dispel it by talking it over with him, all that happened was that he was hurt, and when he was hurt she instantly became perfectly miserable. Seeing, then, that this happened about small things, how impossible it was to talk with him of big things; of, especially, her immense doubt in regard to The Willows. For a long while she was sure he was bearing her feeling in mind, since it couldn't have changed since Christmas, and that when she arrived there she would find that he had had everything altered and all traces of Vera's life there removed. Then, when he began to talk about The Willows, she found that such an idea as alterations hadn't entered his head. She was to sleep in the very room that had been his and Vera's, in the very bed. And positively, so far was it from true that she could tell him every thought and talk everything over with him, when she discovered this she wasn't able to say more than that hesitating remark on the château terrace at Amboise about supposing he was going to change his bedroom.

Yet The Willows haunted her, and what a comfort it would have been to tell him all she felt and let him help her to get rid of her growing obsession by laughing at her. What a comfort if, even if he had thought her too silly and morbid to be laughed at, he had indulged her and consented to alter those rooms. But one learns a lot on a honeymoon, Lucy reflected, and one of the things she had learned was that Wemyss's mind was always made up. There seemed to be no moment when it was in a condition of becoming, and she might have slipped in a suggestion or laid a wish before him; his plans were sprung upon her full fledged, and they were unalterable. Sometimes he said, 'Would you like — ?' and if she didn't like, and answered truthfully, as she answered at first before she learned not to, there was trouble. Silent trouble. A retiring of Wemyss into a hurt aloofness, for his question was only decorative, and his little Love should instinctively, he considered, like what he liked; and there outside this aloofness, after efforts to get at him with fond and anxious questions, she sat like a beggar in patient distress, waiting for him to emerge and be kind to her.

Of course as far as the minor wishes and preferences of every day went it was all quite easy, once she had grasped the right answer to the question, 'Would you like?' She instantly did like. 'Oh yes — very much!' she hastened to assure him; and then his face continued content and happy instead of clouding with aggrievement. But about the big things it wasn't easy, because of the difficulty of getting the right flavour of enthusiasm into her voice, and if she didn't get it in he would put his finger under her chin and turn her to the light and repeat the question in a solemn voice — precursor, she had learned, of the beginning of the cloud on his face.

How difficult it was sometimes. When he said to her, 'You'll like the view from your sitting-room at The Willows,' she naturally wanted to cry out that she wouldn't, and ask him how he could suppose she would like what was to her a view for ever associated with death? Why shouldn't she be able to cry out naturally if she wanted to, to talk to him frankly, to get his help to cure herself of what was so ridiculous by laughing at it with him? She couldn't laugh all alone, though she was always trying to; with him she could have, and so have become quite sensible. For he was so much bigger than she was, so wonderful in the way he had triumphed over diseased thinking, and his wholesomeness would spread over her too, a purging, disinfecting influence, if only he would let her talk, if only he would help her to laugh. Instead, she found herself hurriedly saying in a small, anxious voice, 'Oh yes — very much!'

'Is it possible,' she thought, 'that I am abject?'

Yes, she was extremely abject, she reflected, lying awake at night considering her behaviour during the day. Love had made her so. Love did make one abject, for it was full of fear of hurting the beloved. The assertion of the Scriptures that perfect love casteth out fear only showed, seeing that her love for Everard was certainly perfect, how little the Scriptures really knew what they were talking about.

Well, if she couldn't tell him the things she was feeling, why couldn't she get rid of the sorts of feelings she couldn't tell him, and just be wholesome? Why couldn't she be at least as wholesome about going to that house as Everard? If anybody was justified in shrinking from The Willows it was Everard, not herself. Sometimes Lucy would be sure that deep in his character there was a wonderful store of simple courage. He didn't speak of Vera's death, naturally he didn't wish to speak of that awful afternoon, but how often he must think of it, hiding his thoughts even from her, bearing them altogether alone. Sometimes she was sure of this, and sometimes she was equally sure of the very opposite. From the way he looked, the way he spoke, from those tiny indications that one somehow has noticed without knowing that one has noticed and that are so far more revealing and conclusive than any words, she sometimes was sure he really had forgotten. But this was too incredible. She couldn't believe it. What had perhaps happened, she thought, was that in self-defence, for the preservation of his peace, he had made up his mind never to think of Vera. Only by banishing her altogether from his mind would he be safe. Yet that couldn't be true either, for several times on the honeymoon he had begun talking of her, of things she had said, of things she had liked, and it was she, Lucy, who stopped him. She shrank from hearing anything about Vera. She especially shrank from hearing her mentioned casually. She was ready to brace herself to talk about her if it was to be a serious talk, because she wanted to help and comfort him whenever the remembrance of her death arose to torment him, but she couldn't bear to hear her mentioned casually. In a way she admired this casualness, because it was a proof of the supreme wholesomeness Everard had attained to by sheer courageous determination, but even so she couldn't help thinking that she would have preferred a little less of just this kind of wholesomeness in her beloved. She might be too morbid, but wasn't it possible to be too wholesome? Anyhow she shrank from the intrusion of Vera into her honeymoon. That, at least, ought to be kept free from her. Later on at The Willows . . .

Lucy fought and fought against it, but always at the back of her mind was the thought, not looked at, slunk away from, but nevertheless fixed, that there at The Willows, waiting for her, was Vera.

16

Those who go to Strorley, and cross the bridge to the other side of the river, have only to follow the towpath for a little to come to The Willows. It can also be reached by road, through a white gate down a lane that grows more and more willowy as it gets nearer the river and the house, but is quite passable for carts and even for cars, except when there are floods. When there are floods this lane disappears, and when the floods have subsided it is black and oozing for a long time afterwards, with clouds of tiny flies dancing about in it if the weather is at all warm, and the shoes of those who walk stick in it and come off, and those who drive, especially if they drive a car, have trouble. But all is well once a second white gate is reached, on the other side of which is a gravel sweep, a variety of handsome shrubs, nicely kept lawns, and The Willows. There are no big trees in the garden of The Willows, because it was built in the middle of meadows where there weren't any, but all round the iron railings of the square garden — the house being the centre of the square — and concealing the wire netting which keeps the pasturing cows from thrusting their heads through and eating the shrubs, is a fringe of willows. Hence its name.

'A house,' said Wemyss, explaining its name to Lucy on the morning of their arrival, 'should always be named after whatever most insistently catches the eye.'

'Then oughtn't it to have been called The Cows?' asked Lucy; for the meadows round were strewn thickly as far as she could see with recumbent cows, and they caught her eye much more than the tossing bare willow branches.

'No,' said Wemyss, annoyed. 'It ought not have been called The Cows.'

'No — of course I didn't mean that,' she said hastily.

Lucy was nervous, and said what first came into her head, and had been saying things of this nature the whole journey down. She didn't want to, she knew he didn't like it, but she couldn't stop.

They had just arrived, and were standing on the front steps while the servants unloaded the fly that had brought them from the station, and Wemyss was pointing out what he wished her to look at and admire from that raised-up place before taking her indoors. Lucy was glad of any excuse that delayed going indoors, that kept her on the west side of the house, furthest away from the terrace and the library window. Indoors would be the rooms, the unaltered rooms, the library past whose window . . . , the sitting-room at the top of the house out of whose window . . . , the bedroom she was going to sleep in with the very bed . . . It was too miserably absurd, too unbalanced of her for anything but shame and self-contempt, how she couldn't get away from the feeling that indoors waiting for her would be Vera.

It was a grey, windy morning, with low clouds scurrying across the meadows. The house was raised well above flood level, and standing on the top step she could see how far the meadows stretched beyond the swaying willow hedge. Grey sky, grey water, green fields — it was all grey and green except the house, which was red brick with handsome stone facings, and made, in its exposed position unhidden by any trees, a great splotch of vivid red in the landscape.

'Like blood,' said Lucy to herself; and was immediately ashamed.

'Oh, how bracing!' she cried, spreading out her arms and letting the wind blow her serge wrap out behind her like a flag. It whipped her skirt round her body, showing its slender pretty lines, and the parlourmaid, going in and out with the luggage, looked curiously at this small juvenile new mistress. 'Oh, I love this wind — don't take me indoors yet — '

Wemyss was pleased that she should like the wind, for was it not by the time it reached his house part, too, of his property? His face, which had clouded a little because of The Cows, cleared again.

But she didn't really like the wind at all, she never had liked anything that blustered and was cold, and if she hadn't been nervous the last thing she would have done was to stand there letting it blow her to pieces.

'And what a lot of laurels!' she exclaimed, holding on her hat with one hand and with the other pointing to a corner filled with these shrubs.

'Yes. I'll take you round the garden after lunch,' said Wemyss. 'We'll go in now.'

'And — and laurustinus. I love laurustinus — '

'Yes. Vera planted that. It has done very well. Come in now — '

'And — look, what are those bare things without any leaves yet?'

'I'll show you everything after lunch, Lucy. Come in — ' And he put his arm about her shoulders, and urged her through the door the maid was holding open with difficulty because of the wind.

There she was, then, actually inside The

Willows. The door was shut behind her. She looked about her shrinkingly.

They were in a roomy place with a staircase in it.

'The hall,' said Wemyss, standing still, his arm round her.

'Yes,' said Lucy.

'Oak,' said Wemyss.

'Yes,' said Lucy.

He gazed round him with a sigh of satisfaction at having got back to it.

'All oak,' he said. 'You'll find nothing gimcrack about *my* house, little Love. Where are those flowers?' he added, turning sharply to the parlourmaid. 'I don't see my yellow flowers.'

'They're in the dining-room, sir,' said the parlourmaid.

'Why aren't they where I could see them the first thing?'

'I understood the orders were they were always to be on the breakfast-table, sir.'

'Breakfast-table! When there isn't any breakfast?'

'I understood — '

'I'm not interested in what you understood.'

Lucy here nervously interrupted, for Everard sounded suddenly very angry, by exclaiming, 'Antlers!' and waving her unpinned-down arm in the direction of the —

'Yes,' said Wemyss, his attention called off the parlourmaid, gazing up at his walls with pride.

'What a lot,' said Lucy.

'Aren't there. I always said I'd have a hall with antlers in it, and I've got it.' He hugged her close to his side. 'And I've got you too,' he said. 'I always get what I'm determined to get.'

'Did you shoot them all yourself?' asked Lucy, thinking the parlourmaid would take the opportunity to disappear, and a little surprised that she continued to stand there.

'What? The beasts they belonged to? Not I. If you want antlers the simple way is to go and buy them. Then you get them all at once, and not gradually. The hall was ready for them all at once, not gradually. I got these at Whiteley's. Kiss me.'

This sudden end to his remarks startled Lucy, and she repeated in her surprise — for there still stood the parlourmaid 'Kiss you?'

'I haven't had my birthday kiss yet.'

'Why, the very first thing when you woke up — '

'Not my real birthday kiss in my own home.'

She looked at the parlourmaid, who was quite frankly looking at her. Well, if the parlourmaid didn't mind, and Everard didn't mind, why should she mind?

She lifted her face and kissed him; but she didn't like kissing him or being kissed in public. What was the point of it? Kissing Everard was a great delight to her. A mixture of all sorts of wonderful sensations, and she loved to do it in different ways, tenderly, passionately, lingeringly, dreamily, amusingly, solemnly; each kind in turn, or in varied combinations. But among her varied combinations there was nothing that included a parlourmaid. Consequently her kiss was of the sort that was to be expected, perfunctory and brief, whereupon Wemyss said, 'Lucy — ' in his hurt voice.

She started.

'Oh Everard — what is it?' she asked nervously.

That particular one of his voices always by now made her start, for it always took her by surprise. Pick her way as carefully as she might among his feelings there were always some, apparently, that she hadn't dreamed were there and that she accordingly knocked against. How dreadful if she had hurt him the very first thing on getting into The Willows! And on his birthday too. From the moment he woke that morning, all the way down in the train, all the way in the fly from the station, she had been unremittingly engaged in avoiding hurting him; an activity made extra difficult by the unfortunate way her nervousness about the house at the journey's end impelled her to say the kinds of things she least wanted to. Irreverent things; such as the silly remark on his house's name. She had got on much better the evening before at the house in Lancaster Gate where they had slept, because gloomy as it was it anyhow wasn't The Willows. Also there was no trace in it that she could see of such a thing as a woman ever having lived in it. It was a man's house; the house of a man who has no time for pictures, or interesting books and furniture. It was like a club and an office mixed up together, with capacious leather chairs and solid tables and Turkey carpets and reference books. She found it quite impossible to imagine Vera, or any other woman, in that house. Either Vera had spent most of her time at The Willows, or every trace of her had been very carefully removed. Therefore Lucy, helped besides by extreme fatigue, for she had been sea-sick all the way from Dieppe to Newhaven, Wemyss having crossed that way because he was fond of the sea, had positively been unable to think of Vera in those surroundings and had dropped off to sleep directly she got there and had slept all night; and of course being asleep she naturally hadn't said anything she oughtn't to have said, so that her first appearance in Lancaster Gate was a success; and when she woke next morning, and saw Wemyss's face in such unclouded tranquillity next to hers as he still slept, she lay gazing at it with her heart brimming with tender love and vowed that his birthday should be as unclouded throughout as his dear face was at that moment. She adored him. He was her very life. She wanted nothing in the world except for him to be happy. She would watch every word. She really must see to it that on this day of all days no word should escape her before it had been turned round in her head at least three times, and considered with the utmost care. Such were her resolutions in the morning; and here she was not only saying the wrong things but doing them. It was because she hadn't expected to be told to kiss him in the presence of a parlourmaid. She was always being tripped up by the unexpected. She ought by now to have learned better. How unfortunate.

'Oh Everard — what is it?' she asked nervously; but she knew before he could answer, and throwing her objections to public caresses to the winds, for anything was better than that he should be hurt at just that moment, she put up her free arm and drew his head down and kissed him again — lingeringly this time, a kiss of tender, appealing love. What must it be like, she thought while she kissed him and her heart yearned over him, to be so fearfully sensitive. It made things difficult for her, but how much, much more difficult for him. And how wonderful the way his sensitiveness had developed since marriage. There had been no sign of it before.

Implicit in her kiss was an appeal not to let anything she said or did spoil his birthday, to forgive her, to understand. And at the back of her mind, quite uncontrollable, quite unauthorised, ran beneath these other thoughts this thought: 'I am certainly abject.'

This time he was quickly placated because of his excitement at getting home. 'Nobody can hurt me as you can,' was all he said.

'Oh but as though I ever, ever mean to,' she breathed, her arm round his neck.

Meanwhile the parlourmaid looked on.

'Why doesn't she go?' whispered Lucy, making the most of having got his ear.

'Certainly not,' said Wemyss out loud, raising his head. 'I might want her. Do you like the hall, little Love?'

'Very much,' she said, loosing him.

'Don't you think it's a very fine staircase?'

'Very fine,' she said.

He gazed about him with pride, standing in the middle of the Turkey carpet holding her close to his side.

'Now look at the window,' he said, turning her round when she had had time to absorb the staircase. 'Look — isn't it a jolly window? No nonsense about that window. You can really see out of it, and it really lets in light. Vera' — she winced — 'tried to stuff it all up with curtains. She said she wanted colour, or something. Having got a beautiful garden to look out at, what does she try to do but shut most of it out again by putting up curtains.'

The attempt had evidently not succeeded, for the window, which was as big as a window in the waiting-room of a London terminus, had nothing to interfere with it but the hanging cord of a drawn-up brown holland blind. Through it Lucy could see the whole half of the garden on the right side of the front door with the tossing willow hedge, the meadows, and the cows. The leafless branches of some creeper beat against it and made a loud irregular tapping in the pauses of Wemyss's observations.

'Plate glass,' he said.

'Yes,' said Lucy; and something in his voice made her add in a tone of admiration, 'Fancy.'

Looking at the window they had their backs to the stairs. Suddenly she heard footsteps coming down them from the landing above.

'Who's that?' she said quickly, with a little gasp, before she could think, before she could stop, not turning her head, her eyes staring at the window.

'Who's what?' asked Wemyss. 'You do think it's a jolly window, don't you, little Love?'

The footsteps on the stairs stopped, and a gong she had noticed at the angle of the turn was sounded. Her body, which had shrunk together, relaxed. What a fool she was.

'Lunch,' said Wemyss. 'Come along — but isn't it a jolly window, little Love?'

'Very jolly.'

He turned her round to march her off to the dining-room, while the housemaid, who had come down from the landing, continued to beat the gong, though there they were obeying it under her very nose.

'Don't you think that's a good place to have a gong?' he asked, raising his voice because the gong, which had begun quietly, was getting rapidly louder. 'Then when you're upstairs in your sitting-room you'll hear it just as distinctly as if you were downstairs. Vera — '

But what he was going to say about Vera

184

was drowned this time in the increasing fury of the gong.

'Why doesn't she leave off?' Lucy tried to call out to him, straining her voice to its utmost, for the maid was very good at the gong and was now extracting the dreadfullest din out of it.

'Eh?' shouted Wemyss.

In the dining-room, whither they were preceded by the parlourmaid, who at last had left off standing still and had opened the door for them, as Lucy could hear the gong continuing to be beaten though muffled now by doors and distance, she again said, 'Why doesn't she leave off?'

Wemyss took out his watch.

'She will in another fifty seconds,' he said.

Lucy's mouth and eyebrows became all inquiry.

'It is beaten for exactly two and a half minutes before every meal,' he explained.

'Oh?' said Lucy. 'Even when we're visibly collected?'

'She doesn't know that.'

'But she saw us.'

'But she doesn't know it officially.'

'Oh,' said Lucy.

'I had to make that rule,' said Wemyss, arranging his knives and forks more accurately beside his plate, 'because they would leave off beating it almost as soon as they'd begun, and then Vera was late and her excuse was that she hadn't heard. For a time after that I used to have it beaten all up the stairs right to the door of her sitting-room. Isn't it a fine gong? Listen — ' And he raised his hand.

'Very fine,' said Lucy, who was thoroughly convinced there wasn't a finer, more robust gong in existence.

'There. Time's up,' he said, as three great strokes were followed by a blessed silence.

He pulled out his watch again. 'Let's see. Yes — to the tick. You wouldn't believe the trouble I had to get them to keep time.'

'It's wonderful,' said Lucy.

The dining-room was a narrow room full of a table. It had a window facing west and a window facing north, and in spite of the uninterrupted expanses of plate glass was a bleak, dark room. But then the weather was bleak and dark, and one saw such a lot of it out of the two big windows as one sat at the long table and watched the rolling clouds blowing straight towards one from the north-west; for Lucy's place was facing the north window, on Wemyss's left hand. Wemyss sat at the end of the table facing the west window. The table was so long that if Lucy had sat in the usual seat of wives, opposite her husband, communication would have been difficult — indeed, as she remarked, she would have disappeared below the dip of the horizon.

'I like a long table,' said Wemyss to this. 'It looks so hospitable.'

'Yes,' said Lucy a little doubtfully, but willing to admit that its length at least showed a readiness for hospitality. 'I suppose it does. Or it would if there were people all round it.'

'People? You don't mean to say you want people already?'

'Good heavens no,' said Lucy hastily. 'Of course I don't. Why, of course, Everard, I didn't mean that,' she added, laying her hand on his and smiling at him so as to dispel the gathering cloud on his face; and once more she flung all thoughts of the parlourmaid to the winds. 'You know I don't want a soul in the world but you.'

'Well, that's what I thought,' said Wemyss, mollified. 'I know all I want is you.'

(Was this same parlourmaid here in Vera's time? Lucy asked herself very privately and unconsciously and beneath the concerned attentiveness she was concentrating on Wemyss.)

'What lovely kingcups!' she said aloud.

'Oh yes, there they are — I hadn't noticed them. Yes, aren't they? They're my birthday flowers.' And he repeated his formula: 'It's my birthday and Spring's.'

But Lucy, of course, didn't know the proper ritual, it being her first experience of one of Wemyss's birthdays, besides having wished him his many happy returns hours ago when he first opened his eyes and found hers gazing at him with love; so all she did was to make the natural but unfortunate remark that surely Spring began on the 21st of March — or was it the 25th? No, that was Christmas Day — no, she didn't mean that —

'You're always saying things and then saying you didn't mean them,' interrupted Wemyss, vexed, for he thought that Lucy of all people should have recognised the allegorical nature of his formula. If it had been Vera, now — but even Vera had managed to understand that much. 'I wish you would begin with what you do mean, it would be so much simpler. What, pray, *do* you mean now?'

'I can't think,' said Lucy timidly, for she had offended him again, and this time she couldn't even remotely imagine how.

17

He got over it, however. There was a particularly well-made soufflé, and this helped. Also Lucy kept on looking at him very tenderly, and it was the first time she had sat at his table in his beloved home, realising the dreams of months that she should sit just there with him, his little bobbed-haired Love, and gradually therefore he recovered and smiled at her again.

But what power she had to hurt him, thought Wemyss; it was so great because his love for her was so great. She should be very careful how she wielded it. Her Everard was made very sensitive by his love.

He gazed at her solemnly, thinking this, while the plates were being changed.

'What is it, Everard?' Lucy asked anxiously.

'I'm only thinking that I love you,' he said, laying his hand on hers.

She flushed with pleasure, and her face grew instantly happy. 'My Everard,' she murmured, gazing back at him, forgetful in her pleasure of the parlourmaid. How dear he was. How silly she was to be so much distressed when he was offended. At the core he was so sound and simple. At the core he was utterly her own dear lover. The rest was mere incident, merest indifferent detail.

'We'll have coffee in the library,' he said to the parlourmaid, getting up when he had finished his lunch and walking to the door. 'Come along, little Love,' he called over his shoulder.

The library . . .

'Can't we — don't we — have coffee in the hall?' asked Lucy, getting up slowly.

'No,' said Wemyss, who had paused before an enlarged photograph that hung on the wall between the two windows, enlarged to life size.

He examined it a moment, and then drew his finger obliquely across the glass from top to bottom. It then became evident that the picture needed dusting.

'Look,' he said to the parlourmaid, pointing.

The parlourmaid looked.

'I notice you don't say anything,' he said to her after a silence in which she continued to look, and Lucy, taken aback again, stood uncertain by the chair she had got up from. 'I don't wonder. There's nothing you can possibly say to excuse such carelessness.'

'Lizzie — ' began the parlourmaid.

'Don't put it on to Lizzie.'

The parlourmaid ceased putting it on to Lizzie and was dumb.

'Come along, little Love,' said Wemyss, turning to Lucy and holding out his hand. 'It makes one pretty sick, doesn't it, to see that not even one's own father gets dusted.'

'Is that your father?' asked Lucy, hurrying to his side and offering no opinion about dusting.

It could have been no one else's. It was Wemyss grown very enormous, Wemyss grown very old, Wemyss displeased. The photograph had been so arranged that wherever you moved to in the room Wemyss's father watched you doing it. He had been watching Lucy from between those two windows all through her first lunch, and must, flashed through Lucy's brain, have watched Vera like that all through her last one.

'How long has he been there?' she asked, looking up into Wemyss's father's displeased eyes which looked straight back into hers.

'Been there?' repeated Wemyss, drawing her away for he wanted his coffee. 'How can I remember? Ever since I've lived here, I should think. He died five years ago. He was a wonderful old man, nearly ninety. He used to stay here a lot.'

Opposite this picture hung another, next to

191

the door that led into the hall — also a photograph enlarged to life-size. Lucy had noticed neither of these pictures when she came in, because the light from the windows was in her eyes. Now, turning to go out through the door led by Wemyss, she was faced by this one.

It was Vera. She knew at once; and if she hadn't she would have known the next minute, because he told her.

'Vera,' he said, in a matter-of-fact tone, as it were introducing them.

'Vera,' repeated Lucy under her breath; and she and Vera — for this photograph too followed one about with its eye — stared at each other.

It must have been taken about twelve years earlier, judging from the clothes. She was standing, and in a day dress that yet had a train to it trailing on the carpet, and loose, floppy sleeves and a high collar. She looked very tall, and had long thin fingers. Her dark hair was drawn up from her ears and piled on the top of her head. Her face was thin and seemed to be chiefly eyes — very big dark eyes that stared out of the absurd picture in a kind of astonishment, and her mouth had a little twist in it as though she were trying not to laugh.

Lucy looked at her without moving. So this

was Vera. Of course. She had known, though she had never constructed any image of her in her mind, had carefully avoided doing it, that she would be like that. Only older; the sort of Vera she must have been at forty when she died — not attractive like that, not a young woman. To Lucy at twenty-two, forty seemed very old; at least, if you were a woman. In regard to men, since she had fallen in love with some one of forty-five who was certainly the youngest thing she had ever come across, she had rearranged her ideas of age, but she still thought forty very old for a woman. Vera had been thin and tall and dark in her idea of her, just as this Vera was thin and tall and dark; but thin bonily, tall stoopingly, and her dark hair was turning grey. In her idea of her, too, she was absent-minded and not very intelligent; indeed, she was rather trouble-somely unintelligent, doing obstinate, foolish things, and at last doing that fatal, obstinate, foolish thing which so dreadfully ended her. This Vera was certainly intelligent. You couldn't have eyes like that and be a fool. And the expression of her mouth — what had she been trying not to laugh at that day? Did she know she was going to be enlarged and hang for years in the bleak dining-room facing her father-in-law, each of them eyeing the other from their walls, while three times a day the originals sat down beneath their own pictures at the long table and ate? Perhaps she laughed, thought Lucy, because else she might have cried; only that would have been silly, and she couldn't have been silly — not with those eyes, not with those straight, fine eyebrows. But would she, herself, presently be photographed too and enlarged and hung there? There was room next to Vera, room for just one more before the sideboard began. How very odd it would be if she were hung up next to Vera, and every day three times as she went out of the room was faced by Everard's wives. And how quaint to watch one's clothes as the years went by leaving off being pretty and growing more absurd. Really for such purposes one ought to be just wrapped round in a shroud. Fashion didn't touch shrouds; they always stayed the same. Besides, how suitable, thought Lucy, gazing into her dead predecessor's eyes; one would only be taking time by the forelock . . .

'Come along,' said Wemyss, drawing her away, 'I want my coffee. Don't you think it's a good idea,' he went on, as he led her down the hall to the library door, 'to have life-sized photographs instead of those idiotic portraits that are never the least like people?'

'Oh, a *very* good idea,' said Lucy mechanically, bracing herself for the library.

There was only one room in the house she dreaded going into more than the library, and that was the sitting-room on the top floor — her sitting-room and Vera's.

'Next week we'll go to a photographer's in London and have my little girl done,' said Wemyss, pushing open the library door, 'and then I'll have her exactly as God made her, without some artist idiot or other coming butting-in with his idea of her. God's idea of her is good enough for me. They won't have to enlarge much,' he laughed, 'to get *you* life-size, you midge. Vera was five foot ten. Now isn't this a fine room? Look — there's the river. Isn't it jolly being so close to it? Come round here — don't knock against my writing-table, now. Look — there's only the towpath between the river and the garden. Lord, what a beastly day. It might just as easily have been a beautiful spring day and us having our coffee out on the terrace. Don't you think this is a beautiful look-out — so typically English with the beautiful green lawn and the bit of lush grass along the towpath, and the river. There's no river like it in the world, is there, little Love. Say you think it's the most beautiful river in the world' — he hugged her close — 'say you think it's a hundred times better than that beastly French one we got so sick of with all those châteaux.'

'Oh, a *hundred* times better,' said Lucy.

They were standing at the window, with his arm round her shoulder. There was just room for them between it and the writing-table. Outside was the flagged terrace, and then a very green lawn with worms and blackbirds on it and a flagged path down the middle leading to a little iron gate. There was no willow hedge along the river end of the square garden, so as not to interrupt the view — only the iron railings and wire-netting. Terra-cotta vases, which later on would be a blaze of geraniums, Wemyss explained, stood at intervals on each side of the path. The river, swollen and brown, slid past Wemyss's frontage very quickly that day, for there had been much rain. The clouds scudding across the sky before the wind were not in such a hurry but that every now and then they let loose a violent gust of rain, soaking the flags of the terrace again just as the wind had begun to dry them up. How could he stand there, she thought, holding her tight so that she couldn't get away, making her look out at the very place on those flags not two yards off . . .

But the next minute she thought how right he really was, how absolutely the only way this was to do the thing. Perfect simplicity was the one way to meet this situation successfully; and she herself was so far from simplicity that here she was shrinking, not able to bear to look, wanting only to hide her face — oh, he was wonderful, and she was the most ridiculous of fools.

She pressed very close to him, and put up her face to his, shutting her eyes, for so she shut out the desolating garden with its foreground of murderous flags.

'What is it, little Love?' asked Wemyss.

'Kiss me,' she said; and he laughed and kissed her, but hastily, because he wanted her to go on admiring the view.

She still, however, held up her face. 'Kiss my eyes,' she whispered, keeping them shut. 'They're tired — '

He laughed again, but with a slight impatience, and kissed her eyes; and then, suddenly struck by her little blind face so close to his, the strong light from the big window showing all its delicate curves and delicious softnesses, his Lucy's face, his own little wife's, he kissed her really, as she loved him to kiss her, becoming absorbed only in his love.

'Oh, I love you, love you — ' murmured Lucy, clinging to him, making secret vows of sensibleness, of wholesomeness, of a determined, unfailing future simplicity.

'Aren't we happy,' he said, pausing in his kisses to gaze down at what was now his face, for was it not much more his than hers? Of course it was his. She never saw it, except when she specially went to look, but he saw it all the time; she only had duties in regard to it, but he was on the higher plane of only having joys. She washed it, but he kissed it. And he kissed it when he liked and as much as ever he liked. 'Isn't it wonderful being married,' he said, gazing down at this delightful thing that was his very own for ever.

'Oh — wonderful!' murmured Lucy, opening her eyes and gazing into his.

Her face broke into a charming smile. 'You have the dearest eyes,' she said, putting up her finger and gently tracing his eyebrows with it.

Wemyss's eyes, full at that moment of love and pride, were certainly dear eyes, but a noise at the other end of the room made Lucy jump so in his arms, gave her apparently such a fright, that when he turned his head to see who it was daring to interrupt them, daring to startle his little girl like that, and beheld the parlourmaid, his eyes weren't dear at all but very angry.

The parlourmaid had come in with the coffee; and seeing the two interlaced figures against the light of the big window had pulled up short, uncertain what to do. This pulling up had jerked a spoon off its saucer onto the floor with a loud rattle because of the floor not having a carpet on it and being of polished oak, and it was this noise that made Lucy jump so excessively that her jump actually made Wemyss jump too.

In the parlourmaid's untrained phraseology there had been a good deal of billing and cooing during luncheon, and even in the hall before luncheon there were examples of it, but what she found going on in the library was enough to make anybody stop dead and upset things — it was such, she said afterwards in the kitchen, that if she didn't know for a fact that they were really married she wouldn't have believed it. Married people in the parlourmaid's experience didn't behave like that. What affection there was was exhibited before, and not after, marriage. And she went on to describe the way in which Wemyss — thus briefly and irreverently did they talk of their master in the kitchen — had flown at her for having come into the library. 'After telling me to,' she said. 'After saying, 'We'll 'ave coffee in the library.'' And they all agreed, as they had often before agreed, that if it weren't that he was in London half the time they wouldn't stay in the place five minutes.

Meanwhile Wemyss and Lucy were sitting side by side in two enormous chairs facing the unlit library fire drinking their coffee. The fire was only lit in the evenings, explained Wemyss, after the 1st of April; the weather ought to be warm enough by then to do without fires in the daytime, and if it wasn't it was its own look-out.

'Why did you jump so?' he asked. 'You gave me such a start. I couldn't think what was the matter.'

'I don't know,' said Lucy, faintly flushing. 'Perhaps' — she smiled at him over the arm of the enormous chair in which she almost totally disappeared — 'because the maid caught us.'

'Caught us?'

'Being so particularly affectionate.'

'I like that,' said Wemyss. 'Fancy feeling guilty because you're being affectionate to your own husband.'

'Oh, well,' laughed Lucy, 'don't forget I haven't had him long.'

'You're such a complicated little thing. I shall have to take you seriously in hand and teach you to be natural. I can't have you having all sorts of finicking ideas about not doing this and not doing the other before servants. Servants don't matter. I never consider them.'

'I wish you had considered the poor parlourmaid,' said Lucy, seeing that he was in an unoffended frame of mind. 'Why did you give her such a dreadful scolding?'

'Why? Because she made you jump so. You couldn't have jumped more if you had thought it was a ghost. I won't have your flesh being made to creep.'

'But it crept much worse when I heard the things you said to her.'

'Nonsense. These people have to be kept in order. What did the woman mean by coming in like that?'

'Why, you told her to bring us coffee.'

'But I didn't tell her to make an infernal noise by dropping spoons all over the place.'

'That was because she got just as great a fright when she saw us as I did when I heard her.'

'I don't care what she got. Her business is not to drop things. That's what I pay her for. But look here — don't you go thinking such a lot of tangled-up things and arguing. Do, for goodness sake, try and be simple.'

'I feel *very* simple,' said Lucy, smiling and putting out her hand to him, for his face was clouding. 'Do you know, Everard, I believe what's the matter with me is that I'm *too* simple.'

Wemyss roared, and forgot how near he was getting to being hurt. 'You simple! You're the most complicated — '

'No I'm not. I've got the untutored mind and uncontrolled emotions of a savage. That's really why I jumped.'

'Lord,' laughed Wemyss, 'listen to her how she talks. Anybody might think she was clever, saying such big long words, if they didn't know she was just her Everard's own little wife. Come here, my little savage — come and sit on your husband's knee and tell him all about it.'

He held out his arms, and Lucy got up and went into them and he rocked her and said, 'There, there — was it a little untutored savage then — '

But she didn't tell him all about it, first because by now she knew that to tell him all about anything was asking for trouble, and second because he didn't really want to know. Everard, she was beginning to realise with much surprise, preferred not to know. He was not merely incurious as to other people's ideas and opinions, he definitely preferred to be unconscious of them.

This was a great contrast to the restless curiosity and interest of her father and his friends, to their insatiable hunger for discussion, for argument; and it much surprised Lucy. Discussion was the very salt of life for them — a tireless exploration of each other's ideas, a clashing of them together, and out of that clashing the creation of fresh ones. To Everard, Lucy was beginning to perceive, discussion merely meant contradiction, and he disliked contradiction, he disliked even difference of opinion. 'There's only one way of looking at a thing, and that's the right way,' as he said, 'so what's the good of such a lot of talk?'

The right way was his way; and though he seemed by his direct, unswerving methods to succeed in living mentally in a great calm, and though after the fevers of her father's set this was to her immensely restful, was it really a good thing? Didn't it cut one off from growth? Didn't it shut one in an isolation? Wasn't it, frankly, rather like death? Besides, she had doubts as to whether it were true that there was only one way of looking at a thing, and couldn't quite believe that his way was invariably the right way. But what did it matter after all, thought Lucy, snuggled up on his knee with one arm round his neck, compared to the great, glorious fact of their love? That at least was indisputable and splendid. As to the rest, truth would go on being truth whether Everard saw it or not; and if she were not going to be able to talk

over things with him she could anyhow kiss
him, and how sweet that was, thought Lucy.
They understood each other perfectly when
they kissed. What, indeed, when such sweet
means of communion existed, was the good
of a lot of talk?

'I believe you're asleep' said Wemyss,
looking down at the face on his breast.

'Sound,' said Lucy, smiling, her eyes shut.

'My baby.'

'My Everard.'

18

But this only lasted as long as his pipe lasted. When that was finished he put her off his knee, and said he was now ready to gratify her impatience and show her everything; they would go over the house first, and then the garden and outbuildings.

No woman was ever less impatient than Lucy. However, she pulled her hat straight and tried to seem all readiness and expectancy. She wished the wind wouldn't howl so. What an extraordinary dreary place the library was. Well, any place would be dreary at half-past two o'clock on such an afternoon, without a fire and with the rain beating against the window, and that dreadful terrace just outside.

Wemyss stooped to knock out the ashes of his pipe on the bars of the empty grate, and Lucy carefully kept her head turned away from the window and the terrace towards the other end of the room. The other end was filled with bookshelves from floor to ceiling, and the books, in neat rows and uniform editions, were packed so tightly in the shelves that no one but an unusually determined reader would have the energy to wrench one out. Reading was evidently not encouraged, for not only were the books shut in behind glass doors, but the doors were kept locked and the key hung on Wemyss's watch-chain. Lucy discovered this when Wemyss, putting his pipe in his pocket, took her by the arm and walked her down the room to admire the shelves. One of the volumes caught her eye, and she tried to open the glass door to take it out and look at it. 'Why,' she said surprised, 'it's locked.'

'Of course,' said Wemyss.

'Why but then nobody can get at them.'

'Precisely.'

'But — '

'People are so untrustworthy about books. I took pains to arrange mine myself, and they're all in first-class-bindings and I don't want them taken out and left lying anywhere by Tom, Dick, and Harry. If any one wants to read they can come and ask me. Then I know exactly what is taken, and can see that it is put back.' And he held up the key on his watch-chain.

'But doesn't that rather discourage people?' asked Lucy, who was accustomed to the most careless familiarity in intercourse with books, to books loose everywhere, books overflowing out of their shelves, books in every room, instantly accessible books, friendly books, books used to being read aloud, with their hospitable pages falling open at a touch.

'All the better,' said Wemyss. '*I* don't want anybody to read my books.'

Lucy laughed, though she was dismayed inside. 'Oh Everard — ' she said, 'not even me?'

'You? You're different. You're my own little girl. Whenever you want to, all you've got to do is to come and say, 'Everard, your Lucy wants to read,' and I'll unlock the bookcase.'

'But — I shall be afraid I may be disturbing you.'

'People who love each other can't ever disturb each other.'

'That's true,' said Lucy.

'And they shouldn't ever be afraid of it.'

'I suppose they shouldn't,' said Lucy.

'So be simple, and when you want a thing just say so.' Lucy said she would, and promised with many kisses to be simple, but she couldn't help privately thinking it a difficult way of getting at a book.

'Macaulay, Dickens, Scott, Thackeray, British Poets, English Men of Letters, *Encyclopædia Britannica* — I think there's about everything,' said Wemyss, going over the gilt names on the backs of the volumes with much satisfaction as he stood holding her in front of them. 'Whiteley's did it for me. I said I had room for so and so many of such and such sizes of the best modern writers in good bindings. I think they did it very well, don't you little Love?'

'Very well,' said Lucy, eyeing the shelves doubtfully.

She was of those who don't like the feel of prize books in their hands, and all Wemyss's books might have been presented as prizes to deserving schoolboys. They were handsome; their edges — she couldn't see them, but she was sure — were marbled. They wouldn't open easily, and one's thumbs would have to do a lot of tiring holding while one's eyes tried to peep at the words tucked away towards the central crease. These were books with which one took no liberties. She couldn't imagine idly turning their pages in some lazy position out on the grass. Besides, their pages wouldn't be idly turned; they would be, she was sure, obstinate with expensiveness, stiff with the leather and gold of their covers.

Lucy stared at them, thinking all this so as not to think other things. What she wanted to shut out was the wind sobbing up and down that terrace behind her, and the conscious-ness of the fierce intermittent squalls of rain beating on its flags, and the certainty that upstairs . . . Had Everard *no* imagination, she thought, with a sudden flare of rebellion, that he should expect her to use and to like using the very sitting-room where Vera —

With a quick shiver she grabbed at her thoughts and caught them just in time.

'Do you like Macaulay?' she asked, lingering in front of the bookcase, for he was beginning to move her off towards the door.

'I haven't read him,' said Wemyss, still moving her.

'Which of all these do you like best?' she asked, holding back.

'Oh, I don't know,' said Wemyss, pausing a moment, pleased by her evident interest in his books. 'I haven't much time for reading, you must remember. I'm a busy man. By the time I've finished my day's work, I'm not inclined for much more than the evening paper and a game of bridge.'

'But what will you do with me, who don't play bridge?'

'Lord, you don't suppose I shall want to play bridge now that I've got you?' he said. 'All I shall want is just to sit and look at you.'

She turned red with swift pleasure, and laughed, and hugged the arm that was thrust through hers leading her to the door. How much she adored him; when he said dear,

209

absurd, simple things like that, how much she adored him!

'Come upstairs now and take off your hat,' said Wemyss. 'I want to see what my bobbed hair looks like in my home. Besides, aren't you dying to see our bedroom?'

'Dying,' said Lucy, going up the oak staircase with a stout, determined heart.

The bedroom was over the library, and was the same size and with the same kind of window. Where the bookcase stood in the room below, stood the bed: a double, or even a treble, bed, so very big was it, facing the window past which Vera — it was no use, she couldn't get away from Vera — having slept her appointed number of nights, fell and was finished. But she wasn't finished. If only she had slipped away out of memory, out of imagination, thought Lucy . . . but she hadn't, she hadn't — and this was her room, and that intelligent-eyed thin thing had slept in it for years and years, and for years and years the looking-glass had reflected her while she had dressed and undressed, dressed and undressed before it — regularly, day after day, year after year — oh, what a trouble — and her thin long hands had piled up her hair — Lucy could see her sitting there piling it on the top of her small head — sitting at the dressing-table in the window past which she was at last to drop like a stone — horribly — ignominiously — all anyhow — and everything in the room had been hers, every single thing in it had been Vera's, including Ev —

Lucy made a violent lunge after her thoughts and strangled them.

Meanwhile Wemyss had shut the door and was standing looking at her without moving.

'Well?' he said.

She turned to him nervously, her eyes still wide with the ridiculous things she had been thinking.

'Well?' he said again.

She supposed he meant her to praise the room, so she hastily began, saying what a good view there must be on a fine day, and how very comfortable it was, such a nice big looking-glass — she loved a big looking-glass — and such a nice sofa — she loved a nice sofa — and what a very big bed — and what a lovely carpet —

'Well?' was all Wemyss said when her words came to an end.

'What is it, Everard?'

'I'm waiting,' he said.

'Waiting?'

'For my kiss.'

She ran to him.

'Yes,' he said, when she had kissed him,

looking down at her solemnly, '*I* don't forget these things. *I* don't forget that this is the first time my own wife and I have stood together in our very own bedroom.'

'But Everard I didn't forget — I only — '

She cast about for something to say, her arms still round his neck, for the last thing she could have told him was what she had been thinking — oh, how he would have scolded her for being morbid, and oh, how right he would have been! — and she ended by saying as lamely and as unfortunately as she had said it in the château of Amboise — 'I only didn't remember.'

Luckily this time his attention had already wandered away from her. 'Isn't it a jolly room?' he said. 'Who's got far and away the best bedroom in Strorley? And who's got a sitting-room all for herself, just as jolly? And who spoils his little woman?'

Before she could answer, he loosened her hands from his neck and said, 'Come and look at yourself in the glass. Come and see how small you are compared to the other things in the room.' And with his arms round her shoulders he led her to the dressing-table.

'The other things?' laughed Lucy; but like a flame the thought was leaping in her brain, 'Now what shall I do if when I look into this

I don't see myself but Vera? It's *accustomed* to Vera . . . '

'Why, she's shutting her eyes. Open them, little Love,' said Wemyss, standing with her before the glass and seeing in it that though he held her in front of it she wasn't looking at the picture of wedded love he and she made, but had got her eyes tight shut.

With his free hand he took off her hat and threw it on to the sofa; then he laid his head on hers and said, 'Now look.'

Lucy obeyed; and when she saw the sweet picture in the glass the face of the girl looking at her broke into its funny, charming smile, for Everard at that moment was at his dearest, Everard boyishly loving her, with his good-looking, unlined face so close to hers and his proud eyes gazing at her. He and she seemed to set each other off; they were becoming to each other.

Smiling at him in the glass, a smile tremulous with tenderness, she put up her hand and stroked his face. 'Do you know who you've married?' she asked, addressing the man in the glass.

'Yes,' said Wemyss, addressing the girl in the glass.

'No you don't,' she said. 'But I'll tell you. You've married the completest of fools.'

'Now what has the little thing got into its

head this time?' he said, kissing her hair, and watching himself doing it.

'Everard, you must help me,' she murmured, holding his face tenderly against hers. 'Please, my beloved, help me, teach me — '

'That, Mrs. Wemyss, is a very proper attitude in a wife,' he said. And the four people laughed at each other, the two Lucys a little quiveringly.

'Now come and I'll introduce you to your sitting-room,' he said, disengaging himself. 'We'll have tea up there. The view is really magnificent.'

19

The wind made more noise than ever at the top of the house, and when Wemyss tried to open the door to Vera's sitting-room it blew back on him.

'Well I'm damned,' he said, giving it a great shove.

'Why?' asked Lucy nervously.

'Come in, come in,' he said impatiently, pressing the door open and pulling her through.

There was a great flapping of blinds and rattling of blind cords, a whirl of sheets of notepaper, an extra wild shriek of the wind, and then Wemyss, hanging on to the door, shut it and the room quieted down.

'That slattern Lizzie!' he exclaimed, striding across to the fireplace and putting his finger on the bell-button and keeping it there.

'What has she done?' asked Lucy, standing where he had left her just inside the door.

'Done? Can't you see?'

'You mean' — she could hardly get herself to mention the fatal thing — 'you mean — the window?'

'On a day like this!'

He continued to press the bell. It was a very loud bell, for it rang upstairs as well as down in order to be sure of catching Lizzie's ear in whatever part of the house she might be endeavouring to evade it, and Lucy, as she listened to its strident, persistent summons of a Lizzie who didn't appear, felt more and more on edge, felt at last that to listen and wait any longer was unbearable.

'Won't you wear it out?' she asked, after some moments of nothing happening and Wemyss still ringing.

He didn't answer. He didn't look at her. His finger remained steadily on the button. His face was extraordinarily like the old man's in the enlarged photograph downstairs. Lucy wished for only two things at that moment, one was that Lizzie shouldn't come, and the other was that if she did she herself might be allowed to go and be somewhere else.

'Hadn't — hadn't the window better be shut?' she suggested timidly presently, while he still went on ringing and saying nothing — 'else when Lizzie opens the door won't all the things blow about again?'

He didn't answer, and went on ringing.

Of all the objects in the world that she could think of, Lucy most dreaded and shrank from that window; nevertheless she

216

began to feel that as Everard was engaged with the bell and apparently wouldn't leave it, it behoved her to put into practice her resolution not to be a fool but to be direct and wholesome, and go and shut it herself. There it was, the fatal window, huge as the one in the bedroom below and the one in the library below that, yawning wide open above its murderous low sill, with the rain flying in on every fresh gust of wind and wetting the floor and the cushions of the sofa and even, as she could see, those sheets of notepaper off the writing-table that had flown in her face when she came in and were now lying scattered at her feet. Surely the right thing to do was to shut the window before Lizzie opened the door and caused a second convulsion? Everard couldn't, because he was ringing the bell. She could and she would; yes, she would do the right thing, and at the same time be both simple and courageous.

'I'll shut it,' she said, taking a step forward.

She was arrested by Wemyss's voice. 'Confound it!' he cried. 'Can't you leave it alone?'

She stopped dead. He had never spoken to her like that before. She had never heard that voice before. It seemed to hit her straight on the heart.

'Don't interfere,' he said, very loud.

She was frozen where she stood.

'Tiresome woman,' he said, still ringing.

She looked at him. He was looking at her.

'Who?' she breathed.

'You.'

Her heart seemed to stop beating. She gave a little gasp, and turned her head to right and left like something trapped, something searching for escape. Everard — where was her Everard? Why didn't he come and take care of her? Come and take her away — out of that room — out of that room —

There were sounds of steps hurrying along the passage, and then there was a great scream of the wind and a great whirl of the notepaper and a great blowing up on end off her forehead of her short hair, and Lizzie was there panting on the threshold.

'I'm sorry, sir,' she panted, her hand on her chest, 'I was changing my dress — '

'Shut the door, can't you?' cried Wemyss, about whose ears, too, notepaper was flying. 'Hold on to it — don't let it go, damn you!'

'Oh — oh — ' gasped Lucy, stretching out her hands as though to keep something off, 'I think I — I think I'll go downstairs — '

And before Wemyss realised what she was doing, she had turned and slipped through the door Lizzie was struggling with and was gone.

'Lucy!' he shouted, 'Lucy! Come back at once!' But the wind was too much for Lizzie, and the door dragged itself out of her hands and crashed to.

As though the devil were after her Lucy ran along the passage. Down the stairs she flew, down past the bedroom landing, down past the gong landing, down into the hall and across it to the front door, and tried to pull it open, and found it was bolted, and tugged and tugged at the bolts, tugged frantically, getting them undone at last, and rushing out on to the steps.

There an immense gust of rain caught her full in the face. Splash — bang — she was sobered. The rain splashed on her as though a bucket were being emptied at her, and the door had banged behind her shutting her out. Suddenly horrified at herself she turned quickly, as frantic to get in again as she had been to get out. What was she doing? Where was she running to? She must get in, get in — before Everard could come after her, before he could find her standing there like a drenched dog outside his front door. The wind whipped her wet hair across her eyes. Where was the handle? She couldn't find it. Her hair wouldn't keep out of her eyes; her thin serge skirt blew up like a balloon and got in the way of her trembling fingers searching along the door. She must get in — before he came — what had possessed her? Everard — he couldn't have meant — he didn't mean — what would he think — what *would* he think — oh, where was that handle?

Then she heard heavy footsteps on the other side of the door, and Wemyss's voice, still very loud, saying to somebody he had got with him, 'Haven't I given strict orders that this door is to be kept bolted?' — and then the sound of bolts being shot.

'Everard! Everard!' Lucy cried, beating on the door with both hands, 'I'm here — out here — let me in — Everard! Everard!'

But he evidently heard nothing, for his footsteps went away again.

Snatching her hair out of her eyes, she looked about for the bell and reached up to it and pulled it violently. What she had done was terrible. She must get in at once, face the parlourmaid's astonishment, run to Everard. She couldn't imagine his thoughts. Where did he suppose she was? He must be searching the house for her. He would be dreadfully upset. Why didn't the parlourmaid come? Was she changing her dress too? No — she had waited at lunch all ready in her black afternoon clothes. Then why didn't she come?

Lucy pulled the bell again and again, at last

220

keeping it down, using up its electricity as squanderously as Wemyss had used it upstairs. She was wet to the skin by this time, and you wouldn't have recognised her pretty hair, all dark now and sticking together in lank strands.

Everard — why, of course — Everard had only spoken like that out of fear — fear and love. The window — of course he would be terrified lest she too, trying to shut that fatal window, that great heavy fatal window, should slip . . . Oh, of course, of course — how could she have misunderstood — in moments of danger, of dreadful anxiety for one's heart's beloved, one did speak sharply, one did rap out commands. It was because he loved her so *much* . . . Oh, how lunatic of her to have misunderstood!

At last she heard some one coming, and she let go of the bell and braced herself to meet the astonished gaze of the parlourmaid with as much dignity as was possible in one who only too well knew she must be looking like a drowning cat, but the footsteps grew heavy as they got nearer, and it was Wemyss who, after pulling back the bolts, opened the door.

'Oh Everard!' Lucy exclaimed, running in, pursued to the last by the pelting rain, 'I'm so glad it's you — oh I'm so sorry I — '

Her voice died away; she had seen his face.

He stooped to bolt the lower bolt.

'Don't be angry, darling Everard,' she whispered, laying her arm on his stooping shoulder.

Having finished with the bolt Wemyss straightened himself, and then, putting up his hand to the arm still round his shoulder, he removed it. 'You'll make my coat wet,' he said; and walked away to the library door and went in and shut it.

For a moment she stood where he had left her, collecting her scattered senses; then she went after him. Wet or not wet, soaked and dripping as she was, ridiculous scarecrow with her clinging clothes, her lank hair, she must go after him, must instantly get the horror of misunderstanding straight, tell him how she had meant only to help over that window, tell him how she had thought he was saying dreadful things to her when he was really only afraid for her safety, tell him how silly she had been, silly, silly, not to have followed his thoughts quicker, tell him he must forgive her, be patient with her, help her, because she loved him so much and she knew — oh, she knew — how much he loved her . . .

Across the hall ran Lucy, the whole of her one welter of anxious penitence and longing and love, and when she got to the door and turned the handle it was locked.

He had locked her out.

20

Her hand slid slowly off the knob. She stood quite still. How *could* he . . . And she knew now that he had bolted the front door knowing she was out in the rain. How *could* he? Her body was motionless as she stood staring at the locked door, but her brain was a rushing confusion of questions. Why? Why? This couldn't be Everard. Who was this man — pitiless, cruel? Not Everard. Not her lover. Where was he, her lover and husband? Why didn't he come and take care of her, and not let her be frightened by this strange man . . .

She heard a chair being moved inside the room, and then she heard the creak of leather as Wemyss sat down in it, and then there was the rustle of a newspaper being opened. He was actually settling down to read a newspaper while she, his wife, his love — wasn't he always telling her she was his little Love? — was breaking her heart outside the locked door. Why, but Everard — she and Everard; they understood each other; they had laughed, played together, talked nonsense, been friends . . .

For an instant she had an impulse to cry

out and beat on the door, not to care who heard, not to care that the whole house should come and gather round her naked misery; but she was stopped by a sudden new wisdom. It shuddered down on her heart, a wisdom she had never known or needed before, and held her quiet. At all costs there mustn't be two of them doing these things, at all costs these things mustn't be doubled, mustn't have echoes. If Everard was like this he must be like it alone. She must wait. She must sit quiet till he had finished. Else — but oh, he *couldn't* be like it, it *couldn't* be true that he didn't love her. Yet if he did love her, how could he . . . how could he . . .

She leaned her forehead against the door and began softly to cry. Then, afraid that she might after all burst out into loud, disgraceful sobbing, she turned and went upstairs.

But where could she go? Where in the whole house was any refuge, any comfort? The only person who could have told her anything, who could have explained, who *knew*, was Vera. Yes — she would have understood. Yes, yes — Vera. She would go to Vera's room, get as close to her mind as she could — search, find something, some clue . . .

It seemed now to Lucy, as she hurried upstairs, that the room in the house she had most shrunk from was the one place where she might hope to find comfort. Oh, she wasn't frightened any more. Everything was trying to frighten her, but she wasn't going to be frightened. For some reason or other things were all trying together to-day to see if they could crush her, beat out her spirit. But they weren't going to . . .

She jerked her wet hair out of her eyes as she climbed the stairs. It kept on getting into them and making her stumble. Vera would help her. Vera never was beaten. Vera had had fifteen years of not being beaten before she — before she had that accident. And there must have been heaps of days just like this one, with the wind screaming and Vera up in her room and Everard down in his — locked in, perhaps — and yet Vera had managed, and her spirit wasn't beaten out. For years and years, panted Lucy — her very thoughts came in gasps — Vera lived up here winter after winter, years, years, years, and would have been here now if she hadn't — oh, if only Vera weren't dead! If *only, only* Vera weren't dead! But her mind lived on — her mind was in that room, in every littlest thing in it —

Lucy stumbled up the last few stairs completely out of breath, and opening the sitting-room door stood panting on the threshold much as Lizzie had done, her hand on her chest.

This time everything was in order. The window was shut, the scattered notepaper collected and tidily on the writing-table, the rain on the floor wiped up, and a fire had been lit and the wet cushions were drying in front of it. Also there was Lizzie, engaged in conscience-stricken activities, and when Lucy came in she was on her knees poking the fire. She was poking so vigorously that she didn't hear the door open, especially not with that rattling and banging of the window going on; and on getting up and seeing the figure standing there panting, with strands of lank hair in its eyes and its general air of neglect and weather, she gave a loud exclamation.

'Lumme!' exclaimed Lizzie, whose origin and bringing-up had been obscure.

She had helped carry in the luggage that morning, so she had seen her mistress before and knew what she was like in her dry state. She never could have believed, having seen her then all nicely fluffed out, that there was so little of her. Lizzie knew what long-haired dogs look like when they are being soaped, and she was also familiar with cats as they appear after drowning; yet they too surprised her, in spite of familiarity, each time she saw them in these circumstances by their want of real substance, of stuffing. Her mistress looked just like that — no stuffing at all; and therefore Lizzie, the poker she was holding arrested in mid-air on its way into its corner, exclaimed, 'Lumme!'

Then, realising that this weather-beaten figure must certainly be catching its death of cold, she dropped the poker and hurrying across the room and talking in the stress of the moment like one girl to another, she felt Lucy's sleeve and said, 'Why, you're wet to the bones. Come to the fire and take them sopping clothes off this minute, or you'll be laid up as sure as sure — ' and pulled her over to the fire; and having got her there, and she saying nothing at all and not resisting, Lizzie stripped off her clothes and shoes and stockings, repeating at frequent intervals as she did so, 'Dear, dear,' and repressing a strong desire to beg her not to take on, lest later, perhaps, her mistress mightn't like her to have noticed she had been crying. Then she snatched up a woollen coverlet that lay folded on the end of the sofa, rolled her tightly round in it, sat her in a chair right up close to the fender, and still talking like one girl to another said, 'Now sit there and don't move while I fetch dry things — I won't be above a minute — now you promise, don't you — ' and hurrying to the door never remembered her manners at all till she was through it, whereupon she put in her head again and hastily said, 'Mum,' and disappeared.

She was away, however, more than a minute. Five minutes, ten minutes passed and Lizzie, feverishly unpacking Lucy's clothes in the bedroom below, and trying to find a complete set of them, and not knowing what belonged to which, didn't come back.

Lucy sat quite still, rolled up in Vera's coverlet. Obediently she didn't move, but stared straight into the fire, sitting so close up to it that the rest of the room was shut out. She couldn't see the window, or the dismal rain streaming down it. She saw nothing but the fire, blazing cheerfully. How kind Lizzie was. How comforting kindness was. It was a thing she understood, a normal, natural thing, and it made her feel normal and natural just to be with it. Lizzie had given her such a vigorous rub-down that her skin tingled. Her hair was on ends, for that too had had a vigorous rubbing from Lizzie, who had taken her apron to it feeling that this was an occasion on which one abandoned convention and went in for resource. And as Lucy sat there getting warmer and warmer, and more and more pervaded by the feeling of relief and well-being that even the most wretched feel if they take off all their clothes, her mind gradually calmed down, it left off asking agonised questions, and presently her heart began to do the talking.

She was so much accustomed to find life kind, that given a moment of quiet like this with somebody being good-natured and back she slipped to her usual state, which was one of affection and confidence. Lizzie hadn't been gone five minutes before Lucy had passed from sheer bewildered misery to making excuses for Everard; in ten minutes she was seeing good reasons for what he had done; in fifteen she was blaming herself for most of what had happened. She had been amazingly idiotic to run out of the room, and surely quite mad to run out of the house. It was wrong, of course, for him to bolt her out, but he was angry, and people did things when they were angry that horrified them afterwards. Surely people who easily got angry needed all the sympathy and understanding one could give them — not to be met by despair and the loss of faith in them of the person they had hurt. That only turned passing, temporary bad things into a long unhappiness. She hadn't known he had a temper. She had only, so far, discovered his extraordinary capacity for being offended. Well, if he had a temper how could he help it?

He was born that way, as certainly as if he had been born lame. Would she not have been filled with tenderness for his lameness if he had happened to be born like that? Would it ever have occurred to her to mind, to feel it as a grievance?

The warmer Lucy got the more eager she grew to justify Wemyss. In the middle of the reasons she was advancing for his justification, however, it suddenly struck her that they were a little smug. All that about people with tempers needing sympathy — who was she, with her impulses and impatiences — with her, as she now saw, devastating impulses and impatiences — to take a line of what was very like pity. Pity! Smug, odious word; smug, odious thing. Wouldn't she hate it if she thought he pitied her for her failings? Let him be angry with her failings, but not pity her. She and her man, they needed no pity from each other; they had love. It was impossible that anything either of them did or was should *really* touch that.

Very warm now in Vera's blanket, her face flushed by the fire, Lucy asked herself what could really put out that great, glorious, central blaze. All that was needed was patience when he . . . She gave herself a shake — there she was again, thinking smugly. She wouldn't think at all. She would just take

231

things as they came, and love, and love.

Then the vision of Everard, sitting solitary with his newspaper and by this time, too, probably thinking only of love, and anyhow not happy, caused one of those very impulses to lay hold of her which she had a moment before been telling herself she would never give way to again. She was aware one had gripped her, but this was a good impulse — this wasn't a bad one like running out into the rain: she would go down and have another try at that door. She was warmed through now and quite reasonable, and she felt she couldn't another minute endure not being at peace with Everard. How silly they were. It was ridiculous. It was like two children fighting. Lizzie was so long bringing her clothes; she couldn't wait, she must sit on Everard's knee again, feel his arms round her, see his eyes looking kind. She would go down in her blanket. It wrapped her up from top to toe. Only her feet were bare; but they were quite warm, and anyhow feet didn't matter.

So Lucy padded softly downstairs, making hardly a sound, and certainly none that could be heard above the noise of the wind by Lizzie in the bedroom, frantically throwing clothes about.

She knocked at the library door.

Wemyss's voice said, 'Come in.'

So he had unlocked it. So he had hoped she would come.

He didn't, however, look round. He was sitting with his back to the door at the writing-table in the window, writing.

'I want my flowers in here,' he said, without turning his head.

So he had rung. So he thought it was the parlourmaid. So he hadn't unlocked the door because he hoped she would come.

But his flowers — he wanted his birthday flowers in there because they were all that were left to him of his ruined birthday.

When she heard this order Lucy's heart rushed out to him. She shut the door softly and with her bare feet making no sound went up behind him.

He thought the parlourmaid had shut the door, and gone to carry out his order. Feeling an arm put round his shoulder he thought the parlourmaid hadn't gone to carry out his order, but had gone mad instead.

'Good God!' he exclaimed, jumping up.

At the sight of Lucy in her blanket, with her bare feet and her confused hair, his face changed. He stared at her without speaking.

'I've come to tell you — I've come to tell you — ' she began.

Then she faltered, for his mouth was a mere hard line.

'Everard, darling,' she said entreatingly, lifting her face to his, 'let's be friends — please let's be friends — I'm so sorry — so sorry — '

His eyes ran over her. It was evident that all she had on was that blanket. A strange fury came into his face, and he turned his back on her and marched with a heavy tread to the door, a tread that made Lucy, for some reason she couldn't at first understand, think of Elgar. Why Elgar? part of her asked, puzzled, while the rest of her was blankly watching Wemyss. Of course: the march: *Pomp and Circumstance.*

At the door he turned and said, 'Since you thrust yourself into my room when I have shown you I don't desire your company you force me to leave it.'

Then he added, his voice sounding queer and through his teeth, 'You'd better go and put your clothes on. I assure you I'm proof against sexual allurements.'

Then he went out.

Lucy stood looking at the door. Sexual allurements? What did he mean? Did he think — did he mean —

She flushed suddenly, and gripping her blanket tight about her she too marched to the door, her eyes bright and fixed.

Considering the blanket, she walked

upstairs with a good deal of dignity, and passed the bedroom door just as Lizzie, her arms full of a complete set of clothing, came out of it.

'Lumme!' once more exclaimed Lizzie, who seemed marked down for shocks; and dropped a hairbrush and a shoe.

Disregarding her, Lucy proceeded up the next flight with the same dignity, and having reached Vera's room crossed to the fire, where she stood in silence while Lizzie, who had hurried after her and was reproaching her for having gone downstairs like that, dressed her and brushed her hair.

She was quite silent. She didn't move. She was miles away from Lizzie, absorbed in quite a new set of astonished, painful thoughts. But at the end, when Lizzie asked her if there was anything more she could do, she looked at her a minute and then, having realised her, put out her hand and laid it on her arm.

'Thank you *very* much for everything,' she said earnestly.

'I'm terribly sorry about that window, mum,' said Lizzie, who was sure she had been the cause of trouble. 'I don't know what come over me to forget it.'

Lucy smiled faintly at her. 'Never mind,' she said; and she thought that if it hadn't been for that window she and Everard

— well, it was no use thinking like that; perhaps there would have been something else.

Lizzie went. She was a recent acquisition, and was the only one of the servants who hadn't known the late Mrs. Wemyss, but she told herself that anyhow she preferred this one. She went; and Lucy stood where she had left her, staring at the floor, dropping back into her quite new set of astonished, painful thoughts.

Everard — that was an outrage, that about sexual allurements; just simply an outrage. She flushed at the remembrance of it; her whole body seemed to flush hot. She felt as though never again would she be able to bear him making love to her. He had spoilt that. But that was a dreadful way to feel, that was destructive of the very heart of marriage. No, she mustn't let herself — she must stamp that feeling out; she must forget what he had said. He couldn't really have meant it. He was still in a temper. She oughtn't to have gone down. But how could she know? All this was new to her, a new side of Everard. Perhaps, she thought, watching the reflection of the flames flickering on the shiny, slippery oak floor, only people with tempers should marry people with tempers. They would understand each other, say the same sorts of things, tossing them backwards and forwards like a fiery, hissing ball, know the exact time it would last, and be saved by their vivid emotions from the deadly hurt, the deadly loneliness of the one who couldn't get into a rage.

Loneliness.

She lifted her head and looked round the room.

No, she wasn't lonely. There was still —

Suddenly she went to the bookshelves, and began pulling out the books quickly, hungrily reading their names, turning over their pages in a kind of starving hurry to get to know, to get to understand, Vera . . .

21

Meanwhile Wemyss had gone into the drawing-room till such time as his wife should choose to allow him to have his own library to himself again.

For a long while he walked up and down it thinking bitter things, for he was very angry. The drawing-room was a big gaunt room, rarely used of recent years. In the early days, when people called on the newly arrived Wemysses, there had been gatherings in it — retaliatory festivities to the vicar, to the doctor, to the landlord, with a business acquaintance or two of Wemyss's, wife appended, added to fill out. These festivities, however, died of inanition. Something was wanting, something necessary to nourish life in them. He thought of them as he walked about the echoing room from which the last guest had departed years ago. Vera, of course. Her fault that the parties had left off. She had been so slack, so indifferent. You couldn't expect people to come to your house if you took no pains to get them there. Yet what a fine room for entertaining. The grand piano, too. Never used. And Vera who made such a fuss about music, and pretended she knew all about it.

The piano was clothed from head to foot in a heavy red baize cover, even its legs being buttoned round in what looked like Alpine Sport gaiters, and the baize flap that protected the keys had buttons all along it from one end to the other. In order to play, these buttons had first to be undone — Wemyss wasn't going to have the expensive piano not taken care of. It had been his wedding present to Vera — how he had loved that woman! — and he had had the baize clothes made specially, and had instructed Vera that whenever the piano was not in use it was to have them on, properly fastened.

What trouble he had had with her at first about it. She was always forgetting to button it up again. She would be playing, and get up and go away to lunch, or tea, or out into the garden, and leave it uncovered with the damp and dust getting into it, and not only uncovered but with its lid open. Then, when she found that he went in to see if she had remembered, she did for a time cover it up in the intervals of playing, but never buttoned all its buttons; invariably he found that some had been forgotten. It had cost £150. Women had no sense of property. They were unfit to have the charge of valuables. Besides, they got tired of them. Vera had actually quite soon got tired of the piano. His present. That wasn't very loving of her. And when he said anything about it she wouldn't speak. Sulked. How profoundly he disliked sulking. And she, who had made such a fuss about music when first he met her, gave up playing, and for years no one had touched the piano. Well, at least it was being taken care of.

From habit he stooped and ran his eye up its gaiters.

All buttoned.

Stay — no; one buttonhole gaped.

He stooped closer and put out his hand to button it, and found the button gone. No button. Only an end of thread. How was that?

He straightened himself, and went to the fireplace and rang the bell. Then he waited, looking at his watch. Long ago he had timed the distances between the different rooms and the servants' quarters, allowing for average walking and one minute's margin for getting under way at the start, so that he knew exactly at what moment the parlour-maid ought to appear.

She appeared just as time was up and his finger was moving towards the bell again.

'Look at that piano-leg,' said Wemyss.

The parlourmaid, not knowing which leg, looked at all three so as to be safe.

'What do you see?' he asked.

The parlourmaid was reluctant to say. What she saw was piano-legs, but she felt that wasn't the right answer.

'What do you *not* see?' Wemyss asked, louder.

This was much more difficult, because there were so many things she didn't see; her parents, for instance.

'Are you deaf, woman?' he inquired.

She knew the answer to that, and said it quickly. 'No sir,' she said.

'Look at that piano-leg, I say,' said Wemyss, pointing with his pipe.

It was, so to speak, the off fore-leg at which he pointed, and the parlourmaid, relieved to be given a clue, fixed her eye on it earnestly.

'What do you see?' he asked. 'Or, rather, what do you not see?'

The parlourmaid looked hard at what she saw, leaving what she didn't see to take care of itself. It seemed unreasonable to be asked to look at what she didn't see. But though she looked, she could see nothing to justify speech. Therefore she was silent.

'Don't you see there's a button off?'

The parlourmaid, on looking closer, did see that, and said so.

'Isn't it your business to attend to this room?'

She admitted that it was.

'Buttons don't come off of themselves,' Wemyss informed her.

The parlourmaid, this not being a question, said nothing.

'Do they?' he asked loudly.

'No sir,' said the parlourmaid; though she could have told him many a story of things buttons did do of themselves, coming off in your hand when you hadn't so much as begun to touch them. Cups, too. The way cups would fall apart in one's hand —

She, however, merely said, 'No sir.'

'Only wear and tear makes them come off,' Wemyss announced; and continuing judicially, emphasising his words with a raised forefinger, he said: 'Now attend to me. This piano hasn't been used for years. Do you hear that? Not for years. To my certain knowledge not for years. Therefore the cover cannot have been unbuttoned legitimately, it cannot have been unbuttoned by any one authorised to unbutton it. Therefore — '

He pointed his finger straight at her and paused. 'Do you follow me?' he asked sternly.

The parlourmaid hastily reassembled her wandering thoughts. 'Yes sir,' she said.

'Therefore some one unauthorised has unbuttoned the cover, and some one unauthorised has played on the piano. Do you understand?'

'Yes sir,' said the parlourmaid.

'It is hardly credible,' he went on, 'but nevertheless the conclusion can't be escaped, that some one has actually taken advantage of my absence to play on that piano. Some one in this house has actually dared — '

'There's the tuner,' said the parlourmaid tentatively, not sure if that would be an explanation, for Wemyss's lucid sentences, almost of a legal lucidity, invariably confused her, but giving the suggestion for what it was worth. 'I understood the orders was to let the tuner in once a quarter, sir. Yesterday was his day. He played for a hour. And 'ad the baize and everything off, and the lid leaning against the wall.'

True. True. The tuner. Wemyss had forgotten the tuner. The tuner had standing instructions to come and tune. Well, why couldn't the fool-woman have reminded him sooner? But the tuner having tuned didn't excuse the parlourmaid's not having sewn on the button the tuner had pulled off.

He told her so.

'Yes sir,' she said.

'You will have that button on in five minutes,' he said, pulling out his watch. 'In five minutes exactly from now that button will be on. I shall be staying in this room, so shall see for myself that you carry out my orders.'

'Yes sir,' said the parlourmaid.

He walked to the window and stood staring at the wild afternoon. She remained motionless where she was.

What a birthday he was having. And with what joy he had looked forward to it. It seemed to him very like the old birthdays with Vera, only so much more painful because he had expected so much. Vera had got him used to expecting very little; but it was Lucy, his adored Lucy, who was inflicting this cruel disappointment on him. Lucy! Incredible. And she to come down in that blanket, tempting him, very nearly getting him that way rather than by the only right and decent way of sincere and obvious penitence. Why, even Vera had never done a thing like that, not once in all the years.

'Let's be friends,' says Lucy. Friends! Yes, she did say something about sorry, but what about that blanket? Sorrow with no clothes on couldn't possibly be genuine. It didn't go together with that kind of appeal. It was not the sort of combination one expected in a wife. Why couldn't she come down and apologise properly dressed? God, her little shoulder sticking out — how he had wanted to seize and kiss it . . . but then that would have been giving in, that would have meant her triumph. Her triumph, indeed — when it was she, and she only, who had begun the whole thing, running out of the room like that, not obeying him when he called, humiliating him before that damned Lizzie . . .

He thrust his hands into his pockets and turned away with a jerk from the window.

There, standing motionless, was the parlourmaid

'What? You still here?' he exclaimed. 'Why the devil don't you go and fetch that button?'

'I understood your orders was none of us is to leave rooms without your permission, sir.'

'You'd better be quick then,' he said, looking at his watch. 'I gave you five minutes, and three of them have gone.'

She disappeared; and in the servants' sitting-room, while she was hastily searching for her thimble and a button that would approximately do, she told the others what they already knew but found satisfaction in repeating often, that if it weren't that Wemyss was most of the week in London, not a day, not a minute, would she stay in the place.

'There's the wages,' the cook reminded her.

Yes; they were good; higher than anywhere she had heard of. But what was the making of the place was the complete freedom from Monday morning every week to Friday tea-time. Almost anything could be put up with from Friday tea-time till Monday morning, seeing that the rest of the week they could do exactly as they chose, with the whole place as good as belonging to them; and she hurried away, and got back to the drawing-room thirty seconds over time.

Wemyss, however, wasn't there with his watch. He was on his way upstairs to the top of the house, telling himself as he went that if Lucy chose to take possession of his library he would go and take possession of her sitting-room. It was only fair. But he knew she wasn't now in the library. He knew she wouldn't stay there all that time. He wanted an excuse to himself for going to where she was. She must beg his pardon properly. He could hold out — oh, he could hold out all right for any length of time, as she'd find out very soon if she tried the sulking game with him — but to-day it was their first day in his home; it was his birthday; and though nothing could be more monstrous than the way she had ruined everything, yet if she begged his pardon properly he would forgive her, he was ready to take her back the moment she showed real penitence. Never was a woman loved as he loved Lucy. If only she would be penitent, if only she would properly and sincerely apologise, then he could kiss her again. He would kiss that little shoulder of hers, make her pull her blouse back so that he could see it as he saw it down in the library, sticking out of that damned blanket — God, how he loved her . . .

22

The first thing he saw when he opened the door of the room at the top of the house was the fire.

A fire. He hadn't ordered a fire. He must look into that. That officious slattern Lizzie —

Then, before he had recovered from this, he had another shock. Lucy was on the hearthrug, her head leaning against the sofa, sound asleep.

So that's what she had been doing — just going comfortably to sleep, while he —

He shut the door and walked over to the fireplace and stood with his back to it looking down at her. Even his heavy tread didn't wake her. He had shut the door in the way that was natural, and had walked across the room in the way that was natural, for he felt no impulse in the presence of sleep to go softly. Besides, why should she sleep in broad daylight? Wemyss was of opinion that the night was for that. No wonder she couldn't steep at night if she did it in the daytime. There she was, sleeping soundly, completely indifferent to what he might be doing. Would a really loving woman be able to do that? Would a really devoted wife?

Then he noticed that her face, the side of it he could see, was much swollen, and her nose was red. At least, he thought, she had had some contrition for what she had done before going to sleep. It was to be hoped she would wake up in a proper frame of mind. If so, even now some of the birthday might be saved.

He took out his pipe and filled it slowly, his eyes wandering constantly to the figure on the floor. Fancy that thing having the power to make or mar his happiness. He could pick that much up with one hand. It looked like twelve, with its long-stockinged relaxed legs, and its round, short-haired head, and its swollen face of a child in a scrape. Make or mar. He lit his pipe, repeating the phrase to himself, struck by it, struck by the way it illuminated his position of bondage to love.

All his life, he reflected, he had only asked to be allowed to lavish love, to make a wife happy. Look how he had loved Vera: with the utmost devotion till she had killed it, and nothing but trouble as a reward. Look how he loved that little thing on the floor. Passionately. And in return, the first thing she did on being brought into his home as his bride was to quarrel and ruin his birthday. She knew how keenly he had looked forward to his birthday, she knew how the arrangements of the whole honeymoon, how the very date of the wedding, had hinged on this one day; yet she had deliberately ruined it. And having ruined it, what did she care? Comes up here, if you please, and gets a book and goes comfortably to sleep over it in front of the fire.

His mouth hardened still more. He pulled the arm-chair up and sat down noisily in it, his eyes cold with resentment.

The book Lucy had been reading had dropped out of her hand when she fell asleep, and lay open on the floor at his feet. If she used books in such a way, Wemyss thought, he would be very careful how he let her have the key of his bookcase. This was one of Vera's — Vera hadn't taken any care of her books either; she was always reading them. He slanted his head sideways to see the title, to see what it was Lucy had considered more worth her attention than her conduct that day towards her husband. *Wuthering Heights.* He hadn't read it, but he fancied he had heard of it as a morbid story. She might have been better employed, on their first day at home, than in shutting herself away from him reading a morbid story.

It was while he was looking at her with these thoughts stonily in his eyes that Lucy, wakened by the smell of his pipe, opened hers. She saw Everard sitting close to her, and had one of those moments of instinctive happiness, of complete restoration to unshadowed contentment, which sometimes follow immediately on waking up, before there has been time to remember. It seems for a wonderful instant as though all in the world were well. Doubts have vanished. Pain is gone. And sometimes the moment continues even beyond remembrance.

It did so now with Lucy. When she opened her eyes and saw Everard, she smiled at him a smile of perfect confidence. She had forgotten everything. She woke up after a deep sleep and saw him, her dear love, sitting beside her. How natural to be happy. Then, the expression on his face bringing back remembrance, it seemed to her in that first serene sanity, that clear-visioned moment of spirit unfretted by body, that they had been extraordinarily silly, taking everything the other one said and did with a tragicness . . .

Only love filled Lucy after the deep, restoring sleep. 'Dearest one,' she murmured drowsily, smiling at him, without changing her position.

He said nothing to that; and presently,

having woken up more, she got on to her knees and pulled herself across to him and curled up at his feet, her head against his knee.

He still said nothing. He waited. He would give her time. Her words had been familiar, but not penitent. They had hardly been the right beginning for an expression of contrition; but he would see what she said next.

What she said next was, 'Haven't we been silly,' — and, more familiarity, she put one arm round his knees and held them close against her face.

'We?' said Wemyss. 'Did you say we?'

'Yes,' said Lucy, her cheek against his knee. 'We've been wasting time.'

Wemyss paused before he made his comment on this. 'Really,' he then said, 'the way you include me shows very little appreciation of your conduct.'

'Well, *I've* been silly then,' she said, lifting her head and smiling up at him.

She simply couldn't go on with indignations. Perhaps they were just ones. It didn't matter if they were. Who wanted to be in the right in a dispute with one's lover? Everybody, oh, but everybody who loved, would passionately want always to have been in the wrong, never, never to have been right. That one's beloved should have been unkind — who wanted that to be true? Who wouldn't do anything sooner than have not been mistaken about it? Vividly she saw Everard as he was before their marriage; so dear, so boyish, such fun, her playmate. She could say anything to him then. She had been quite fearless. And vividly, too, she saw him as he was when first they met, both crushed by death — how he had comforted her, how he had been everything that was wonderful and tender. All that had happened since, all that had happened on this particular and most unfortunate day, was only a sort of excess of boyishness: boyishness on its uncontrolled side, a wave, a fit of bad temper provoked by her not having held on to her impulses. That locking her out in the rain — a schoolboy might have done that to another schoolboy. It meant nothing, except that he was angry. That about sexual allure — oh, well.

'I've been very silly,' she said earnestly.

He looked down at her in silence. He wanted more than that. That wasn't nearly enough. He wanted much more of humbleness before he could bring himself to lift her on to his knee, forgiven. And how much he wanted her on his knee.

'Do you realise what you've done?' he asked.

'Yes,' said Lucy. 'And I'm so sorry. Won't we kiss and be friends?'

'Not yet, thank you. I must be sure first that you understand how deliberately wicked you've been.'

'Oh, but I haven't been deliberately wicked!' exclaimed Lucy, opening her eyes wide with astonishment. 'Everard, how can you say such a thing?'

'Ah, I see. You are still quite impenitent, and I am sorry I came up.'

He undid her arm from round his knees, put her on one side, and got out of the chair. Rage swept over him again.

'Here I've been sitting watching you like a dog,' he said, towering over her, 'like a faithful dog while you slept, waiting patiently till you woke up and only wanting to forgive you, and you not only callously sleep after having behaved outrageously and allowed yourself to exhibit temper before the whole house on our very first day together in my home — well knowing, mind you, what day it is — but when I ask you for some sign, some word, some assurance that you are ashamed of yourself and will not repeat your conduct, you merely deny that you have done anything needing forgiveness.'

He knocked the ashes out of his pipe, his face twitching with anger, and wished to God

254

he could knock the opposition out of Lucy as easily.

She, on the floor, sat looking up at him, her mouth open. What could she do with Everard? She didn't know. Love had no effect; saying she was sorry had no effect.

She pushed her hair nervously behind her ears with both hands. 'I'm sick of quarrels,' she said.

'So am I,' said Wemyss, going towards the door thrusting his pipe into his pocket. 'You've only got yourself to thank for them.'

She didn't protest. It seemed useless. She said, 'Forgive me, Everard.'

'Only if you apologise.'

'Yes.'

'Yes what?' He paused for her answer.

'I do apologise.'

'You admit you've been deliberately wicked?'

'Oh yes.'

He continued towards the door.

She scrambled to her feet and ran after him. 'Please don't go,' she begged, catching his arm. 'You know I can't bear it, I can't bear it if we quarrel — '

'Then what do you mean by saying 'Oh yes,' in that insolent manner?'

'Did it seem insolent? I didn't mean — oh, I'm so tired of this — '

'I daresay. You'll be tireder still before you've done. *I* don't get tired, let me tell you. You can go on as long as you choose — it won't affect me.'

'Oh do, do let's be friends. I don't want to go on. I don't want anything in the world except to be friends. Please kiss me, Everard, and say you forgive me — '

He at least stood still and looked at her.

'And do believe I'm so, so sorry — '

He relented. He wanted, extraordinarily, to kiss her. 'I'll accept it if you assure me it is so,' he said.

'And do, do let's be happy. It's your birthday — '

'As though I've forgotten that.'

He looked at her upturned face; her arm was round his neck now. 'Lucy, I don't believe you understand my love for you,' he said solemnly.

'No,' said Lucy truthfully, 'I don't think I do.'

'You'll have to learn.'

'Yes,' said Lucy; and sighed faintly.

'You mustn't wound such love.'

'No,' said Lucy. 'Don't let us wound each other ever any more, darling Everard.'

'I'm not talking of each other. I'm talking at this moment of myself in relation to you. One thing at a time, please.'

'Yes,' said Lucy. 'Kiss me, won't you, Everard? Else I shan't know we're really friends.'

He took her head in his hands, and bestowed a solemn kiss of pardon on her brow.

She tried to coax him back to cheerfulness. 'Kiss my eyes too,' she said, smiling at him, 'or they'll feel neglected.'

He kissed her eyes.

'And now my mouth, please, Everard.'

He kissed her mouth, and did at last smile.

'And now won't we go to the fire and be cosy?' she asked, her arm in his.

'By the way, who ordered the fire?' he inquired in his ordinary voice.

'I don't know. It was lit when I came up. Oughtn't it to have been?'

'Not without orders. It must have been that Lizzie. I'll ring and find out — '

'Oh, don't ring!' exclaimed Lucy, catching his hand — she felt she couldn't bear any more ringing. 'If you do she'll come, and I want us to be alone together.'

'Well, whose fault is it we haven't been alone together all this time?' he asked.

'Ah, but we're friends now — you mustn't go back to that any more,' she said, anxiously smiling and drawing his hand through her arm.

He allowed her to lead him to the arm-chair, and sitting in it did at last feel justified in taking her on his knee.

'How my own Love spoils things,' he said, shaking his head at her with fond solemnity when they were settled in the chair.

And Lucy, very cautious now, only said gently, 'But I never *mean* to.'

23

She sat after that without speaking on his knee, his arms round her, her head on his breast.

She was thinking.

Try as she might to empty herself of everything except acceptance and love, she found that only her body was controllable. That lay quite passive in Wemyss's arms; but her mind refused to lie passive, it would think. Strange how tightly one's body could be held, how close to somebody else's heart, and yet one wasn't anywhere near the holder. They locked you up in prisons that way, holding your body tight and thinking they had got you, and all the while your mind — you — was as free as the wind and the sunlight. She couldn't help it, she struggled hard to feel as she had felt when she woke up and saw him sitting near her; but the way he had refused to be friends, the complete absence of any readiness in him to meet her, not half, nor even a quarter, but a little bit of the way, had for the first time made her consciously afraid of him.

She was afraid of him, and she was afraid

of herself in relation to him. He seemed outside anything of which she had experience. He appeared not to be — he anyhow had not been that day — generous. There seemed no way, at any point, by which one could reach him. What was he *really* like? How long was it going to take her really to know him? Years? And she herself — she now knew, now that she had made their acquaintance, that she couldn't at all bear scenes. Any scenes. Either with herself, or in her presence with other people. She couldn't bear them while they were going on, and she couldn't bear the exhaustion of the long drawn-out making up at the end. And she not only didn't see how they were to be avoided — for no care, no caution would for ever be able to watch what she said, or did, or looked, or, equally important, what she didn't say, or didn't do, or didn't look — but she was afraid, afraid with a most dismal foreboding, that some day after one of them, or in the middle of one of them, her nerve would give out and she would collapse. Collapse deplorably; into just something that howled and whimpered.

This, however, was horrible. She mustn't think like this. Sufficient unto the day, she thought, trying to make herself smile, is the whimpering thereof. Besides, she wouldn't whimper, she wouldn't go to pieces, she would discover a way to manage. Where there was so much love there must be a way to manage.

He had pulled her blouse back, and was kissing her shoulder and asking her whose very own wife she was. But what was the good of love-making if it was immediately preceded or followed or interrupted by anger? She was afraid of him. She wasn't in this kissing at all. Perhaps she had been afraid of him unconsciously for a long while. What was that abjectness on the honeymoon, that anxious desire to please, to avoid offending, but fear? It was love afraid; afraid of getting hurt, of not going to be able to believe whole-heartedly, of not going to be able — this was the worst — to be proud of its beloved. But now, after her experiences today, she had a fear of him more separate, more definite, distinct from love. Strange to be afraid of him and love him at the same time. Perhaps if she didn't love him she wouldn't be afraid of him. No, she didn't think she would then, because then nothing that he said would reach her heart. Only she couldn't imagine that. He *was* her heart.

'What are you thinking of?' asked Wemyss, who having finished with her shoulder noticed how quiet she was.

She could tell him truthfully; a moment sooner and she couldn't have. 'I was thinking,' she said, 'that you are my heart.'

'Take care of your heart then, won't you?' said Wemyss.

'We both will,' said Lucy.

'Of course,' said Wemyss. 'That's understood. Why state it?'

She was silent a minute. Then she said, 'Isn't it nearly tea-time?'

'By Jove, yes,' he exclaimed, pulling out his watch. 'Why, long past. I wonder what that fool — get up, little Love — ' he brushed her off his lap — 'I'll ring and find out what she means by it.'

Lucy was sorry she had said anything about tea. However, he didn't keep his finger on the bell this time, but rang it normally. Then he stood looking at his watch.

She put her arm through his. She longed to say, 'Please don't scold her.'

'Take care,' he said, his eyes on his watch. 'Don't shake me — '

She asked what he was doing.

'Timing her,' he said. 'Sh — sh — don't talk. I can't keep count if you talk.'

She became breathlessly quiet and expectant. She listened anxiously for the sound of footsteps. She did hope Lizzie would come in time. Lizzie was so nice — it would be dreadful if she got a scolding. Why didn't she come? There — what was that? A door going somewhere. Would she do it? Would she?

Running steps came along the passage outside. Wemyss put his watch away. 'Five seconds to spare,' he said. 'That's the way to teach them to answer bells,' he added with satisfaction.

'Did you ring, sir?' inquired Lizzie, opening the door.

'Why is tea late?'

'It's in the library, sir.'

'Kindly attend to my question. I asked why tea was late.'

'It wasn't late to begin with, sir,' said Lizzie.

'Be so good as to make yourself clear.'

Lizzie, who had felt quite clear, here became befogged. She did her best, however. 'It's got late through waiting to be 'ad, sir,' she said.

'I'm afraid I don't follow you. Do you?' he asked, turning to Lucy.

She started. 'Yes,' she said.

'Really. Then you are cleverer than I am,' said Wemyss.

Lizzie at this — for she didn't want to make any more trouble for the young lady — made a further effort to explain. 'It was punctual in the library, sir, at 'alf-past four if you'd been there to 'ave it. The tea was punctual, sir, but there wasn't no one to 'ave it.'

'And pray by whose orders was it in the library?'

'I couldn't say, sir. Chesterton — '

'Don't put it on to Chesterton.'

'I was thinking,' said Lizzie, who was more stout-hearted than the parlourmaid and didn't take cover quite so frequently in dumbness, 'I was thinking p'raps Chesterton knew. I don't do the tea, sir.'

'Send Chesterton,' said Wemyss.

Lizzie disappeared with the quickness of relief. Lucy, with a nervous little movement, stooped and picked up *Wuthering Heights*, which was still lying face downward on the floor.

'Yes,' said Wemyss. 'I like the way you treat books.'

She put it back on its shelf. 'I went to sleep, and it fell down,' she said. 'Everard,' she went on quickly, 'I must go and get a handkerchief. I'll join you in the library.'

'I'm not going into the library. I'm going to have tea here. Why should I have tea in the library?'

'I only thought as it was there — '

'I suppose I can have tea where I like in my own house?'

'But of course. Well, then, I'll go and get a

264

handkerchief and come back here.'

'You can do that some other time. Don't be so restless.'

'But I — I *want* a handkerchief this minute,' said Lucy.

'Nonsense; here, have mine,' said Wemyss; and anyhow it was too late to escape, for there in the door stood Chesterton.

She was the parlourmaid. Her name has not till now been mentioned. It was Chesterton.

'Why is tea in the library?' Wemyss asked.

'I understood, sir, tea was always to be in the library,' said Chesterton.

'That was while I was by myself. I suppose it wouldn't have occurred to you to inquire whether I still wished it there now that I am not by myself.'

This floored Chesterton. Her ignorance of the right answer was complete. She therefore said nothing, and merely stood.

But he didn't let her off. 'Would it?' he asked suddenly.

'No sir,' she said, dimly feeling that 'Yes sir' would land her in difficulties.

'No. Quite so. It wouldn't. Well, you will now go and fetch that tea and bring it up here. Stop a minute, stop a minute — don't be in such a hurry, please. How long has it been made?'

'Since half-past four, sir.'

'Then you will make fresh tea, and you will make fresh toast, and you will cut fresh bread and butter.'

'Yes sir.'

'And another time you will have the goodness to ascertain my wishes before taking upon yourself to put the tea into any room you choose to think fit.'

'Yes sir.'

She waited.

He waved.

She went.

'That'll teach her,' said Wemyss, looking refreshed by the encounter. 'If she thinks she's going to get out of bringing tea up here by putting it ready somewhere else she'll find she's mistaken. Aren't they a set? *Aren't they a set*, little Love?'

'I — don't know,' said Lucy nervously.

'You don't know!'

'I mean, I don't know them yet. How can I know them when I've only just come?'

'You soon will, then. A lazier set of careless, lying — '

'Do tell me what that picture is, Everard,' she interrupted, quickly crossing the room and standing in front of it. 'I've been wondering and wondering.'

'You can see what it is. It's a picture.'

266

'Yes. But where's the place?'

'I've no idea. It's one of Vera's. She didn't condescend to explain it.'

'You mean she painted it?'

'I daresay. She was always painting.'

Wemyss, who had been filling his pipe, lit it and stood smoking in front of the fire, occasionally looking at his watch, while Lucy stared at the picture. Lovely, lovely to run through that door out into the open, into the warmth and sunshine, further and further away . . .

It was the only picture in the room; indeed, the room was oddly bare — a thin room, with no carpet on its slippery floor, only some infrequent rugs, and no curtains. But there had been curtains, for there were the rods with rings on them, so that somebody must have taken Vera's curtains away. Lucy had been strangely perturbed when she noticed this. It was Vera's room. Her curtains oughtn't to have been touched.

The long wall opposite the fireplace had nothing at all on its sand-coloured surface from the door to the window except a tall narrow looking-glass in a queerly-carved black frame, and the picture. But how that one picture glowed. What glorious weather they were having in it! It wasn't anywhere in England, she was sure. It was a brilliant, sunlit place, with a lot of almond trees in full blossom — an orchard of them, apparently, standing in grass that was full of little flowers, very gay little flowers, of kinds she didn't know. And through the open door in the wall there was an amazing stretch of hot, vivid country. It stretched on and on till it melted into an ever so far away lovely blue. There was an effect of immense spaciousness, of huge freedom. One could feel oneself running out into it with one's face to the sun, flinging up one's arms in an ecstasy of release, of escape . . .

'It's somewhere abroad,' she said, after a silence.

'I daresay,' said Wemyss.

'Used you to travel much?' she asked, still examining the picture, fascinated.

'She refused to.'

'She refused to?' echoed Lucy, turning round.

She looked at him wonderingly. That seemed not only unkind of Vera, but extraordinarily — yes, energetic. The exertion required for refusing Everard something he wanted was surely enormous, was surely greater than any but the most robust-minded wife could embark upon. She had had one small experience of what disappointing him meant in that question of Christmas, and she hadn't been living with him then, and she had had all the nights to recover in; yet the effect of that one experience had been to make her give in at once when next he wanted something, and it was because of last Christmas that she was standing married in that room instead of being still, as both she and her Aunt Dot had intended, six months off it.

'Why did she refuse?' she asked, wondering.

Wemyss didn't answer for a moment. Then he said, 'I was going to say you had better ask her, but you can't very well do that, can you.'

Lucy stood looking at him. 'Yes,' she said, 'she does seem extraordinarily near, doesn't she. This room is full — '

'Now Lucy I'll have none of that. Come here.'

He held out his hand. She crossed over obediently and took it.

He pulled her close and ruffled her hair. He was in high spirits again. His encounters with the servants had exhilarated him.

'Who's my duddely-umpty little girl?' he asked. 'Tell me who's my duddely-umpty little girl. Quick. Tell me — ' And he caught her round the waist and jumped her up and down.

Chesterton, bringing in the tea, arrived in the middle of a jump.

24

There appeared to be no tea-table. Chesterton, her arms stretched taut holding the heavy tray, looked round. Evidently tea up there wasn't usual.

'Put it in the window,' said Wemyss, jerking his head towards the writing-table.

'Oh — ' began Lucy quickly; and stopped.

'What's the matter?' asked Wemyss.

'Won't it — be draughty?'

'Nonsense. Draughty. Do you suppose I'd tolerate windows in my house that let in draughts?'

Chesterton, resting a corner of the tray on the table, was sweeping a clear space for it with her hand. Not that much sweeping was needed, for the table was big and all that was on it was the notepaper which earlier in the afternoon had been scattered on the floor, a rusty pen or two, some pencils whose ends had been gnawed as the pencils of a child at its lessons are gnawed, a neglected-looking inkpot, and a grey book with *Household Accounts* in dark lettering on its cover.

Wemyss watched her while she arranged the tea-things.

'Take care, now — take care,' he said, when a cup rattled in its saucer.

Chesterton, who had been taking care, took more of it; and *le trop* being *l'ennemi du bien* she was so unfortunate as to catch her cuff in the edge of the plate of bread and butter.

The plate tilted up; the bread and butter slid off; and only by a practised quick movement did she stop the plate from following the bread and butter and smashing itself on the floor.

'There now,' said Wemyss. 'See what you've done. Didn't I tell you to be careful? It isn't,' he said, turning to Lucy, 'as if I hadn't *told* her to be careful.'

Chesterton, on her knees, was picking up the bread and butter which lay — a habit she had observed in bread and butter under circumstances of this kind — butter downwards.

'You will fetch a cloth,' said Wemyss.

'Yes sir.'

'And you will cut more bread and butter.'

'Yes sir.'

'That makes two plates of bread and butter wasted to-day entirely owing to your carelessness. They shall be stopped out of your — Lucy, where are you going?'

'To fetch a handkerchief. I must have a

handkerchief, Everard. I can't for ever use yours.'

'You'll do nothing of the kind. Lizzie will bring you one. Come back at once. I won't have you running in and out of the room the whole time. I never knew any one so restless. Ring the bell and tell Lizzie to get you one. What is she for, I should like to know?'

He then resumed and concluded his observations to Chesterton. 'They shall be stopped out of your wages. That,' he said, 'will teach you.'

And Chesterton, who was used to this, and had long ago arranged with the cook that such stoppages should be added on to the butcher's book, said, 'Yes sir.'

When she had gone — or rather withdrawn, for a plain word like gone doesn't justly describe the noiseless decorum with which Chesterton managed the doors of her entrances and exits — and when Lizzie, too, had gone after bringing a handkerchief, Lucy supposed they would now have tea; she supposed the moment had at last arrived for her to go and sit in that window.

The table was at right angles to it, so that sitting at it you had nothing between one side of you and the great pane of glass that reached nearly to the floor. You could look sheer down on to the flags below. She thought it horrible, gruesome to have tea there, and the very first day, before she had had a moment's time to get used to things. Such detachment on the part of Everard was either just stark wonderful — she had already found noble explanations for it — or it was so callous that she had no explanation for it at all; none, that is, that she dared think of. Once more she decided that his way was really the best and simplest way to meet the situation. You took the bull by the horns. You seized the nettle. You cleared the air. And though her images, she felt, were not what they might be, neither was anything else that day what it might be. Everything appeared to reflect the confusion produced by Wemyss's excessive lucidity of speech.

'Shall I pour out the tea?' she asked presently, preparing, then, to take the bull by the horns; for he remained standing in front of the fire smoking in silence. 'Just think,' she went on, making an effort to be gay, 'this is the first time I shall pour out tea in my — '

She was going to say 'My own home,' but the words wouldn't come off her tongue. Wemyss had repeatedly during the day spoken of his home, but not once had he said 'our' or 'your'; and if ever a house didn't feel as if it in the very least belonged, too, to her, it was this one.

'Not yet,' he said briefly.

She wondered. 'Not yet?' she repeated.

'I'm waiting for the bread and butter.'

'But won't the tea get cold?'

'No doubt. And it'll be entirely that fool's fault.'

'But — ' began Lucy, after a silence.

'Buts again?'

'I was only thinking that if we had it now it wouldn't be cold.'

'She must be taught her lesson.'

Again she wondered. 'Won't it rather be a lesson to us?' she asked.

'For God's sake, Lucy, don't argue. Things have to be done properly in my house. You've had no experience of a properly managed household. All that set you were brought up in — why, one only had to look at them to see what a hugger-mugger way they probably lived. It's entirely the careless fool's own fault that the tea will be cold. *I* didn't ask her to throw the bread and butter on the floor, did I?'

And as she said nothing, he asked again. 'Did I?' he asked.

'No,' said Lucy.

'Well then,' said Wemyss.

They waited in silence.

Chesterton arrived. She put the fresh bread and butter on the table, and then wiped the floor with a cloth she had brought.

Wemyss watched her closely. When she had done — and Chesterton being good at her work, scrutinise as he might he could see no sign on the floor of overlooked butter — he said, 'You will now take the teapot down and bring some hot tea.'

'Yes sir,' said Chesterton, removing the teapot.

A line of a hymn her nurse used to sing came into Lucy's head when she saw the teapot going. It was:

What various hindrances we meet —

and she thought the next line, which she didn't remember, must have been:

Before at tea ourselves we seat.

But though one portion of her mind was repeating this with nervous levity, the other was full of concern for the number of journeys up and down all those stairs the parlourmaid was being obliged to make. It was — well, thoughtless of Everard to make her go up and down so often. Probably he didn't realise — of course he didn't — how very many stairs there were. When and how could she talk to him about things like this? When would he be in such a mood that she would be able to do so without making them worse? And how, in what words sufficiently tactful, sufficiently gentle, would she be able to avoid his being offended? She must manage somehow. But tact — management — prudence — all these she had not yet in her life needed. Had she the smallest natural gift for them? Besides, each of them applied to love seemed to her an insult. She had supposed that love, real love, needed none of these protections. She had thought it was a simple, sturdy growth that could stand anything . . . Why, here was the parlourmaid already, teapot and all. How very quick she had been!

Chesterton, however, hadn't so much been quick as tactful, managing, and prudent. She had been practising these qualities on the other side of the door, whither she had taken the teapot and quietly waited with it a few minutes, and whence she now brought it back. She placed it on the table with admirable composure; and when Wemyss, on her politely asking whether there were anything else he required, said, 'Yes. You will now take away that toast and bring fresh,' she took the toast also only as far as the other side of the door, and waited with it there a little.

Lucy now hoped they would have tea. 'Shall I pour it out?' she asked after a moment a little anxiously, for he still didn't move and she began to be afraid the toast might be going to be the next hindrance; in which case they would go round and round for the rest of the day, never catching up the tea at all.

But he did go over and sit down at the table, followed by her who hardly now noticed its position, so much surprised and absorbed was she by his methods of housekeeping.

'Isn't it monstrous,' he said, sitting down heavily, 'how we've been kept waiting for such a simple thing as tea. I tell you they're the most slovenly — '

There was Chesterton again, bearing the toast-rack balanced on the tip of a respectful ringer.

This time even Lucy realised that it must be the same toast, and her hand, lifted in the act of pouring out tea, trembled, for she feared the explosion that was bound to come.

How extraordinary. There was no explosion. Everard hadn't — it seemed incredible — noticed. His attention was so much fixed on what she was doing with his cup, he was watching her so carefully lest she should fill it a hair's-breadth fuller than he liked, that all he said to Chesterton as she put the toast on the table was, 'Let this be a lesson to you.' But there was no gusto in it; it was quite mechanical.

'Yes sir,' said Chesterton.

She waited.

He waved.

She went.

The door hadn't been shut an instant before Wemyss exclaimed, 'Why, if that slovenly hussy hasn't forgotten — ' And too much incensed to continue he stared at the tea-tray.

'What? What?' asked Lucy startled, also staring at the tea-tray.

'Why, the sugar.'

'Oh, I'll call her back — she's only just gone — '

'Sit down, Lucy.'

'But she's just outside — '

'Sit *down*, I tell you.'

Lucy sat.

Then she remembered that neither she nor Everard ever had sugar in their tea, so naturally there was no point in calling Chesterton back.

'Oh, of course,' she said, smiling nervously, for what with one thing and another she was feeling shattered, 'how stupid of me. We don't want sugar.'

Wemyss said nothing. He was studying his watch, timing Chesterton. Then when the number of seconds needed to reach the kitchen had run out, he got up and rang the bell.

In due course Lizzie appeared. It seemed that the rule was that this particular bell should be answered by Lizzie.

'Chesterton,' said Wemyss.

In due course Chesterton appeared. She was less composed than when she brought back the teapot, than when she brought back the toast. She tried to hide it, but she was out of breath.

'Yes sir?' she said.

Wemyss took no notice, and went on drinking his tea.

Chesterton stood.

After a period of silence Lucy thought that perhaps it was expected of her as mistress of the house to tell her about the sugar; but then as they neither of them wanted any . . .

After a further period of silence, during which she anxiously debated whether it was this that they were all waiting for, she thought that perhaps Everard hadn't heard the parlourmaid come in; so she said — she was ashamed to hear how timidly it came out — 'Chesterton is here, Everard.'

He took no notice, and went on eating bread and butter.

After a further period of anxious inward debate she concluded that it must after all be expected of her, as mistress of the house, to talk of the sugar; and the sugar was to be talked of not because they needed it but on principle. But what a roundabout way; how fatiguing and difficult. Why didn't Everard say what he wanted, instead of leaving her to guess?

'I think — ' she stammered, flushing, for she was now very timid indeed, 'you've forgotten the sugar, Chesterton.'

'Will you not interfere!' exclaimed Wemyss very loud, putting down his cup with a bang.

The flush on Lucy's face vanished as if it had been knocked out. She sat quite still. If she moved, or looked anywhere but at her plate, she knew she would begin to cry. The scenes she had dreaded had not included any with herself in the presence of servants. It hadn't entered her head that these, too, were possible. She must hold on to herself; not move; not look. She sat absorbed in that one necessity, fiercely concentrated. Chesterton must have gone away and come back again, for presently she was aware that sugar was being put on the tea-tray; and then she was aware that Everard was holding out his cup.

'Give me some more tea, please,' he said, 'and for God's sake don't sulk. If the servants forget their duties it's neither your nor my business to tell them what they've forgotten — they've just got to look and see, and if they don't see they've just got to stand there looking till they do. It's the only way to teach them. But for you to get sulking on the top of it — '

She lifted the teapot with both hands, because one hand by itself too obviously shook. She succeeded in pouring out the tea without spilling it, and in stopping almost at the very moment when he said, 'Take care, take care — you're filling it too full.' She even succeeded after a minute or two in saying, holding carefully on to her voice to keep it steady, 'I'm not — sulking. I've — got a headache.'

And she thought desperately, 'The only thing to be done with marriage is to let it wash over one.'

25

For the rest of that day she let it wash; unresistingly. She couldn't think any more. She couldn't feel any more — not that day. She really had a headache; and when the dusk came, and Wemyss turned on the lights, it was evident even to him that she had, for there was no colour at all in her face and her eyes were puffed and leaden.

He had one of his sudden changes. 'Come here,' he said, reaching out and drawing her on to his knee; and he held her face against his breast, and felt full of maternal instincts, and crooned over her. 'Was it a poor little baby,' he crooned. 'Did it have a headache then — ' And he put his great cool hand on her hot forehead and kept it there.

Lucy gave up trying to understand anything at all any more. These swift changes — she couldn't keep up with them; she was tired, tired . . .

They sat like that in the chair before the fire, Wemyss holding his hand on her forehead and feeling full of maternal instincts, and she an unresisting blank, till he suddenly remembered he hadn't shown her the drawing-room yet. The afternoon had not proceeded on the lines laid down for it in his plans, but if they were quick there was still time for the drawing-room before dinner.

Accordingly she was abruptly lifted off his knee. 'Come along, little Love,' he said briskly. 'Come along. Wake up. I want to show you something.'

And the next thing she knew was that she was going downstairs, and presently she found herself standing in a big cold room, blinking in the bright lights he had switched on at the door.

'This,' he said, holding her by the arm, 'is the drawing-room. Isn't it a fine room.' And he explained the piano, and told her how he had found a button off, and he pointed out the roll of rugs in a distant corner which, unrolled, decorated the parquet floor, and he drew her attention to the curtains — he had no objections to curtains in a drawing-room, he said, because a drawing-room was anyhow a room of concessions; and he asked her at the end, as he had asked her at the beginning, if she didn't think it a fine room.

Lucy said it was a very fine room.

'You'll remember to put the cover on properly when you've finished playing the piano, won't you,' he said.

'Yes I will,' said Lucy. 'Only I don't play,'

she added, remembering she didn't.

'That's all right then,' he said, relieved.

They were still standing admiring the proportions of the room, its marble fireplace and the brilliancy of its lighting — 'The test of good lighting,' said Wemyss, 'is that there shouldn't be a corner of a room in which a man of eighty can't read his newspaper' — when the gong began.

'Good Lord,' he said, looking at his watch, 'it'll be dinner in ten minutes. Why, we've had nothing at all of the afternoon, and I'd planned to show you so many things. Ah,' he said, turning and shaking his head at her, his voice changing to sorrow, 'whose fault has that been?'

'Mine,' said Lucy.

He put his hand under her chin and lifted her face, gazing at it and shaking his head slowly. The light, streaming into her swollen eyes, hurt them and made her blink.

'Ah, my Lucy,' he said fondly, 'little waster of happiness — isn't it better simply to love your Everard than make him unhappy?'

'Much better,' said Lucy, blinking.

There was no dressing for dinner at The Willows, for that, explained Wemyss, was the great joy of home, that you needn't ever do anything you don't want to in it, and therefore, he said, ten minutes' warning was ample for just washing one's hands. They washed their hands together in the big bedroom, because Wemyss disapproved of dressing-rooms at home even more strongly than on honeymoons in hotels. 'Nobody's going to separate me from my own woman,' he said, drying his hands and eyeing her with proud possessiveness while she dried hers; their basins stood side by side on the brown mottled marble of the washstand. 'Are they,' he said, as she dried in silence.

'No,' said Lucy.

'How's the head?' he said.

'Better,' she said.

'Who's got a forgiving husband?' he said.

'I have,' she said.

'Smile at me,' he said.

She smiled at him.

At dinner it was Vera who smiled, her changeless little strangled smile, with her eyes on Lucy. Lucy's seat had its back to Vera, but she knew she had only to turn her head to see her eyes fixed on her, smiling. No one else smiled; only Vera.

Lucy bent her head over her plate, trying to escape the unshaded light that beat down on her eyes, sore with crying, and hurt. In front of her was the bowl of kingcups, the birthday flowers. Just behind Wemyss stood Chesterton, in an attitude of strained attention. Dimly through Lucy's head floated thoughts: Seeing that Everard invariably spent his birthdays at The Willows, on that day last year at that hour Vera was sitting where she, Lucy, now was, with the kingcups glistening in front of her, and Everard tucking his table napkin into his waistcoat, and Chesterton waiting till he was quite ready to take the cover off the soup; just as Lucy was seeing these things this year Vera saw them last year; Vera still had three months of life ahead of her then, three more months of dinners, and Chesterton, and Everard tucking in his napkin. How queer. What a dream it all was. On that last of his birthdays at which Vera would ever be present, did any thought of his next birthday cross her mind? How strange it would have seemed to her if she could have seen ahead, and seen her, Lucy, sitting in her chair. The same chair; everything just the same; except the wife. 'Souvent femme varie,' floated vaguely across her tired brain. She ate her soup sitting all crooked with fatigue . . . life was exactly like a dream . . .

Wemyss, absorbed in the scrutiny of his food and the behaviour of Chesterton, had no time to notice anything Lucy might be doing. It was the rule that Chesterton, at meals, should not for an instant leave the room. The furthest she was allowed was a door in the dark corner opposite the door into the hall, through which at intervals Lizzie's arm thrust dishes. It was the rule that Lizzie shouldn't come into the room, but, stationary on the other side of this door, her function was to thrust dishes through it; and to her from the kitchen, pattering ceaselessly to and fro, came the tweeny bringing the dishes. This had all been thought out and arranged very carefully years ago by Wemyss, and ought to have worked without a hitch; but sometimes there were hitches, and Lizzie's arm was a minute late thrusting in a dish. When this happened Chesterton, kept waiting and conscious of Wemyss enormously waiting at the end of the table, would put her head round the door and hiss at Lizzie, who then hurried to the kitchen and hissed at the tweeny, who for her part didn't dare hiss at the cook.

To-night, however, nothing happened that was not perfect. From the way Chesterton had behaved about the tea, and the way Lizzie had behaved about the window, Wemyss could see that during his four weeks' absence his household had been getting out of hand, and he was therefore more watchful than ever, determined to pass nothing over. On this occasion he watched in vain. Things went smoothly from start to finish. The tweeny ran, Lizzie thrust, Chesterton deposited, dead on time. Every dish was hot and punctual, or cold and punctual, according to what was expected of it; and Wemyss going out of the dining-room at the end, holding Lucy by the arm, couldn't but feel he had dined very well. Perhaps, though, his father's photograph hadn't been dusted — it would be just like them to have disregarded his instructions. He went back to look, and Lucy, since he was holding her by the arm, went too. No, they had even done that; and there was nothing further to be said except, with great sternness to Chesterton, eyeing her threateningly, 'Coffee at once.'

The evening was spent in the library reading Wemyss's school reports, and looking at photographs of him in his various stages — naked and crowing; with ringlets, in a frock; in knickerbockers, holding a hoop; a stout schoolboy; a tall and slender youth; thickening; still thickening; thick — and they went to bed at ten o'clock.

Somewhere round midnight Lucy discovered that the distances of the treble bed softened sound; either that, or she was too tired to hear anything, for she dropped out of consciousness with the heaviness of a released stone.

Next day it was finer. There were gleams of

sun; and though the wind still blew, the rain held off except for occasional spatterings. They got up very late — breakfast on Sundays at The Willows was not till eleven — and went and inspected the chickens. By the time they had done that, and walked round the garden, and stood on the edge of the river throwing sticks into it and watching the pace at which they were whirled away on its muddy and disturbed surface, it was luncheon time. After luncheon they walked along the towpath, one behind the other because it was narrow and the grass at the sides was wet. Wemyss walked slowly, and the wind was cold. Lucy kept close to his heels, seeking shelter under, as it were, his lee. Talk wasn't possible because of the narrow path and the blustering wind, but every now and then Wemyss looked down over his shoulder at her. 'Still there?' he asked; and Lucy said she was.

They had tea punctually at half-past four up in Vera's sitting-room, but without, this time, a fire — Wemyss had rectified Lizzie's tendency to be officious — and after tea he took her out again to show her how his electricity was made, while the gardener who saw to the machinery, and the boy who saw to the gardener, stood by in attendance.

There was a cold sunset — a narrow strip

of gold below heavy clouds, like a sullen, half-open eye. The prudent cows dotted the fields motionlessly, lying on their dry bite of grass. The wind blew straight across from the sunset through Lucy's coat, wrap herself in it as tightly as she might, while they loitered among outhouses and examined the durability of the railings. Her headache, in spite of her good night, hadn't gone, and by dinner time her throat felt sore. She said nothing to Wemyss, because she was sure she would be well in the morning. Her colds never lasted. Besides she knew, for he had often told her, how much he was bored by the sick.

At dinner her cheeks were very red and her eyes very bright.

'Who's my pretty little girl,' said Wemyss, struck by her.

Indeed he was altogether pleased with her. She had been his own Lucy throughout the day, so gentle and sweet, and hadn't once said But, or tried to go out of rooms. Unquestioningly acquiescent she had been; and now so pretty, with the light full on her, showing up her lovely colouring.

'Who's my pretty little girl,' he said again, laying his hand on hers, while Chesterton looked down her nose.

Then he noticed she had a knitted scarf round her shoulders, and he said, 'Whatever have you got that thing on in here for?'

'I'm cold,' said Lucy.

'Cold! Nonsense. You're as warm as a toast. Feel my hand compared to yours.'

Then she did tell him she thought she had caught cold, and he said, withdrawing his hand and his face falling, 'Well, if you have it's only what you deserve when you recollect what you did yesterday.'

'I suppose it is,' agreed Lucy; and assured him her colds were all over in twenty-four hours.

Afterwards in the library when they were alone, she asked if she hadn't better sleep by herself in case he caught her cold, but Wemyss wouldn't hear of such a thing. Not only, he said, he never caught colds and didn't believe any one else who was sensible ever did, but it would take more than a cold to separate him from his wife. Besides, though of course she richly deserved a cold after yesterday — 'Who's a shameless little baggage,' he said, pinching her ear, 'coming down with only a blanket on — ' somehow, though he had been so angry at the time, the recollection of that pleased him — he could see no signs of her having got one. She didn't sneeze, she didn't blow her nose —

Lucy agreed, and said she didn't suppose it was anything really, and she was sure she would be all right in the morning.

'Yes — and you know we catch the early train up,' said Wemyss. 'Leave here at nine sharp, mind.'

'Yes,' said Lucy. And presently, for she was feeling very uncomfortable and hot and cold in turns, and had a great longing to creep away and be alone for a little while, she said that perhaps, although she knew it was very early, she had better go to bed.

'All right,' said Wemyss, getting up briskly. 'I'll come too.'

26

He found her, however, very trying that night, the way she would keep on turning round, and it reached such a pitch of discomfort to sleep with her, or rather endeavour to sleep with her, for as the night went on she paid less and less attention to his requests that she should keep still, that at about two o'clock, staggering with sleepiness, he got up and went into a spare room, trailing the quilt after him and carrying his pillows, and finished the night in peace.

When he woke at seven he couldn't make out at first where he was, nor why, on stretching out his arm, he found no wife to be gathered in. Then he remembered, and he felt most injured that he should have been turned out of his own bed. If Lucy imagined she was going to be allowed to develop the same restlessness at night that was characteristic of her by day, she was mistaken; and he got up to go and tell her so.

He found her asleep in a very untidy position, the clothes all dragged over to her side of the bed and pulled up round her. He pulled them back again, and she woke up, and he got into bed and said, 'Come here,' stretching out his arm, and she didn't come.

Then he looked at her more closely, and she, looking at him with heavy eyes, said something husky. It was evident she had a very tiresome cold.

'What an untruth you told me,' he exclaimed, 'about not having a cold in the morning!'

She again said something husky. It was evident she had a very tiresome sore throat.

'It's getting on for half-past seven,' said Wemyss. 'We've got to leave the house at nine sharp, mind.'

Was it possible that she wouldn't leave the house at nine sharp? The thought that she wouldn't was too exasperating to consider. He go up to London alone? On this the first occasion of going up after his marriage? He be alone in Lancaster Gate, just as if he hadn't a wife at all? What was the good of a wife if she didn't go up to London with one? And all this to come upon him because of her conduct on his birthday.

'Well,' he said, sitting up in bed and looking down at her, 'I hope you're pleased with the result of your behaviour.'

But it was no use saying things to somebody who merely made husky noises.

He got out of bed and jerked up the blinds.

'Such a beautiful day, too,' he said indignantly.

When at a quarter to nine the station cab arrived, he went up to the bedroom hoping that he would find her after all dressed and sensible and ready to go, but there she was just as he had left her when he went to have his breakfast, dozing and inert in the tumbled bed.

'You'd better follow me by the afternoon train,' he said, after staring down at her in silence. 'I'll tell the cab. But in any case,' he said, as she didn't answer, 'in *any* case, Lucy, I expect you to-morrow.'

She opened her eyes and looked at him languidly.

'Do you hear?' he said.

She made a husky noise.

'Good-bye,' he said shortly, stooping and giving the top of her head a brief, disgusted kiss. The way the consequences of folly fell always on somebody else and punished him . . . Wemyss could hardly give his *Times* the proper attention in the train for thinking of it.

That day Miss Entwhistle, aware of the return from the honeymoon on the Friday, and of the week-end to be spent at The Willows, and of the coming up to Lancaster Gate early on the Monday morning for the inside of the week, waited till twelve o'clock, so as to allow plenty of time for Wemyss no longer to be in the house, and then telephoned. Lucy and she were to lunch together. Lucy had written to say so, and Miss Entwhistle wanted to know if she wouldn't soon be round. She longed extraordinarily to fold that darling little child in her arms again. It seemed an eternity since she saw her radiantly disappearing in the taxi; and the letters she had hoped to get during the honeymoon hadn't been letters at all, but picture postcards.

A man's voice answered her — not Wemyss's. It was, she recognised, the voice of the pale servant, who with his wife attended to the Lancaster Gate house. They inhabited the basement, and emerged from it up into the light only if they were obliged. Bells obliged them to emerge, and Wemyss's bath and breakfast, and after his departure to his office the making of his bed; but then the shades gathered round them again till next morning, because for a long while now once he had left the house he hadn't come back till after they were in bed. His re-marriage was going to disturb them, they were afraid, and the pale wife had forebodings about meals to be cooked; but at the worst the disturbance would only be for the three inside days of the week, and anything could be borne when one had from Friday to Monday to oneself; and as the morning went on, and no one arrived from Strorley, they began to take heart, and had almost quite taken it when the telephone bell rang.

It didn't do it very often, for Wemyss had his other addresses, at the office, at the club, so that Twite, wanting in practice, was not very good at dealing with it. Also the shrill bell vibrating through the empty house, so insistent, so living, never failed to agitate both Twites. It seemed to them uncanny; and Mrs. Twite, watching Twite being drawn up by it out of his shadows, like some quiet fish sucked irresistibly up to gasp on the surface, was each time thankful that she hadn't been born a man.

She always went and listened at the bottom of the kitchen stairs, not knowing what mightn't happen to Twite up there alone with that voice, and on this occasion she heard the following:

'No, ma'am, not yet, ma'am.'

'I couldn't say, ma'am.'

'No, no news, ma'am.'

'Oh yes, ma'am, on Friday night.'

'Yes, ma'am, first thing Saturday.'

'Yes, it is, ma'am — very strange, ma'am.'

And then there was silence. He was writing, she knew, on the pad provided by

Wemyss for the purpose.

This was the most trying part of Twite's duties. Any message had to be written down and left on the hall table, complete with the time of its delivery, for Wemyss to see when he came in at night. Twite was not a facile writer. Words confused him. He was never sure how they were spelt. Also he found it very difficult to remember what had been said, for there was a hurry and an urgency about a voice on the telephone that excited him and prevented his giving the message his undivided attention. Besides, when was a message not a message? Wemyss's orders were to write down messages. Suppose they weren't messages, must he still write? Was this, for instance, a message?

He thought he had best be on the safe side, and laboriously wrote it down.

Miss Henwissel rang up sir to know if you was come and if so when you was coming and what orders we ad and said it was very strange 12.15.

He had only just put this on the table and was about to descend to his quiet shades when off the thing started again.

This time it was Wemyss.

'Back to-night late as usual,' he said.

'Yes sir,' said Twite. 'There's just been a — '

But he addressed emptiness.

Meanwhile Miss Entwhistle, after a period of reflection, was ringing up Strorley 19. The voice of Chesterton, composed and efficient, replied; and the effect of her replies was to make Miss Entwhistle countermand lunch and pack a small bag and go to Paddington.

Trains to Strorley at that hour were infrequent and slow, and it wasn't till nearly five that she drove down the oozy lane in the station cab and, turning in at the white gate, arrived at The Willows. That sooner or later she would have to arrive at The Willows now that she was related to it by marriage was certain, and she had quite made up her mind, during her four weeks' peace since the wedding, that she was going to dismiss all foolish prejudices against the place from her mind and arrive at it, when she did arrive, with a stout heart and an unclouded countenance. After all, there was much in that *mot* of her nephew's: 'Somebody has died everywhere.' Yet, as the cab heaved her nearer to the place along the oozy lane, she did wish that it wasn't in just this house that Lucy lay in bed. Also she had misgivings at being there uninvited. In a case of serious illness naturally such misgivings wouldn't exist; but the maid's voice on the telephone had only said Mrs. Wemyss had a cold and was staying in bed, and Mr. Wemyss had gone up to London by the usual train. It couldn't be much that was wrong, or he wouldn't have gone. Hadn't she, she thought uneasily as she found herself uninvited within Wemyss's gates, perhaps been a little impulsive? Yet the idea of that child alone in the sinister house —

She peered out of the cab window. Not at all sinister, she said, correcting herself severely; all most neat. Perfect order. Shrubs as they should be. Strong railings. Nice cows.

The cab stopped. Chesterton came down the steps and opened its door. Nice parlourmaid. Most normal.

'How is Mrs. Wemyss?' asked Miss Entwhistle.

'About the same I believe, ma'am,' said Chesterton; and inquired if she should pay the man.

Miss Entwhistle paid the man, and then proceeded up the steps followed by Chesterton carrying her bag. Fine steps. Handsome house.

'Does she know I'm coming?'

'I believe the housemaid did mention it, ma'am.'

Nice roomy hall. With a fire it might be

quite warm. Fine windows. Good staircase.

'Do you wish for tea, ma'am?'

'No thank you. I should like to go up at once, if I may.'

'If you please, ma'am.'

At the turn of the stairs, where the gong was, Miss Entwhistle stood aside and let Chesterton precede her. 'Perhaps you had better go and tell Mrs. Wemyss I am here,' she said.

'If you please, ma'am.'

Miss Entwhistle waited, gazing at the gong with the same benevolence she had brought to bear on everything else. Fine gong. She also gazed at the antlers on the wall, for the wall continued to bristle with antlers right up to the top of the house. Magnificent collection.

'If you please, ma'am,' said Chesterton, reappearing, tiptoeing gingerly to the head of the stairs.

Miss Entwhistle went up. Chesterton ushered her into the bedroom, closing the door softly behind her.

Miss Entwhistle knew Lucy was small, but not how small till she saw her in the treble bed. There really did appear to be nothing of her except a little round head. 'Why, but you've shrunk!' was her first exclamation.

Lucy, who was tucked up to her chin by

Lizzie, besides having a wet bandage encased in flannel round her throat, could only move her eyes and smile. She was on the side of the bed farthest from the door, and Miss Entwhistle had to walk round it to reach her. She was still hoarse, but not as voiceless as when Wemyss left in the morning, for Lizzie had been diligently plying her with things like hot honey, and her face, as her eyes followed Miss Entwhistle's approach, was one immense smile. It really seemed too wonderful to be with Aunt Dot again; and there was a peace about being ill, a relaxation from strain, that had made her quiet day, alone in bed, seem sheer bliss. It was so plain that she couldn't move, that she couldn't do anything, couldn't get up and go in trains, that her conscience was at rest in regard to Everard; and she lay in the blessed silence after he left, not minding how much her limbs ached because of the delicious tranquillity of her mind. The window was open, and in the garden the birds were busy. The wind had dropped. Except for the birds there was no sound. Divine quiet. Divine peace. The luxury of it after the week-end, after the birthday, after the honeymoon, was extraordinary. Just to be in bed by oneself seemed an amazingly felicitous condition.

'Lovely of you to come,' she said hoarsely,

smiling broadly and looking so unmistakably contented that Miss Entwhistle, as she bent over her and kissed her hot forehead, thought, 'It's a success. He's making her happy.'

'You darling little thing,' she said, smoothing back her hair. 'Fancy seeing you again like this!'

'Yes,' said Lucy, heavy-eyed and smiling. 'Lovely,' she whispered, 'to see you. Tea, Aunt Dot?'

It was evidently difficult for her to speak, and her forehead was extremely hot.

'No, I don't want tea.'

'You'll stay?'

'Yes,' said Miss Entwhistle, sitting down by the pillow and continuing to smooth back her hair. 'Of course I'll stay. How did you manage to catch such a cold, I wonder?'

She was left to wonder, undisturbed by any explanations of Lucy's. Indeed it was as much as Lucy could manage to bring out the most necessary words. She lay contentedly with her eyes shut, having her hair stroked back, and said as little as possible.

'Everard — ' said Miss Entwhistle, stroking gently, 'is he coming back to-night?'

'No,' whispered Lucy contentedly.

Aunt Dot stroked in silence.

'Has your temperature been taken?' she asked presently.

'No,' whispered Lucy contentedly.

'Oughtn't you — ' after another pause 'to see a doctor?'

'No,' whispered Lucy contentedly. Delicious, simply delicious, to lie like that having one's hair stroked back by Aunt Dot, the dear, the kind, the comprehensible.

'So sweet of you to come,' she whispered again.

Well, thought Miss Entwhistle as she sat there softly stroking and watching Lucy's face of complete content while she dozed off; even after she was asleep the corners of her mouth still were tucked up in a smile — it was plain that Everard was making the child happy. In that case he certainly must be all that Lucy had assured her he was, and she, Miss Entwhistle, would no doubt very quickly now get fond of him. Of course she would. No doubt whatever. And what a comfort, what a relief, to find the child happy. Backgrounds didn't matter where there was happiness. Houses, indeed. What did it matter if they weren't the sort of houses you would, left to yourself, choose so long as in them dwelt happiness? What did it matter what their past had been so long as their present was illuminated by contentment? And as for furniture, why, that only became of interest, of importance, when life had nothing else in it. Loveless lives, empty lives, filled themselves in their despair with beautiful furniture. If you were really happy you had antlers.

In this spirit, while she stroked and Lucy slept, Miss Entwhistle's eye, full of benevolence, wandered round the room. The objects in it, after her own small bedroom in Eaton Terrace and its necessarily small furniture, all seemed to her gigantic. Especially the bed. She had never seen a bed like it before, though she had heard of such beds in history. Didn't Og the King of Bashan have one? But what an excellent plan, for then you could get away from each other. Most sensible. Most wholesome. And a certain bleakness about the room would soon go when Lucy's little things got more strewn about — her books, and photographs, and pretty dressing-table silver.

Miss Entwhistle's eye arrived at and dwelt on the dressing-table. On it were two oval wooden-backed brushes without handles. Hairbrushes. Men's. Also shaving things. And, hanging over one side of the looking-glass, were three neckties.

She quickly recovered. Most friendly. Most companionable. But a feeling of not being in Lucy's room at all took possession of her, and she fidgeted a little. With no business to be there whatever, she was in a strange man's bedroom. She averted her eyes from Wemyss's toilet arrangements, they were the last things she wanted to see; and, in averting them, they fell on the washstand with its two basins and on an enormous red-brown India-rubber sponge. No such sponge was ever Lucy's. The conclusion was forced upon her that Lucy and Everard washed side by side.

From this, too, she presently recovered. After all, marriage was marriage, and you did things in marriage that you would never dream of doing single. She averted her eyes from the washstand. The last thing she wanted to do was to become familiar with Wemyss's sponge.

Her eyes, growing more and more determined in their benevolence, gazed out of the window. How the days were lengthening. And really a beautiful look-out, with the late afternoon light reflected on the hills across the river. Birds, too, twittering in the garden — everything most pleasant and complete. And such a nice big window. Lots of air and light. It reached nearly to the floor. Two housemaids at least, and strong ones, would be needed to open or shut it — ah no, there were cords. A thought struck her: This couldn't be the room, that couldn't be the window, where —

She averted her eyes from the window, and fixed them on what seemed to be the only satisfactory resting-place for them, the contented face on the pillow. Dear little loved face. And the dear, pretty hair — how pretty young hair was, so soft and thick. No, of course it wasn't the window; that tragic room was probably not used at all now. How in the world had the child got such a cold. She could hear by her breathing that her chest was stuffed up, but evidently it wasn't worrying her, or she wouldn't in her sleep look so much pleased. Yes; that room was either shut up now and never used, or — she couldn't help being struck by yet another thought — it was a spare room. If so, Miss Entwhistle said to herself, it would no doubt be her fate to sleep in it. Dear me, she thought, taken aback.

But from this also she presently recovered; and remembering her determination to eject all prejudices merely remarked to herself, 'Well, well.' And, after a pause, was able to add benevolently, 'A house of varied interest.'

27

Later on in the dining-room, when she was reluctantly eating the meal prepared for her — Lucy still slept, or she would have asked to be allowed to have a biscuit by her bedside — Miss Entwhistle said to Chesterton, who attended her, Would she let her know when Mr. Wemyss telephoned, as she wished to speak to him.

She was feeling more and more uneasy as time passed as to what Everard would think of her uninvited presence in his house. It was natural; but would he think so? What wasn't natural was for her to feel uneasy, seeing that the house was also Lucy's, and that the child's face had hardly had room enough on it for the width of her smile of welcome. There, however, it was — Miss Entwhistle felt like an interloper. It was best to face things. She not only felt like an interloper but, in Everard's eyes, she was an interloper. This was the situation: His wife had a cold — a bad cold, but not anything serious; nobody had sent for his wife's aunt; nobody had asked her to come; and here she was. If that, in Everard's eyes, wasn't being an interloper

Miss Entwhistle was sure he wouldn't know one if he saw one.

In her life she had read many books, and was familiar with those elderly relatives frequently to be met in them, and usually female, who intrude into a newly married ménage and make themselves objectionable to one of the parties by sympathising with the other one. There was no cause for sympathy here, and if there ever should be Miss Entwhistle would certainly never sympathise except from a neutral place. She wouldn't come into a man's house, and in the very act of being nourished by his food sympathise with his wife; she would sympathise from London. Her honesty of intention, her single-mindedness, were, she knew, complete. She didn't feel, she knew she wasn't, in the least like these relatives in books, and yet as she sat in Everard's chair — obviously it was his; the upholstered seat was his very shape, inverted — she was afraid, indeed she was certain, he would think she was one of them.

There she was, she thought, come unasked, sitting in his place, eating his food. He usedn't to like her; would he like her any the better for this? From a desire not to have meals of his she had avoided tea, but she hadn't been able to avoid dinner, and with each dish set before her — dishes produced surprisingly, as she couldn't but observe, at the end of an arm thrust to the minute through a door — she felt more and more acutely that she was in his eyes, if he could only see her, an interloper. No doubt it was Lucy's house too, but it didn't feel as if it were, and she would have given much to be able to escape back to London that night.

But whatever Everard thought of her intrusion she wasn't going to leave Lucy. Not alone in that house; not to wake up to find herself alone in that house. Besides, who knew how such a chill would develop? There ought of course to have been a doctor. When Everard rang up, as he would be sure to the last thing to ask how Lucy was, she would go to the telephone, announce her presence, and inquire whether it wouldn't be as well to have a doctor round in the morning.

Therefore she asked Chesterton to let her know when Mr. Wemyss telephoned; and Chesterton, surprised, for it was not Wemyss's habit to telephone to The Willows, all his communications coming on postcards, paused just an instant before replying, 'If you please, ma'am.'

Chesterton wondered what Wemyss was expected to telephone about. It wouldn't have occurred to her that it might be about the new Mrs. Wemyss's health, because he had not within her recollection ever telephoned about the health of a Mrs. Wemyss. Sometimes the previous Mrs. Wemyss's health gave way enough for her to stay in bed, but no telephoning from London had in consequence taken place. Accordingly she wondered what message could be expected.

'What time would Mr. Wemyss be likely to ring up?' asked Miss Entwhistle presently, more for the sake of saying something than from a desire to know. She was going to that telephone, but she didn't want to, she was in no hurry for it, it wasn't impatience to meet Wemyss's voice making her talk to Chesterton; what was making her talk was the dining-room.

For not only did its bareness afflict her, and its glaring light, and its long empty table, and the way Chesterton's footsteps echoed up and down the uncarpeted floor, but there on the wall was that poor thing looking at her, she had no doubt whatever as to who it was standing up in that long slim frock looking at her, and she was taken aback. In spite of her determination to like all the arrangements, it did seem to her tactless to have her there, especially as she had that trick of looking so very steadily at one; and when she turned her eyes away from the queer, suppressed smile, she didn't like what she saw on the other wall either — that enlarged old man, that obvious progenitor.

Having caught sight of both these pictures, which at night were much more conspicuous than by day, owing to the brilliant unshaded lighting, Miss Entwhistle had no wish to look at them again, and carefully looked either at her plate or at Chesterton's back as she hurried down the room to the dish being held out at the end of the remarkable arm; but being nevertheless much disturbed by their presence, and by the way she knew they weren't taking their eyes off her however carefully she took hers off them, she asked Chesterton what time Wemyss would be likely to telephone merely in order to hear the sound of a human voice.

Chesterton then informed her that her master never did telephone to The Willows, so that she was unable to say what time he would.

'But,' said Miss Entwhistle, surprised, 'you have a telephone.'

'If you please, ma'am,' said Chesterton.

Miss Entwhistle didn't like to ask what, then, the telephone was for, because she didn't wish to embark on anything even remotely approaching a discussion of Everard's habits, so she wondered in silence.

Chesterton, however, presently elucidated.

She coughed a little first, conscious that to volunteer a remark wasn't quite within her idea of the perfect parlourmaid, and then she said, 'It's owing to local convenience, ma'am. We find it indispensable in the isolated situation of the 'ouse. We gives our orders to the tradesmen by means of the telephone. Mr. Wemyss installed it for that purpose, he says, and objects to trunk calls because of the charges and the waste of Mr. Wemyss's time at the other end, ma'am.'

'Oh,' said Miss Entwhistle.

'If you please, ma'am,' said Chesterton.

Miss Entwhistle said nothing more. With her eyes fixed on her plate in order to avoid those other eyes, she wondered what she had better do. It was half-past eight, and Everard hadn't rung up. If he were going to be anxious enough not to mind the trunk-call charge he would have been anxious enough before this. That he hadn't rung up showed he regarded Lucy's indisposition as slight. What, then, would he say to her uninvited presence there? Nothing, she was afraid, that would be really hospitable. And she had just eaten a pudding of his. It seemed to curdle up within her.

'No, no coffee, thank you,' she said hastily, on Chesterton's inquiring if she wished it served in the library. She had had dinner because she couldn't help herself, urged to it by the servants, but she needn't proceed to extras. And the library — wasn't it in the library that Everard was sitting the day that poor smiling thing . . . yes, she remembered Lucy telling her so. No, she would not have coffee in the library.

But now about telephoning. Really the only thing to do, the only way of dignity, was to ring him up. Useless waiting any more for him to do it; evidently he wasn't going to. She would ring him up, tell him she was there, and ask — she clung particularly to the doctor idea, because his presence would justify hers if the doctor hadn't better look in in the morning.

Thus it was that, sitting quiet in their basement, the Twites were startled about nine o'clock that evening by the telephone bell. It sounded more uncanny than ever up there, making all that noise by itself in the dark; and when, hurrying up anxiously to it, Twite applied his ear, all that happened was that an extremely short-tempered voice told him to hold on.

Twite held on, listening hard and hearing nothing.

'Say 'Ullo, Twite,' presently advised Mrs. Twite from out of the anxious silence at the foot of the kitchen stairs.

314

' 'Ullo,' said Twite half-heartedly.

'Must be a wrong number,' said Mrs. Twite, after more silence. ' 'Ang it up, and come and finish your supper.'

A very small voice said something very far away. Twite strained every nerve to hear. He hadn't yet had to face a trunk call, and he thought the telephone was fainting.

' 'Ullo?' he said anxiously, trying to make the word sound polite.

'It's a wrong number,' said Mrs. Twite, after further waiting. ' 'Ang it up.'

The voice, incredibly small, began to talk again, and Twite, unable to hear a word, kept on saying with increasing efforts to sound polite, ' 'Ullo?' 'Ullo?'

' 'Ang it up,' said Mrs. Twite, who from the bottom of the stairs was always brave.

'That's what it is,' said Twite at last, exhausted. 'It's a wrong number.' And he went to the writing-pad and wrote:

A wrong number rang up sir believed to be a lady 9.10.

So Miss Entwhistle at the other end was defeated, and having done her best and not succeeded she decided to remain quiescent, at any rate till the morning. Quiescent and uncritical. She wouldn't worry; she wouldn't criticise; she would merely think of Everard in those terms of amiability which were natural to her.

But while she was waiting for the call in the cold hall there had been a moment when her fixed benevolence did a little loosen. Chesterton, seeing that she shivered, had suggested the library for waiting in, where she said there was a fire, but Miss Entwhistle preferred to be cold in the hall than warm in the library; and standing in that bleak place she saw a line of firelight beneath a door, which she then knew must be the library. Accordingly she then also knew that Lucy's bedroom was exactly above the library, for looking up she could see its door from where she stood; so that it was out of that window ... Her benevolence for a moment did become unsteady. He let the child sleep there, he made the child sleep there ...

She soon, however, had herself in hand again. Lucy didn't mind, so why should she? Lucy was asleep there at that moment, with a look of complete content on her face. But there was one thing Miss Entwhistle decided she would do: Lucy shouldn't wake up by any chance in the night and find herself in that room alone — window or no window, she would sleep there with her.

This was a really heroic decision, and only

love for Lucy made it possible. Apart from the window and what she believed had happened at it, apart from the way that poor thing's face in the photograph haunted her, there was the feeling that it wasn't Lucy's bedroom at all but Everard's. It was oddly disagreeable to Miss Entwhistle to spend the night, for instance, with Wemyss's sponge. She debated in the spare-room when she was getting ready for bed — a small room on the other side of the house, with a nice high window-sill — whether she wouldn't keep her clothes on. At least then she would feel less strange, at least she would feel more at home. But how tiring. At her age, if she sat up all night — and in her clothes no lying down could be comfortable — she would be the merest rag next morning, and quite unable to cope on the telephone with Everard. And she really must take out her hairpins; she couldn't sleep a wink with them all pressing on her head. Yet the familiarity of being in that room among the neckties without her hairpins . . . She hesitated, and argued, and all the while she was slowly taking out her hairpins and taking off her clothes.

At the last moment, when she was in her nightgown and her hair was neatly plaited and she was looking the goodest of tidy little women, her courage failed her. No, she

317

couldn't go. She would stay where she was, and ring and ask that nice housemaid to sleep with Mrs. Wemyss in case she wanted anything in the night.

She did ring; but by the time Lizzie came Miss Entwhistle, doubting the sincerity of her motives, had been examining them. Was it really the neckties? Was it really the sponge? Wasn't it, at bottom, really the window?

She was ashamed. Where Lucy could sleep she could sleep. 'I rang,' she said, 'to ask you to be so kind as to help me carry my pillow and blankets into Mrs. Wemyss's room. I'm going to sleep on the sofa there.'

'Yes ma'am,' said Lizzie, picking them up. 'The sofa's very short and 'aid, ma'am. Adn't you better sleep in the bed?'

'No,' said Miss Entwhistle.

'There's plenty of room, ma'am. Mrs. Wemyss wouldn't know you was in it, it's such a large bed.'

'I will sleep on the sofa,' said Miss Entwhistle.

28

In London Wemyss went through his usual day, except that he was kept longer than he liked at his office by the accumulation of business and by having a prolonged difference of opinion, ending in dismissal, with a typist who had got out of hand during his absence to the extent of answering him back. It was five before he was able to leave — and even then he hadn't half finished, but he declined to be sacrificed further — and proceed as usual to his club to play bridge. He had a great desire for bridge after not having played for so long, and it was difficult, doing exactly the things he had always done, for him to remember that he was married. In fact he wouldn't have remembered if he hadn't felt so indignant; but all day underneath everything he did, everything he said and thought, lay indignation, and so he knew he was married.

Being extremely methodical he had long ago divided his life inside and out into compartments, each strictly separate, each, as it were, kept locked till the proper moment for its turn arrived, when he unlocked it and took out its contents — work, bridge, dinner, wife, sleep, Paddington, The Willows, or whatever it was that it contained. Having finished with the contents, the compartment was locked up and dismissed from his thoughts till its turn came round again. A honeymoon was a great shake-up, but when it occurred he arranged the date of its cessation as precisely as the date of its inauguration. On such a day, at such an hour, it would come to an end, the compartments would once more be unlocked, and regularity resumed. Bridge was the one activity which, though it was taken out of its compartment at the proper time, didn't go into it again with any sort of punctuality. Everything else, including his wife, was locked up to the minute; but bridge would stay out till any hour. On each of the days in London, the Mondays to Fridays, he proceeded punctually to his office, and from thence punctually to his club and bridge. He always lunched and dined at his club. Other men, he was aware, dined not infrequently at home, but the explanation of that was that their wives weren't Vera.

The moment, then, that Wemyss found himself once more doing the usual things among the usual surroundings, he felt so exactly as he used to that he wouldn't have remembered Lucy at all if it hadn't been for that layer of indignation at the bottom of his mind. Going up the steps of his club he was conscious of a sense of hard usage, and searching for its cause remembered Lucy. His wife now wasn't Vera, and yet he was to dine at his club exactly as if she were. His wife was Lucy; who, instead of being where she ought to be, eagerly awaiting his return to Lancaster Gate — it was one of his legitimate grievances against Vera that she didn't eagerly await — she was having a cold at Strorley. And why was she having a cold at Strorley? And why was he, a newly-married man, deprived of the comfort of his wife and going to spend the evening exactly as he had spent all the evenings for months past?

Wemyss was very indignant, but he was also very desirous of bridge. If Lucy had been waiting for him he would have had to leave off bridge before his desire for it had been anything like sated — whatever wives one had they shackled one — and as it was he could play as long as he wanted to and yet at the same time remain justly indignant. Accordingly he wasn't nearly as unhappy as he thought he was; not, at any rate, till the moment came for going solitary to bed. He detested sleeping by himself. Even Vera had always slept with him.

Altogether Wemyss felt that he had had a bad day, what with the disappointment of its beginning, and the extra work at the office, and no decent lunch. 'Positively only time to snatch a bun and a glass of milk,' he announced, amazed, to the first acquaintance he met in the club. 'Just fancy, only time to snatch — ' but the acquaintance had melted away and losing rather heavily at bridge, and going back to Lancaster Gate to find from the message left by Twite that that annoying aunt of Lucy's had cropped up already.

Usually Wemyss was amused by Twite's messages, but nothing about this one amused him. He threw down the wrong number one impatiently — Twite was really a hopeless imbecile; he would dismiss him; but the other one he read again. 'Wanted to know all about us, did she. Said it was very strange, did she. Like her impertinence,' he thought. She had lost no time in cropping up, he thought. Of how completely Miss Entwhistle had, in fact, cropped he was of course unaware.

Yes, he had had a bad day, and he was going to have a lonely night. He went upstairs feeling deeply hurt, and winding his watch.

But after much solid sleep he felt better; and at breakfast he said to Twite, who always jumped when he addressed him, 'Mrs. Wemyss will be coming up to-day.'

Twite's brain didn't work very fast owing to the way it spent most of its time dormant in a basement, and for a moment he thought — it startled him that his master had forgotten the lady was dead. Ought he to remind him? What a painful dilemma ... However, he remembered the new Mrs. Wemyss just in time not to remind him, and to say 'Yes sir,' without too perceptible a pause. His mind hadn't room in it to contain much, and it assimilated slowly that which it contained. He had only been in Wemyss's service three months before the Mrs. Wemyss he found there died. He was just beginning to assimilate her when she ceased to be assimilatable, and to him and his wife in their quiet subterraneous existence it had seemed as if not more than a week had passed before there was another Mrs. Wemyss. Far was it from him to pass opinions on the rapid marriages of gentlemen, but he couldn't keep up with these Mrs. Wemysses. His mind, he found, hadn't yet really realised the new one. He knew she was there somewhere, for he had seen her briefly on the Saturday morning, and he knew she would presently begin to disturb him by needing meals, but he easily forgot her. He forgot her now, and consequently for a moment had the dreadful thought described above.

'I shall be in to dinner,' said Wemyss.

'Yes sir,' said Twite.

Dinner. There usedn't to be dinner. His master hadn't been in once to dinner since Twite knew him. A tray for the lady, while there was a lady; that was all. Mrs. Twite could just manage a tray. Since the lady had left off coming up to town owing to her accident, there hadn't been anything. Only quiet.

He stood waiting, not having been waved out of the room, and anxiously watching Wemyss's face, for he was a nervous man.

Then the telephone bell rang.

Wemyss, without looking up, waved him out to it and went on with his breakfast; and after a minute, noticing that he neither came back nor could be heard saying anything beyond a faint, propitiatory ''Ullo,' called out to him.

'What is it?' Wemyss called out.

'I can't hear, sir,' Twite's distressed voice answered from the hall.

'Fool,' said Wemyss, appearing, table-napkin in hand.

'Yes sir,' said Twite.

He took the receiver from him, and then the Twites — Mrs. Twite from the foot of the kitchen stairs and Twite lingering in the background because he hadn't yet been waved away — heard the following:

'Yes yes. Yes, speaking. Hullo. Who is it?'

'What? I can't hear. What?'

'Miss who? En — oh, good-morning, How distant your voice sounds.'

'What? Where? *Where?*'

'Oh really.'

Here the person at the other end talked a great deal.

'Yes. Quite. But then you see she wasn't.'

More prolonged talk from the other end.

'What? She isn't coming up? Indeed she is. She's expected. I've ordered — '

'What? I can't hear. The doctor? You're sending for the doctor?'

'I daresay. But then you see I consider it isn't.'

'I daresay, I daresay. No, of course I can't. How can I leave my work — '

'Oh, very well, very well. I daresay. No doubt. She's to come up for all that as arranged, tell her, and if she needs doctors there are more of them here anyhow than — what? Can't possibly?'

'I suppose you know you're taking a great deal upon yourself unasked — '

'What? What?'

A very rapid clear voice cut in. 'Do you want another three minutes?' it asked.

He hung up the receiver with violence. 'Oh,

damn the woman, damn the woman,' he said, so loud that the Twites shook like reeds to hear him.

At the other end Miss Entwhistle was walking away lost in thought. Her position was thoroughly unpleasant. She disliked extraordinarily that she should at that moment contain an egg and some coffee which had once been Wemyss's. She would have breakfasted on a cup of tea only, if it hadn't been that Lucy was going to need looking after that day, and the looker-after must be nourished. As she went upstairs again, a faint red spot on each cheek, she couldn't help being afraid that she and Everard would have to exercise patience before they got to be fond of each other. On the telephone he hardly did himself justice, she thought.

Lucy hadn't had a good night. She woke up suddenly from what was apparently a frightening dream soon after Miss Entwhistle had composed herself on the sofa, and had been very restless and hot for a long time. There seemed to be a great many things about the room that she didn't like. One of them was the bed. Probably the poor little thing was bemused by her dream and her feverishness, but she said several things about the bed which showed that it was on her mind. Miss Entwhistle had warmed some milk on a spirit-lamp provided by Lizzie, and had given it to her and soothed her and petted her. She didn't mention the window, for which Miss Entwhistle was thankful; but when first she woke up from her frightening dream and her aunt hurried across to her, she had stared at her and actually called her Everard — her, in her meek plaits. When this happened Miss Entwhistle made up her mind that the doctor should be sent for the first thing in the morning. About six she tumbled into an uncomfortable sleep again, and Miss Entwhistle crept out of the room and dressed. Certainly she was going to have a doctor round, and hear what he had to say; and as soon as she was strengthened by breakfast she would do her duty and telephone to Everard.

This she did, with the result that she returned to Lucy's room with a little red spot on each cheek; and when she looked at Lucy, still uneasily sleeping and breathing as though her chest were all sore, the idea that she was to get up and travel to London made the red spots on Miss Entwhistle's cheeks burn brighter. She calmed down, however, on remembering that Everard couldn't see how evidently poorly the child was, and told herself that if he could he would be all tenderness. She told herself this, but she didn't believe it; and then she was vexed that she didn't believe it. Lucy loved him. Lucy had looked perfectly pleased and content yesterday before she became so ill. One mustn't judge a man by his way with a telephone.

At ten o'clock the doctor came. He had been in Strorley for years, and was its only doctor. He was one of those guests who used to dine at The Willows in the early days of Wemyss's possession of it. Occasionally he had attended the late Mrs. Wemyss; and the last time he had been in the house was when he was sent for suddenly on the day of her death. He, in common with the rest of Strorley, had heard of Wemyss's second marriage, and he shared the general shocked surprise. Strorley, which looked such an unconscious place, such a torpid, unconscious riverside place, was nevertheless intensely sensitive to shocks, and it hadn't at all recovered from the shock of that poor Mrs. Wemyss's death and the very dreadful inquest, when the fresh shock of another Mrs. Wemyss arriving on the scene made it, as it were, reel anew, and made it reel worse. Marriage so quickly on the heels of that terrible death? The Wemysses were only week-enders and summer holiday people, so that it wasn't quite so scandalous to have them in Strorley as it would have been if they were unintermittent residents, yet it was serious enough. That inquest had been in all the newspapers. To have a house in one's midst which produced doubtful coroner's verdicts was a blot on any place, and the new Mrs. Wemyss couldn't possibly be anything but thoroughly undesirable. Of course no one would call on her. Impossible. And when the doctor was rung up and asked to come round, he didn't tell his wife where he was going, because he didn't wish for trouble.

Chesterton — how well he remembered Chesterton; but after all, it was only the other day that he was there last — ushered him into the library, and he was standing gloomily in front of the empty grate, looking neither to the right nor to the left for he disliked the memories connected with the flags outside the window, and wishing he had a partner because then he would have sent him instead, when a spare little lady, bland and pleasant, came in and said she was the patient's aunt. An educated little lady; not at all the sort of relative he would have expected the new Mrs. Wemyss to have.

There was a general conviction in Strorley that the new Mrs. Wemyss must have been a barmaid, a typist, or a nursery governess — was, that is, either very bold, very poor, or very meek. Else how could she have married Wemyss? And this conviction had reached and infected even the doctor, who was a busy man off whom gossip usually slid. When, however, he saw Miss Entwhistle he at once was sure that there was nothing in it. This wasn't the aunt of either the bold, the poor, or the meek; this was just a decent gentlewoman. He shook hands with her, really pleased to see her. Everybody was always pleased to see Miss Entwhistle, except Wemyss.

'Nothing serious, I hope?' asked the doctor.

Miss Entwhistle said she didn't think there was, but that her nephew —

'You mean Mr. Wemyss?'

She bowed her head. She did mean Mr. Wemyss. Her nephew. Her nephew, that is, by marriage.

'Quite,' said the doctor.

Her nephew naturally wanted his wife to go up and join him in London.

'Naturally,' said the doctor.

And she wanted to know when she would be fit to go.

'Then let us go upstairs and I'll tell you,' said the doctor.

This was a very pleasant little lady, he thought as he followed her up the well-known stairs, to have become related to Wemyss immediately on the top of all that affair. Now he would have said himself that after such a ghastly thing as that most women —

But here they arrived in the bedroom and his sentence remained unfinished, because on seeing the small head on the pillow of the treble bed he thought, 'Why, he's married a child. What an extraordinary thing.'

'How old is she?' he asked Miss Entwhistle, for Lucy was still uneasily sleeping; and when she told him he was surprised.

'It's because she's out of proportion to the bed,' explained Miss Entwhistle in a whisper. 'She doesn't usually look so inconspicuous.'

The whispering and being looked at woke Lucy, and the doctor sat down beside her and got to business. The result was what Miss Entwhistle expected: she had a very violent feverish cold, which might turn into anything if she were not kept in bed. If she were, and with proper looking after, she would be all right in a few days. He laughed at the idea of London.

'How did you come to get such a violent chill?' he asked Lucy.

'I don't — know,' she answered.

'Well, don't talk,' he said, laying her hand down on the quilt — he had been holding it while his sharp eyes watched her — and giving it a brief pat of farewell. 'Just lie there

331

and get better. I'll send something for your throat, and I'll look in again to-morrow.'

Miss Entwhistle went downstairs with him feeling as if she had buckled him on as a shield, and would be able, clad in such armour, to face anything Everard might say.

'She likes that room?' he asked abruptly, pausing a moment in the hall.

'I can't quite make out,' said Miss Entwhistle. 'We haven't had any talk at all yet. It was from that window, wasn't it, that — ?'

'No. The one above;'

'The one above? Oh really.'

'Yes. There's a sitting-room. But I was thinking whether being in the same bed — well, good-bye. Cheer her up. She'll want it when she's better. She'll feel weak. I'll be round to-morrow.'

He went out pulling on his gloves, followed to the steps by Miss Entwhistle.

On the steps he paused again. 'How does she like being here?' he asked.

'I don't know,' said Miss Entwhistle. 'We haven't talked at all yet.'

She looked at him a moment, and then added, 'She's very much in love.'

'Ah. Yes. Really. I see. Well, good-bye.'

He turned to go.

'It's wonderful, wonderful,' he said, pausing once more.

'What is wonderful?'

'What love will do.'

'It is indeed,' agreed Miss Entwhistle, thinking of all it had done to Lucy.

He seemed as if he were going to say something more, but thought better of it and climbed into his dogcart and was driven away.

29

Two days went by undisturbed by the least manifestation from Wemyss. Miss Entwhistle wrote to him on each of the afternoons, telling him of Lucy's progress and of what the doctor said about her, and on each of the evenings she lay down on the sofa to sleep feeling excessively insecure, for how very likely that he would come down by some late train and walk in, and then there she would be. In spite of that, she would have been very glad if he had walked in, it would have seemed more natural; and she couldn't help wondering whether the little thing in the bed wasn't thinking so too. But nothing happened. He didn't come, he didn't write, he made no sign of any sort. 'Curious,' said Miss Entwhistle to herself; and forbore to criticise further.

They were peaceful days. Lucy was getting better all the time, though still kept carefully in bed by the doctor, and Miss Entwhistle felt as much justified in being in the house as Chesterton or Lizzie, for she was performing duties under a doctor's directions. Also the weather was quiet and sunshiny. In fact, there was peace.

On Thursday the doctor said Lucy might get up for a few hours and sit on the sofa; and there, its asperities softened by pillows, she sat and had tea, and through the open window came the sweet smells of April. The gardener was mowing the lawn, and one of the smells was of the cut grass; Miss Entwhistle had been out for a walk, and found some windflowers and some lovely bright green moss, and put them in a bowl; the doctor had brought a little bunch of violets out of his garden; the afternoon sun lay beautifully on the hills across the river; the river slid past the end of the garden tranquilly; and Miss Entwhistle, pouring out Lucy's tea and buttering her toast, felt that she could at that moment very nearly have been happy, in spite of its being The Willows she was in, if there hadn't, in the background, brooding over her day and night, been that very odd and disquieting silence of Everard's.

As if Lucy knew what she was thinking, she said — it was the first time she had talked of him — 'You know, Aunt Dot, Everard will have been fearfully busy this week, because of having been away so long.'

'Oh of course,' agreed Miss Entwhistle with much heartiness. 'I'm sure the poor dear has been run off his legs.'

'He didn't — he hasn't — '

Lucy flushed and broke off.

'I suppose,' she began again after a minute, 'there's been nothing from him? No message, I mean? On the telephone or anything?'

'No, I don't think there has — not since our talk the first day,' said Miss Entwhistle.

'Oh? Did he telephone the first day?' asked Lucy quickly. 'You never told me.'

'You were asleep nearly all that day. Yes,' said Miss Entwhistle, clearing her throat, 'we had a — we had quite a little talk.'

'What did he say?'

'Well, he naturally wanted you to be well enough to go up to London, and of course he was very sorry you couldn't.'

Lucy looked suddenly much happier.

'Yes,' said Miss Entwhistle, as though in answer to the look.

'He hates writing letters, you know, Aunt Dot,' Lucy said presently.

'Men do,' said Miss Entwhistle. 'It's very curious,' she continued brightly, 'but men do.'

'And he hates telephoning. It was wonderful for him to have telephoned that day.'

'Men,' said Miss Entwhistle, 'are very funny about some things.'

'To-day is Thursday, isn't it,' said Lucy. 'He ought to be here by one o'clock to-morrow.'

Miss Entwhistle started. 'To-morrow?' she repeated. 'Really? Does he? I mean, ought he? Somehow I had supposed Saturday. The week-end somehow suggests Saturdays to me.'

'No. He — we,' Lucy corrected herself, 'come down on Fridays. He's sure to be down in time for lunch.'

'Oh is he?' said Miss Entwhistle, thinking a great many things very quickly. 'Well, if it is his habit,' she went on, 'I am sure too that he will. Do you remember how we set our clocks by him when he came to tea in Eaton Terrace?'

Lucy smiled, and the remembrance of those days of love, and of all his dear, funny ways, flooded her heart and washed out for a moment the honeymoon, the birthday, everything that had happened since.

Miss Entwhistle couldn't but notice the unmistakable love-look. '*Oh* I'm so glad you love each other so much,' she said with all her heart. 'You know, Lucy, I was afraid that perhaps this house — '

She stopped, because adequately to discuss The Willows in all its aspects needed, she felt, perfect health on both sides.

'Yes, I don't think a house matters when people love each other,' said Lucy.

'Not a bit. Not a bit,' agreed Miss

Entwhistle. Not even, she thought robustly, when it was a house with a recent dreadful history. Love — she hadn't herself experienced it, but what was an imagination for except to imagine with? — love was so strong an armour that nothing could reach one and hurt one through it. That was why lovers were so selfish. They sat together inside their armour perfectly safe, entirely untouchable, completely uninterested in what happened to the rest of the world. 'Besides,' she went on aloud, 'you'll alter it.'

Lucy's smile at that was a little sickly. Aunt Dot's optimism seemed to her extravagant. She was unable to see herself altering The Willows.

'You'll have all your father's furniture and books to put about,' said Aunt Dot, continuing in optimism. 'Why, you'll be able to make the place really quite — quite — '

She was going to say habitable, but ate another piece of toast instead.

'Yes, I expect I'll have the books here, anyhow,' said Lucy. 'There's a sitting-room upstairs with room in it.'

'Is there?' said Miss Entwhistle, suddenly very attentive.

'Lots of room. It's to be my sitting-room, and the books could go there. Except that — except that — '

'Except what?' asked Miss Entwhistle.

'I don't know. I don't much want to alter that room. It was Vera's.'

'I should alter it beyond recognition,' said Miss Entwhistle firmly.

Lucy was silent. She felt too flabby, after her three days with a temperature, to engage in discussion with anybody firm.

'That's to say,' said Miss Entwhistle, 'if you like having the room at all. I should have thought — '

'Oh yes, I like having the room,' said Lucy, flushing.

Then it was Miss Entwhistle who was silent; and she was silent because she didn't believe Lucy really could like having the actual room from which that unfortunate Vera met her death. It wasn't natural. The child couldn't mean it. She needed feeding up. Perhaps they had better not talk about rooms; not till Lucy was stronger. Perhaps they had better not talk at all, because everything they said was bound in the circumstances to lead either to Everard or Vera.

'Wouldn't you like me to read aloud to you a little while before you go back to bed?' she asked, when Lizzie came in to clear away the tea-things.

Lucy thought this a very good idea. 'Oh do, Aunt Dot,' she said; for she too was afraid of what talking might lead to. Aunt Dot was phenomenally quick. Lucy felt she couldn't bear it, she simply couldn't bear it, if Aunt Dot were to think that perhaps Everard . . . So she said quite eagerly, 'Oh do, Aunt Dot,' and not until she had said it did she remember that the books were locked up, and the key was on Everard's watch-chain. Then she sat looking up at Aunt Dot with a startled, conscience-stricken face.

'What is it, Lucy?' asked Miss Entwhistle, wondering why she had turned red.

Just in time Lucy remembered that there were Vera's books. 'Do you mind very much going up to the sitting-room?' she asked. 'Vera's books — '

Miss Entwhistle did mind very much going up to the sitting-room, and saw no reason why Vera's books should be chosen. Why should she have to read Vera's books? Why did Lucy want just those, and look so odd and guilty about it? Certainly the child needed feeding up. It wasn't natural, it was unwholesome, this queer attraction she appeared to feel towards Vera.

She didn't say anything of this, but remarked that there was a room called the library in the house which suggested books, and hadn't she better choose something from out of that — go down, instead of go up.

Lucy, painfully flushed, looked at her. Nothing would induce her to tell her about the key. Aunt Dot would think it so ridiculous.

'Yes, but Everard — ' she stammered. 'They're rather special books — he doesn't like them taken out of the room — '

'Oh,' said Miss Entwhistle, trying hard to avoid any opinion of any sort.

'But I don't see why you should go up all those stairs, Aunt Dot darling,' Lucy went on. 'Lizzie will, won't you, Lizzie? Bring down some of the books — any of them. An armful.'

Lizzie, thus given *carte blanche*, brought down the six first books from the top shelf, and set them on the table beside Lucy.

Lucy recognised the cover of one of them at once, it was *Wuthering Heights*.

Miss Entwhistle took it up, read its title in silence, and put it down again.

The next one was Emily Brontë's collected poems.

Miss Entwhistle took it up, read its title in silence, and put it down again.

The third one was Thomas Hardy's *Time's Laughing-Stocks*.

Miss Entwhistle took it up, read its title in silence, and put it down again.

The other three were Baedekers.

'Well, I don't think there's anything I want to read here,' she said.

Lizzie asked if she should take them away then, and bring some more; and presently she reappeared with another armful.

These were all Baedekers.

'Curious,' said Miss Entwhistle.

Then Lucy remembered that she, too, beneath her distress on Saturday when she pulled out one after the other of Vera's books in her haste to understand her, to get comfort, to get, almost she hoped, counsel, had felt surprise at the number of Baedekers. The greater proportion of the books in Vera's shelves were guide-books and time-tables. But there had been other things — 'If you were to bring some out of a different part of the bookcase,' she suggested to Lizzie; who thereupon removed the Baedekers, and presently reappeared with more books.

This time they were miscellaneous, and Miss Entwhistle turned them over with a kind of reverential reluctance. That poor thing; this day last year she was probably reading them herself. It seemed sacrilege for two strangers ... Merciful that one couldn't see into the future. What would the poor creature have thought of the picture presented at that moment — the figure in the blue dressing-gown, sitting in the middle of all the things that had been hers such a very little while before? Well, perhaps she would have been glad they weren't hers any longer, glad that she had finished, was done with them. These books suggested such tiredness, such a — yes, such a wish for escape . . . There was more Hardy — all the poems this time in one volume. There was Pater — *The Child in the House* and *Emerald Uthwart* — Miss Entwhistle, familiar with these, shook her head: that peculiar dwelling on death in them, that queer, fascinated inability to get away from it, that beautiful but sick wistfulness no, she certainly wouldn't read these. There was a book called *In the Strange South Seas*; and another about some island in the Pacific; and another about life in the desert; and one or two others, more of the flamboyant guide-book order, describing remote, glowing places . . .

Suddenly Miss Entwhistle felt uncomfortable. She put down the book she was holding, and folded her hands in her lap and gazed out of the window at the hills on the other side of the river. She felt as if she had been prying, and prying unpardonably. The books people read — was there ever anything more revealing? No, she refused to examine Vera's books further. And apart from that horrible feeling of prying upon somebody defenceless, upon somebody pitiful, she didn't wish to allow the thought these books suggested to get any sort of hold on her mind. It was essential, absolutely essential, that it shouldn't. And if Lucy ever —

She got up and went to the window. Lucy's eyes followed her, puzzled. The gardener was still mowing the lawn, working very hard at it as though he were working against time. She watched his back, bent with hurry as he and the boy laboriously pushed and pulled the machine up and down; and then she caught sight of the terrace just below, and the flags.

This was a dreadful house. Whichever way one looked one was entangled in a reminder. She turned away quickly, and there was that little loved thing in her blue wrapper, propped up on Vera's pillows, watching her with puzzled anxiety. Nothing could harm that child, she was safe, so long as she loved and believed in Everard; but suppose some day — suppose gradually — suppose a doubt should creep into her mind whether perhaps, after all, Vera's fall . . . suppose a question should get into her head whether perhaps, after all, Vera's death — ?

Aunt Dot knew Lucy's face so well that it seemed absurd to examine it now, searching for signs in its features and expression of enough character, enough nerves, enough

— this, if there were enough of it, might by itself carry her through — sense of humour. Yes, she had a beautiful sweep of forehead; all that part of her face was lovely — so calm and open, with intelligent, sweet eyes. But were those dear eyes intelligent enough? Was not sweetness really far more manifest in them than intelligence? After that her face went small, and then, looking bigger than it was because of her little face, was her kind, funny mouth. Generous; easily forgiving; quick to be happy; quick to despair — Aunt Dot, looking anxiously at it, thought she saw all this in the shape of Lucy's mouth. But had the child strength? Had she the strength that would be needed equally — supposing that doubt and that question should ever get into her head — for staying or for going; for staying or for running . . . oh, but running, running, for her very *life* . . .

With a violent effort Miss Entwhistle shook herself free from these thoughts. Where in heaven's name was her mind wandering to? It was intolerable, this tyranny of suggestion in everything one looked at here, in everything one touched. And Lucy, who was watching her and who couldn't imagine why Aunt Dot should be so steadfastly gazing at her mouth, naturally asked, 'Is anything the matter with my face?'

Then Miss Entwhistle managed to smile, and came and sat down again beside the sofa. 'No,' she said, taking her hand. 'But I don't think I want to read after all. Let us talk.'

And holding Lucy's hand, who looked a little afraid at first but soon grew content on finding what the talk was to be about, she proceeded to discuss supper, and whether a poached egg or a cup of beef-tea contained the greater amount of nourishment.

30

Also she presently told her, approaching it with caution, for she was sure Lucy wouldn't like it, that as Everard was coming down next day she thought it better to go back to Eaton Terrace in the morning.

'You two love-birds won't want me,' she said gaily, expecting and prepared for opposition; but really, as the child was getting well so quickly, there was no reason why she and Everard should be forced to begin practising affection for each other here and now. Besides, in the small bag she brought there had only been a nightgown and her washing things, and she couldn't go on much longer on only that.

To her surprise Lucy not only agreed but looked relieved. Miss Entwhistle was greatly surprised, and also greatly pleased. 'She adores him,' she thought, 'and only wants to be alone with him. If Everard makes her as happy as all that, who cares what he is like to me or to anybody else in the world?'

And all the horrible, ridiculous things she had been thinking half an hour before were blown away like so many cobwebs.

Just before half-past seven, while she was in her room on the other side of the house tidying herself before facing Chesterton and the evening meal — she had reduced it to the merest skeleton of a meal, but Chesterton insisted on waiting, and all the usual ceremonies were observed — she was startled by the sound of wheels on the gravel beneath the window. It could only be Everard. He had come.

'Dear me,' said Miss Entwhistle to herself — and she who had planned to be gone so neatly before his arrival!

It would be idle to pretend that she wasn't very much perturbed — she was; and the brush with which she was tidying her pretty grey hair shook in her hand. Dinner alone with Everard — well, at least let her be thankful that he hadn't arrived a few minutes later and found her actually sitting in his chair. What would have happened if he had? Miss Entwhistle, for all her dismay, couldn't help laughing. Also, she encouraged herself for the encounter by remembering the doctor. Behind his authority she was secure. She had developed, since Tuesday, from an uninvited visitor into an indispensable adjunct. Not a nurse; Lucy hadn't at any moment been positively ill enough for a nurse; but an adjunct.

She listened, her brush suspended. There was no mistaking it: it was certainly Everard, for she heard his voice. The wheels of the cab, after the interval necessary for ejecting him, turned round again on the drive, crunching much less, and went away, and presently there was his well-known deliberate, heavy tread coming up the uncarpeted staircase. Thank God for bedrooms, thought Miss Entwhistle, fervently brushing. Where would one be without them and bathrooms — places of legitimate lockings-in, places even the most indignant host was bound to respect?

Now this wasn't the proper spirit in which to go down and begin getting fond of Everard and giving him the opportunity of getting fond of her, as she herself presently saw. Besides, at that very moment Lucy was probably in his arms, all alight with joyful surprise, and if he could make Lucy so happy there must he enough of good in him to enable him to fulfil the very mild requirements of Lucy's aunt. Just bare pleasantness, bare decency would be enough. She stoutly assured herself of her certainty of being fond of Everard if only he would let her. Sufficiently fond of him, that is; she didn't suppose any affection she was going to feel for him would ever be likely to get the better of her reason.

Immediately on Wemyss's arrival the silent house had burst into feverish life. Doors banged, feet ran; and now Lizzie came hurrying along the passage, and knocked at the door and told her breathlessly that dinner would be later — not for at least another half hour, because Mr. Wemyss had come unexpectedly, and cook had to —

She didn't finish the sentence, she was in such a hurry to be off.

Miss Entwhistle, her simple preparations being complete, had nothing left to do but sit in one of those wicker work chairs with thin, hard, cretonne-covered upholstery, which are sometimes found in inhospitable spare-rooms and wait.

She found this bad for her *morale*. There wasn't a book in the room, or she would have distracted her thoughts by reading. She didn't want dinner. She would have best liked to get into the bed she hadn't yet slept once in, and stay there till it was time to go home, but her pride blushed scarlet at such a cowardly desire. She arranged herself, therefore, in the chair, and, since she couldn't read, tried to remember something to say over to herself instead, some poem, or verse of a poem, to take her attention off the coming dinner; and she was shocked to find, as she sat there with her eyes shut to keep out the light that glared on her from the middle of the ceiling, that she could remember nothing but fragments: loose bits floating derelict round her mind, broken spars that didn't even belong, she was afraid, to any really magnificent whole. How Jim would have scolded her — Jim who forgot nothing that was beautiful.

> *By nature cool, in pious habits bred,*
> *She looked on husbands with a virgin's*
> *dread . . .*

Now where did that come from? And why should it come at all?

> *Such was the tone and manners of*
> *them all*
> *No married lady at the house would*
> *call . . .*

And that, for instance? She couldn't remember ever having read any poem that could contain these lines, yet she must have; she certainly hadn't invented them.

And this — an absurd German thing Jim used to quote and laugh at:

> *Der Sultan winkt, Zuleika schweigt,*
> *Und zeigt sich gänzlich abgeneigt . . .*

Why should a thing like that rise now to the surface of her mind and float round on it, while all the noble verse she had read and enjoyed, which would have been of such use and support to her at this juncture, was no where to be found, not a shred of it, in any corner of her brain?

What a brain, thought Miss Entwhistle, disgusted, sitting up very straight in the wickerwork chair, her hands folded in her lap, her eyes shut; what a contemptible, anæmic brain, deserting her like this, only able to throw up to the surface when stirred, out of all the store of splendid stuff put so assiduously into it during years and years of life, couplets.

A sound she hadn't yet heard began to crawl round the house, and, even while she wondered what it was, increased and increased till it seemed to her at last as if it must fill the universe and reach to Eaton Terrace.

It was that gong. Become active. Heavens, and what activity. She listened amazed. The time it went on! It went on and on, beating in her ears like the crack of doom.

When the three great final strokes were succeeded by silence, she got up from her chair. The moment had come. A last couplet floated through her brain — her brain seemed to clutch at it:

Betwixt the stirrup and the ground
She mercy sought, she mercy found . . .

Now where did that come from? she asked
herself distractedly, nervously passing one
hand over her already perfectly tidy hair and
opening the door with the other.

There was Wemyss, opening Lucy's door at
the same moment.

'Oh how do you do, Everard,' said Miss
Entwhistle, advancing with all the precipitate
and affectionate politeness of one who is
greeting not only a host but a nephew.

'Quite well thank you,' was Everard's
slightly unexpected reply; but logical, perfectly logical.

She held out her hand and he shook it, and
then proceeded past her to her bedroom
door, which she had left open, and switched
off the light, which she had left on.

'Oh I'm sorry,' said Miss Entwhistle.

'That,' she thought, 'is one to Everard.'

She waited for his return, and then walked,
followed by him in silence, down the stairs.

'How do you find Lucy?' she asked when
they had got to the bottom. She didn't like
Everard's silences; she remembered several of
them during that difference of opinion he and
she had had about where Christmas should
be spent. They weighed on her; and she had

the sensation of wriggling beneath them like an earwig beneath a stone, and it humiliated her to wriggle.

'Just as I expected,' he said. 'Perfectly well.'

'Oh no — not perfectly well,' exclaimed Miss Entwhistle, a vision of the blue-wrapped little figure sitting weakly up against the pillows that afternoon before her eyes. 'She is better to-day, but not nearly well.'

'You asked me what I thought, and I've told you,' said Wemyss.

No, it wouldn't be an impulsive affection, hers and Everard's, she felt; it would, when it did come, be the result of slow and careful preparation — line upon line, here a little and there a little.

'Won't you go in?' he asked; and she perceived he had pushed the dining-room door open and was holding it back with his arm while she, thinking this, lingered.

'That,' she thought, 'is another to Everard,' — her second bungle; first the light left on in her room, now keeping him waiting.

She hurried through the door, and then, vexed with herself for hurrying, walked to her chair with almost an excess of deliberation.

'The doctor — ' she began, when they were in their places, and Chesterton was hovering in readiness to snatch the cover off the soup the instant Wemyss had finished arranging his table-napkin.

'I wish to hear nothing about the doctor,' he interrupted.

Miss Entwhistle gave herself pains to be undaunted, and said with almost an excess of naturalness, 'But I'd like to tell you.'

'It is no concern of mine,' he said.

'But you're her husband, you know,' said Miss Entwhistle, trying to sound pleasant.

'I gave no orders,' said Wemyss.

'But he had to be sent for. The child — '

'So you say. So you said on the telephone. And I told you then you were taking a great deal on yourself, unasked.'

Miss Entwhistle hadn't supposed that any one ever talked like this before servants. She now knew that she had been mistaken.

'He's your doctor,' said Wemyss.

'My doctor?'

'I regard him entirely as your doctor.'

'I wish, Everard,' said Miss Entwhistle politely, after a pause, 'that I understood.'

'You sent for him on your own responsibility, unasked. You must take the consequences.'

'I don't know what you mean by the consequences,' said Miss Entwhistle, who was getting further and further away from that beginning of affection for Everard to which she had braced herself.

'The bill,' said Wemyss.

'Oh,' said Miss Entwhistle.

She was so much surprised that she could only ejaculate just that. Then the idea that she was in the act of being nourished by Wemyss's soup seemed to her so disagreeable that she put down her spoon.

'Certainly if you wish it,' she said.

'I do,' said Wemyss.

The conversation flagged.

Presently, sitting up very straight, refusing to take any notice of the variety and speed of the thoughts rushing round inside her and determined to behave as if she weren't minding anything, she said in a very clear little voice which she strove to make sound pleasant, 'Did you have a good journey down?'

'No,' said Wemyss, waving the soup away.

This as an answer, though no doubt strictly truthful, was too bald for much to be done with it. Miss Entwhistle therefore merely echoed, as she herself felt foolishly, 'No?'

And Wemyss confirmed his first reply by once more saying, 'No.'

The conversation flagged.

'I suppose,' she then said, making another effort, 'the train was very full.'

As this was not a question he was silent, and allowed her to suppose.

The conversation flagged.

'Why is there no fish?' he asked Chesterton, who was offering him cutlets.

'There was no time to get any, sir,' said Chesterton.

'He might have known that,' thought Miss Entwhistle.

'You will tell the cook that I consider I have not dined unless there is fish.'

'Yes sir,' said Chesterton.

'Goose,' thought Miss Entwhistle.

It was easier, and far less nerve-racking, to regard him indulgently as a goose than to let oneself get angry. He was like a great cross schoolboy, she thought, sitting there being rude; but unfortunately a schoolboy with power.

He ate the cutlets in silence. Miss Entwhistle declined them. She had missed her chance, she thought, when the cab was beneath her window and all she had to do was to lean out and say, 'Wait a minute.' But then Lucy — ah yes, Lucy. The minute she thought of Lucy she felt she absolutely must be friends with Everard. Incredible as it seemed to her, and always had seemed from the first, that Lucy should love him, there it was — she did. It couldn't be possible to love him without any reason. Of course not. The child knew. The child was wise and tender. Therefore Miss Entwhistle made another attempt at resuscitating conversation.

Watching her opportunity when Chesterton's back was receding down the room towards the outstretched arm at the end, for she didn't mind what Wemyss said quite so acutely if Chesterton wasn't looking, she said with as natural a voice as she could manage, 'I'm very glad you've come, you know. I'm sure Lucy has been missing you very much.'

'Lucy can speak for herself,' he said.

Then Miss Entwhistle concluded that conversation with Everard was too difficult. Let it flag. She couldn't, whatever he might feel able to do, say anything that wasn't polite in the presence of Chesterton. She doubted whether, even if Chesterton were not there, she would be able to; and yet continued politeness appeared in the face of his answers impossible. She had best be silent, she decided; though to withdraw into silence was of itself a humiliating defeat.

When she was little Miss Entwhistle used to be rude. Between the ages of five and ten she frequently made faces at people. But not since then. Ten was the latest. After that good manners descended upon her, and had enveloped her ever since. Nor had any occasion arisen later in her life in which she had even been tempted to slough them. Urbane herself, she dwelt among urbanities;

kindly, she everywhere met kindliness. But she did feel now that it might, if only she could so far forget herself, afford her solace were she able to say, straight at him, 'Wemyss.'

Just that word. No more. For some reason she was dying to call him Wemyss without any Mr. She was sure that if she might only say that one word, straight at him, she would feel better; as much relieved as she did when she was little and made faces.

Dreadful; dreadful. She cast down her eyes, overwhelmed by the nature of her thoughts, and said No thank you to the pudding.

'It is clear,' thought Wemyss, observing her silence and her refusal to eat, 'where Lucy gets her sulking from.'

No more words were spoken till, dinner being over, he gave the order for coffee in the library.

'I'll go and say good-night to Lucy,' said Miss Entwhistle as they got up.

'You'll be so good as to do nothing of the sort,' said Wemyss.

'I — beg your pardon?' inquired Miss Entwhistle, not quite sure she could have heard right.

At this point they were both just in front of Vera's portrait on their way to the door, and she was looking at each of them, impartially strangling her smile.

'I wish to speak to you in the library,' said Wemyss.

'But suppose I don't wish to be spoken to in the library?' leapt to the tip of Miss Entwhistle's tongue.

There, however, was Chesterton — checking, calming.

So she said, instead, 'Do.'

31

She hadn't been into the library yet. She knew the dining-room, the hall, the staircase, Lucy's bedroom, the spare-room, the antlers, and the gong; but she didn't know the library. She had hoped to go away without knowing it. However, she was not to be permitted to.

The newly-lit wood fire blazed cheerfully when they went in, but its amiable light was immediately quenched by the electric light Wemyss switched on at the door. From the middle of the ceiling it poured down so strongly that Miss Entwhistle wished she had brought her sun-shade. The blinds were drawn, and there in front of the window was the table where Everard had sat writing — she remembered every word of Lucy's account of it on that July afternoon of Vera's death. It was now April; still well over three months to the first anniversary of that dreadful day, and here he was married again, and to, of all people in the world, her Lucy. There were so many strong, robust-minded young women in the world, so many hardened widows, so many thick-skinned persons of mature years wanting a comfortable home, who wouldn't mind Everard because they wouldn't love him and therefore wouldn't feel — why should Fate have ordered that it should just be her Lucy? No, she didn't like him, she couldn't like him. He might, and she hoped he was, be all Lucy said, be wonderful and wholesome and natural and all the rest of it, but if he didn't seem so to her what, as far as she was concerned, was the good of it?

The fact is that by the time Miss Entwhistle got into the library she was very angry. Even the politest worm, she said to herself, the most conciliatory, sensible worm, fully conscious that wisdom points to patience, will nevertheless turn on its niece's husband if trodden on too heavily. The way Wemyss had ordered her not to go up to Lucy . . . Particularly enraging to Miss Entwhistle was the knowledge of her weak position, uninvited in his house.

Wemyss, standing on the hearthrug in front of the blaze, filled his pipe. How well she knew that attitude and that action. How often she had seen both in her drawing-room in London. And hadn't she been kind to him? Hadn't she always, when she was hostess and he was guest, been hospitable and courteous? No, she didn't like him.

She sat down in one of the immense chairs,

and had the disagreeable sensation that she was sitting down in Wemyss hollowed out. The two little red spots were brightly on her cheekbones — had been there, indeed, ever since the beginning of dinner.

Wemyss filled his pipe with his customary deliberation, saying nothing. 'I believe he's enjoying himself,' flashed into her mind. 'Enjoying being in a temper, and having me to bully.'

'Well?' she asked, suddenly unbearably irritated.

'Oh it's no good taking that tone with me,' he said, continuing carefully to fill his pipe.

'Really, Everard,' she said, ashamed of him, but also ashamed of herself. She oughtn't to have let go her grip on herself and said, 'Well?' with such obvious irritation.

The coffee came.

'No thank you,' said Miss Entwhistle.

He helped himself.

The coffee went.

'Perhaps,' said Miss Entwhistle in a very polite voice when the door had been shut by Chesterton, 'you'll tell me what it is you wish to say.'

'Certainly. One thing is that I've ordered the cab to come round for you to-morrow in time for the early train.'

'Oh thank you, Everard. That is most

thoughtful,' said Miss Entwhistle. 'I had already told Lucy, when she said you would be down to-morrow, that I would go home early.'

'That's one thing,' said Wemyss, taking no notice of this and going on carefully filling his pipe. 'The other is, that I don't wish you to see Lucy again, either to-night or before you go.'

She looked at him in astonishment. 'But why not?' she asked.

'I'm not going to have her upset.'

'But my dear Everard, don't you see it will upset her much more if I don't say good-bye to her? It won't upset her at all if I do, because she knows I'm going to-morrow anyhow. Why, what will the child think?'

'Oblige me by allowing me to be the best judge of my own affairs.'

'Do you know I very much doubt if you're that,' said Miss Entwhistle earnestly, really moved by his inability to perceive consequences. Here he had got everything, everything to make him happy for the rest of his life — the wife he loved adoring him, believing in him, blotting out by her mere marrying him every doubt as to the exact manner of Vera's death, and all he had to do was to be kind and ordinarily decent. And poor Everard — it was absurd of her to mind for him, but she did in fact at that moment mind for him, he seemed such a pathetic human being, blindly bent on ruining his own happiness — would spoil it all, inevitably smash it all sooner or later, if he wasn't able to see, wasn't able to understand . . .

Wemyss considered her remark so impertinent that he felt he would have been amply justified in requesting her to leave his house then and there, dark or no dark, train or no train. And so he would have done, if he hadn't happened to prefer a long rather than a short scene.

'I didn't ask you into my library to hear your opinion of my character,' he said, lighting his pipe.

'Well then,' said Miss Entwhistle, for there was too much at stake for her to allow herself either to be silenced or goaded, 'let me tell you a few things about Lucy's.'

'About Lucy's?' echoed Wemyss, amazed at such effrontery. 'About my wife's?'

'Yes,' said Miss Entwhistle, very earnestly. 'It's the sort of character that takes things to heart, and she'll be miserable — miserable, Everard, and worry and worry if I just disappear as you wish me to without a word. Of course I'll go, and I promise I'll never come again unless you ask me to. But don't, because you're angry, insist on something that will make Lucy extraordinarily unhappy. Let me say good-night to her now, and good-bye to-morrow morning. I tell you she'll be terribly worried if I don't. She'll think' — Miss Entwhistle tried to smile — 'that you've turned me out. And then, you see, if she thinks that, she won't be able — ' Miss Entwhistle hesitated. 'Well, she won't be able to be proud of you. And that, my dear Everard — ' she looked at him with a faint smile of deprecation and apology that she, a spinster, should talk of this — 'gives love its deepest wound.'

Wemyss stared at her, too much amazed to speak. In his house . . . In his own house!

'I'm sorry,' she said, still more earnestly, 'if this annoys you, but I do want — I really do think it is very important.'

There was then a silence during which they looked at each other, he at her in amazement, she at him trying to hope — hope that he would take what she had said in good part. It was so vital that he should understand, that he should get an idea of the effect on Lucy of just that sort of unkind, even cruel behaviour. His own happiness was involved as well. Tragic, tragic for every one if he couldn't be got to see . . .

'Are you aware,' he said, 'that this is my house?'

'Oh Everard — ' she said at that, with a movement of despair.

'Are you aware,' he continued, 'that you are talking to a husband of his wife?'

Miss Entwhistle said nothing, but leaning her head on her hand looked at the fire.

'Are you aware that you thrust yourself into my house uninvited directly my back was turned, and have been living in it, and would have gone on indefinitely living in it, without any sanction from me unless I had come down, as I did come down, on purpose to put an end to such an outrageous state of affairs?'

'Of course,' she said, 'that is one way of describing it.'

'It is the way of every reasonable and decent person,' said Wemyss.

'Oh no,' said Miss Entwhistle. 'That is precisely what it isn't. But,' she added, getting up from the chair and holding out her hand, 'it is your way, and so I think, Everard, I'll say good-night. And good-bye too, for I don't expect I'll see you in the morning.'

'One would suppose,' he said, taking no notice of her proffered hand, for he hadn't nearly done, 'from your tone that this was your house and I was your servant.'

'I assure you I could never imagine it to be my house or you my servant.'

'You made a great mistake, I can tell you,

when you started interfering between husband and wife. You have only yourself to thank if I don't allow you to continue to see Lucy.'

She stared at him.

'Do you mean,' she said, after a silence, 'that you intend to prevent my seeing her later on too? In London?'

'That, exactly, is my intention.'

Miss Entwhistle stared at him, lost in thought; but he could see he had got her this time, for her face had gone visibly pale.

'In that case, Everard,' she said presently, 'I think it my duty — '

'Don't begin about duties. You have no duties in regard to me and my household.'

'I think it my duty to tell you that from my knowledge of Lucy — '

'Your knowledge of Lucy! What is it compared to mine, I should like to know?'

'Please listen to me. It's most important. From my knowledge of her, I'm quite sure she hasn't the staying power of Vera.'

It was now his turn to stare. She was facing him, very pale, with shining, intrepid eyes. He had got her in her vulnerable spot he could see, or she wouldn't be so white, but she was going to do her utmost to annoy him up to the last.

'The staying power of — ?' he repeated.

'I'm sure of it. And you must be wise, you must positively have the wisdom to take care of your own happiness — '

'Oh good God, you preaching woman!' he burst out. 'How dare you stand there in my own house talking to me of Vera?'

'Hush,' said Miss Entwhistle, her eyes shining brighter and brighter in her white face. 'Listen to me. It's atrocious that I should have to, but nobody ever seems to have told you a single thing in your life. You don't seem to know anything at all about women, anything at all about human beings. How could you bring a girl like Lucy — any young wife — to this house? But here she is, and it still may be all right because she loves you so, if you take care, if you are tender and kind. I assure you it is nothing to me how angry you are with me, or how completely you separate me from Lucy, if only you are kind to her. Don't you realise, Everard, that she may soon begin to have a baby, and that then she — '

'You indelicate woman! You incredibly indecent, improper — '

'I don't in the least mind what you say to me, but I tell you that unless you take care, unless you're kinder than you're being at this moment, it won't be anything like fifteen years this time.'

He repeated, staring, 'Fifteen years this time?'

'Yes. Good-bye.'

And she was gone, and had shut the door behind her before her monstrous meaning dawned on him.

Then, when it did, he strode out of the room after her.

She was going up the stairs very slowly.

'Come down,' he said.

She went on as if she hadn't heard him.

'Come down. If you don't come down at once I'll fetch you.'

This, through all her wretchedness, through all her horror, for beating in her ears were two words over and over again, *Lucy, Vera — Lucy, Vera* struck her as so absurd, the vision of herself, more naturally nimble, going on up the stairs just out of Wemyss's reach, with him heavily pursuing her, till among the attics at the top he couldn't but run her to earth in a cistern, that she had great difficulty in not spilling over into a ridiculous, hysterical laugh.

'Very well then,' she said, stopping and speaking in a low voice so that Lucy shouldn't be disturbed by unusual sounds, 'I'll come down.' And shining, quivering with indomitableness, she did.

She arrived at the bottom of the stairs where he was standing and faced him. What was he going to do? Take her by the shoulders and turn her out? Not a sign, not the smallest sign of distress or fear should he get out of her. Fear of him in relation to herself was the last thing she would condescend to feel, but fear for Lucy — for Lucy . . . She could very easily have cried out because of Lucy, entreated to be allowed to see her sometimes, humbled herself, if she hadn't gripped hold of the conviction of his delight if she broke down, of his delight at having broken her down, at refusing. The thought froze her serene.

'You will now leave my house,' said Wemyss through his teeth.

'Without my hat, Everard?' she inquired mildly.

He didn't answer. He would gladly at that moment have killed her, for he thought he saw she was laughing at him. Not openly. Her face was serious and her voice polite; but he thought he saw she was laughing at him, and beyond anything that could happen to him he hated being defied.

He walked to the front door, reached up and undid the top bolt, stooped down and undid the bottom bolt, turned the key, took the chain off, pulled the door open, and said, 'There now. Go. And let this be a lesson to you.'

'I am glad to see,' said Miss Entwhistle, going out on to the steps with dignity, and surveying the stars with detachment, 'that it is a fine night.'

He shut and bolted and locked and chained her out, and as soon as he had done, and she heard his footsteps going away, and her eyes were a little accustomed to the darkness, she went round to the back entrance, rang the bell, and asked the astonished tweeny, who presently appeared, to send Lizzie to her; and when Lizzie came, also astonished, she asked her to be so kind as to go up to her room and put her things in her bag and bring her her hat and cloak and purse.

'I'll wait here in the garden,' said Miss Entwhistle, 'and it would be most kind, Lizzie, if you were rather quick.'

Then, when she had got her belongings, and Lizzie had put her cloak round her shoulders and tried to express, by smoothings and brushings of it, her understanding and sympathy, for it was clear to Lizzie and to all the servants that Miss Entwhistle was being turned out, she went away; she went away past the silent house, through the white gate, up through the darkness of the sunken oozy lane, out on to the road where the stars gave light, across the bridge, into the village, along the road to the station, to wait for whatever train should come.

She walked slower and slower.

She was extraordinarily tired.

32

Wemyss went back into the library, and seeing his coffee still on the chimney-piece he drank it, and then sat down in the chair Miss Entwhistle had just left, and smoked.

He wouldn't go up to Lucy yet; not till he was sure the woman wasn't going to try any tricks of knocking at the front door or ringing bells. He actually, so inaccurate was his perception of Miss Entwhistle's character and methods, he actually thought she might perhaps throw stones at the windows, and he decided to remain downstairs guarding his premises till this possibility became, with the lapse of time, more remote.

Meanwhile the fury of his indignation at the things she had said was immensely tempered by the real satisfaction he felt in having turned her out. That was the way to show people who was master, and meant to be master, in his own house. She had supposed she could do as she liked with him, use his house, be waited on by his servants, waste his electric light, interfere between him and his wife, say what she chose, lecture him, stand there and insult him, and he had showed her very quickly and clearly that she couldn't. As to her final monstrous suggestion, it merely proved how completely he had got her, how accurately he had hit on the punishment she felt most, that she should have indulged in such ravings. The ravings of impotence, that's what that was. For the rest of his life, he supposed, whenever people couldn't get their own way with him, were baffled by his steadfastness and consequently became vindictive, they would throw that old story up against him. Let them. It wouldn't make him budge, not a hair's-breadth, in any direction he didn't choose. Master in his own house — that's what he was.

Curious how women invariably started by thinking they could do as they liked with him. Vera had thought so, and behaved accordingly; and she had been quite surprised, and even injured, when she discovered she couldn't. No doubt this woman was feeling considerably surprised too now; no doubt she never dreamt he would turn her out. Women never believed he would do the simple, obvious thing. And even when he warned them that he would, as he could remember on several occasions having warned Vera — indeed, it was recorded in his diary — they still didn't believe it. Daunted themselves by convention and the fear of what people might think, they imagined that he would be daunted too. Then, when he wasn't, and it happened, they were surprised; and they never seemed to see that they had only themselves to thank.

He sat smoking and thinking a long time, one ear attentive to any sounds which might indicate that Miss Entwhistle was approaching hostilely from outside. Chesterton found him sitting like that when she came in to remove the coffee cup, and she found him still sitting like that when she came in an hour later with his whisky.

It was nearly eleven before he decided that the danger of attack was probably over; but still, before he went upstairs, he thought it prudent to open the window and step over the sill on to the terrace and just look round.

All was as quiet as the grave. It was so quiet that he could hear a little ripple where the water was split by a dead branch as the river slid gently along. There were stars, so that it was not quite dark; and although the April air was moist it was dry under foot. A pleasant night for a walk. Well, he would not grudge her that.

He went along the terrace, and round the clump of laurustinus bushes which cloaked the servants' entrance, to the front of the house.

Empty. Nobody still lingering on the steps.

He then proceeded as far as the white gate, holding her capable of having left it open on purpose — 'In order to aggravate me,' as he put it to himself.

It was shut.

He stood leaning on it a minute listening, in case she should be lurking in the lane.

Not a sound.

Satisfied that she had really gone, he returned to the terrace and re-entered the library, fastening the window carefully and pulling down the blind.

What a relief, what an extraordinary relief, to have got rid of her; and not just for this once, but for good. Also she was Lucy's only relation, so there were no more of them to come and try to interfere between man and wife. He was very glad she had behaved so outrageously at the end saying that about Vera, for it justified him completely in what he had done. A little less bad behaviour, and she would have had to be allowed to stay the night; still a little less, and she would have had to come to The Willows again, let alone having a free hand in London to influence Lucy when he was at his club playing bridge and unable to look after her. Yes; it was very satisfactory, and well worth coming down a day earlier for.

He wound up his watch, standing before the last glimmerings of the fire, and felt quite good-humoured again. More than good-humoured — refreshed and exhilarated, as though he had had a cold bath and a thorough rub-down. Now for bed and his little Love. What simple things a man wanted — only his woman and peace.

Wemyss finished winding his watch, stretched himself, yawned, and then went slowly upstairs, switching off the lights as he went.

In the bedroom there was a night-light burning, and Lucy had fallen asleep, tired of waiting for Aunt Dot to come and say good-night, but she woke when he came in.

'Is that you, Aunt Dot?' she murmured, even through her sleepiness sure it must be, for Everard would have turned on the light.

Wemyss, however, didn't want her to wake up and begin asking questions, so he refrained from turning on the light.

'No, it's your Everard,' he said, moving about on tiptoe. 'Sh-sh, now. Go to sleep again like a good little girl.'

Through her sleepiness she knew that voice of his; it meant one of his pleased moods. How sweet of him to be taking such care not to disturb her . . . dear Everard . . . she and Aunt Dot must have made friends then

378

. . . how glad she was . . . wonderful little Aunt Dot . . . before dinner he was angry, and she had been so afraid . . . afraid . . . what a relief . . . how glad . . .

But Lucy was asleep again, and the next thing she knew was Everard's arm being slid under her shoulders and she being drawn across the bed and gathered to his breast.

'Who's my very own baby?' she heard him saying; and she woke up just enough sleepily to return his kiss.

We do hope that you have enjoyed reading this large print book.

Did you know that all of our titles are available for purchase?

We publish a wide range of high quality large print books including:
Romances, Mysteries, Classics
General Fiction
Non Fiction and Westerns

Special interest titles available in large print are:
The Little Oxford Dictionary
Music Book
Song Book
Hymn Book
Service Book

Also available from us courtesy of Oxford University Press:
Young Readers' Dictionary
(large print edition)
Young Readers' Thesaurus
(large print edition)

For further information or a free brochure, please contact us at:
Ulverscroft Large Print Books Ltd.,
The Green, Bradgate Road, Anstey,
Leicester, LE7 7FU, England.
Tel: (00 44) 0116 236 4325
Fax: (00 44) 0116 234 0205

Other titles published by Ulverscroft:

THE DAUGHTER OF THE COMMANDANT

Alexander Pushkin

The only child of a retired army officer, Pyotr Andreyich Grinyov is already enrolled in the Semenofsky regiment, due to assume his position as sergeant of the Guard once his education has finished. By the age of seventeen, he is keen to take up the mantle of military service, anticipating the liberties and pleasures of duty in Petersburg. But his father has other ideas: his son will be no preening idler of a Guard, but an active soldier. Indignant and resentful, Pyotr is assigned to garrison duty at the remote Fort Belogorsk. And there he meets Marya, the Commandant's daughter . . .

THE DUEL AND
COLONEL CHABERT

Joseph Conrad & Honoré de Balzac

When Lieutenant D'Hubert is sent to arrest Lieutenant Feraud for wounding a civilian in a duel, Feraud truculently insists on fighting the other officer — sparking a deadly feud between the two Hussars which will erupt in recurrent duels across many miles and many years . . . The japes of the law-clerks in the office of M. Derville are interrupted by the arrival of an old man in a tattered box-coat, seeking the attorney. He claims he is Chabert — the brave cavalry Colonel, beloved by Napoleon, who was presumed slain at Eylau. And he wants M. Derville to win back the money and honour stolen away from him . . .

THE PASSENGER FROM CALAIS

Arthur Griffiths

After crossing from Dover, Colonel Basil Annesley finds himself to be the only passenger on the Engadine express from Calais to Lucerne. That is, the only passenger until a woman shows up at the last minute to book a compartment for her servant, an infant, and herself. Through the open window of his compartment, the colonel overhears their private conversation on the station platform, and is intrigued. The mysterious woman — a self-confessed thief, carrying something she refers to as 'our treasure' — fears she is being followed. Who is after her? What is her secret? And is she a criminal or a victim?

THE HOUSE BEHIND THE CEDARS

Charles W. Chesnutt

North Carolina, 1860s: Ten years ago, John Walden, of mixed racial ancestry and light-skinned, left his home and family to forge a new life for himself as a white lawyer in Clarence, South Carolina. Now the widowed John returns, asking his sister Rena to join him and help to care for his baby son. Rena, also able to pass as white, seizes this opportunity with alacrity. But both Waldens know that the truth of their bloodline can never be revealed. And when Rena begins to fall in love with George Tryon, she finds herself burdened by the family secret . . .